The Girl With
The Make-Believe
Husband

BY JULIA QUINN

The Girl With The Make-Believe Husband

Because of Miss Bridgerton

The Bridgerton Series

The Duke and I

The Viscount Who Loved Me

An Offer From a Gentleman

Romancing Mister Bridgerton

To Sir Phillip, With Love

When He Was Wicked

It's In His Kiss

On the Way to the Wedding

The Bridgertons: Happily Ever After

The Smythe-Smith Quartet

Just Like Heaven

A Night Like This

The Sum of All Kisses

The Secrets of Sir Richard Kenworthy

The Girl With The Make-Believe Husband

A Bridgertons Prequel

Julia Quinn

HARPER LUXE

An Imprint of HarperCollinsPublishers

THE GIRL WITH THE MAKE-BELIEVE HUSBAND. Copyright © 2017 by Julie Cotler Pottinger. All rights reserved. Printed in the United States of America. No part of this book may be used or reproduced in any manner whatsoever without written permission except in the case of brief quotations embodied in critical articles and reviews. For information address HarperCollins Publishers, 195 Broadway, New York, NY 10007.

HarperCollins books may be purchased for educational, business, or sales promotional use. For information please e-mail the Special Markets Department at SPsales@harpercollins.com.

FIRST HARPERLUXE EDITION

ISBN: 978-0-06-267033-5

HarperLuxe™ is a trademark of HarperCollins Publishers.

17 18 19 20 21   ID/LSC   10 9 8 7 6 5 4 3 2 1

For Nana Vaz de Castro,
who created a movement.
It's probably a good thing
I can't get Bob's Ovomaltine shakes
in the United States.

And also for Paul.
There's got to be some irony in the fact that
I wrote about a make-believe husband
while you were gone for three months
climbing Mount Everest.
But that mountain is <u>real</u>. And so are you.
And so are we.

The Girl With
The Make-Believe
Husband

Chapter 1

Manhattan Island
June 1779

H is head hurt.

Correction, his head *really* hurt.

It was hard to tell, though, just what sort of pain it was. He *might* have been shot through the head with a musket ball. That seemed plausible, given his current location in New York (or was it Connecticut?) and his current occupation as a captain in His Majesty's Army.

There was a war going on, in case one hadn't noticed.

But this particular pounding—the one that felt more like someone was bashing his skull with a cannon (not a cannon*ball*, mind you, but an actual cannon)—seemed to indicate that he had been attacked with a blunter instrument than a bullet.

An anvil, perhaps. Dropped from a second-story window.

But if one cared to look on the bright side, a pain such as this did seem to indicate that he wasn't dead, which was also a plausible fate, given all the same facts that had led him to believe he might have been shot.

That war he'd mentioned . . . people did die.

With alarming regularity.

So he wasn't dead. That was good. But he also wasn't sure where he was, precisely. The obvious next step would be to open his eyes, but his eyelids were translucent enough for him to realize that it was the middle of the day, and while he did like to look on the metaphorical bright side, he was fairly certain that the literal one would prove blinding.

So he kept his eyes closed.

But he listened.

He wasn't alone. He couldn't make out any actual conversation, but a low buzz of words and activity filtered through the air. People were moving about, setting objects on tables, maybe pulling a chair across the floor.

Someone was moaning in pain.

Most of the voices were male, but there was at least one lady nearby. She was close enough that he could hear her breathing. She made little noises as she went about her business, which he soon realized included tucking blankets around him and touching his forehead with the back of her hand.

He liked these little noises, the tiny little *mmm*s and sighs she probably had no idea she was making. And she smelled nice, a bit like lemons, a bit like soap.

And a bit like hard work.

He knew that smell. He'd worn it himself, albeit usually only briefly until it turned into a full-fledged stink.

On her, though, it was more than pleasant. Perhaps a little earthy. And he wondered who she was, to be tending to him so diligently.

"How is he today?"

Edward held himself still. This male voice was new, and he wasn't sure he wanted anyone to know he was awake yet.

Although he wasn't sure *why* he felt this hesitancy.

"The same," came the woman's reply.

"I am concerned. If he doesn't wake up soon . . ."

"I know," the woman said. There was a touch of irritation in her voice, which Edward found curious.

"Have you been able to get him to take broth?"

"Just a few spoonfuls. I was afraid he would choke if I attempted any more than that."

The man made a vague noise of approval. "Remind me how long he has been like this?"

"A week, sir. Four days before I arrived, and three since."

A week. Edward thought about this. A week meant it must be . . . March? April?

No, maybe it was only February. And this was probably New York, not Connecticut.

But that still didn't explain why his head hurt so bloody much. Clearly he'd been in some sort of an accident. Or had he been attacked?

"There has been no change at all?" the man asked, even though the lady had just said as much.

But she must have had far more patience than Edward, because she replied in a quiet, clear voice, "No, sir. None."

The man made a noise that wasn't quite a grunt. Edward found it impossible to interpret.

"Er . . ." The woman cleared her throat. "Have you any news of my brother?"

Her brother? Who was her brother?

"I am afraid not, Mrs. Rokesby."

Mrs. Rokesby?

"It has been nearly three months," she said quietly.

Mrs. Rokesby? Edward really wanted them to get back to that point. There was only one Rokesby in North America as far as he knew, and that was he. So if she was Mrs. Rokesby . . .

"I think," the male voice said, "that your energies would be better spent tending to your husband."

Husband?

"I assure you," she said, and there was that touch of irritation again, "that I have been caring for him most faithfully."

Husband? They were calling him her *husband?* Was he married? He couldn't be married. How could he be married and not remember it?

Who was this woman?

Edward's heart began to pound. What the devil was happening to him?

"Did he just make a noise?" the man asked.

"I . . . I don't think so."

She moved then, quickly. Hands touched him, his cheek, then his chest, and even through her obvious concern, there was something soothing in her motions, something undeniably right.

"Edward?" she asked, taking his hand. She stroked it several times, her fingers brushing lightly over his skin. "Can you hear me?"

He ought to respond. She was worried. What kind of gentleman did not act to relieve a lady's distress?

"I fear he may be lost to us," the man said, with far less gentleness than Edward thought appropriate.

"He still breathes," the woman said in a steely voice.

The man said nothing, but his expression must have been one of pity, because she said it again, more loudly this time.

"*He still breathes.*"

"Mrs. Rokesby . . ."

Edward felt her hand tighten around his. Then she placed her other on top, her fingers resting lightly on his knuckles. It was the smallest sort of embrace, but Edward felt it down to his soul.

"He still breathes, Colonel," she said with quiet resolve. "And while he does, I will be here. I may not be able to help Thomas, but—"

Thomas. Thomas Harcourt. *That* was the connection. This must be his sister. Cecilia. He knew her well.

Or not. He'd never actually met the lady, but he *felt* like he knew her. She wrote to her brother with a diligence that was unmatched in the regiment. Thomas received twice as much mail as Edward, and Edward had four siblings to Thomas's one.

Cecilia Harcourt. What on earth was she doing in North America? She was supposed to be in Derbyshire, in that little town Thomas had been so eager to leave. The one with the hot springs. Matlock. No, Matlock Bath.

Edward had never been, but he thought it sounded charming. Not the way Thomas described it, of course; he liked the bustle of city life and couldn't wait to take a commission and depart his village. But Cecilia was different. In her letters, the small Derbyshire town came alive, and Edward almost felt that he would recognize her neighbors if he ever went to visit.

She was witty. Lord, she was witty. Thomas used to laugh so much at her missives that Edward finally made him read them out loud.

Then one day, when Thomas was penning his response, Edward interrupted so many times that Thomas finally shoved out his chair and held forth his quill.

"You write to her," he'd said.

So he did.

Not on his own, of course. Edward could never have written to her directly. It would have been the worst sort of impropriety, and he would not have insulted her in such a manner. But he took to scribbling a few lines at the end of Thomas's letters, and whenever she replied, she had a few lines for him.

Thomas carried a miniature of her, and even though he said it was several years old, Edward had found himself staring at it, studying the small portrait of the young woman, wondering if her hair really was that remarkable golden color, or if she really did smile that way, lips closed and mysterious.

Somehow he thought not. She did not strike him as a woman with secrets. Her smile would be sunny and free. Edward had even thought he'd like to meet her once this godforsaken war was over. He'd never said anything to Thomas, though.

That would have been strange.

Now Cecilia was here. In the colonies. Which made absolutely no sense, but then again, what did? Edward's head was injured, and Thomas seemed to be missing, and . . .

Edward thought hard.

. . . and he seemed to have married Cecilia Harcourt.

He opened his eyes and tried to focus on the green-eyed woman peering down at him.

"Cecilia?"

Cecilia had had three days to imagine what Edward Rokesby might say when he finally woke up. She'd come up with several possibilities, the most likely of which was: "Who the hell are you?"

It would not have been a silly question.

Because no matter what Colonel Stubbs thought—

no matter what everyone at this rather poorly outfitted military hospital thought, her name was not Cecilia Rokesby, it was Cecilia Harcourt, and she most definitely was not married to the rather handsome dark-haired man lying in the bed at her side.

As for how the misunderstanding had come about . . .

It might have been something to do with her declaring that she was his wife in front of his commanding officer, two soldiers, and a clerk.

It had seemed a good idea at the time.

She'd not come to New York lightly. She was well aware of the dangers of traveling to the war-torn colonies, to say nothing of the voyage across the temperamental North Atlantic. But her father had died, and then she'd received word that Thomas was injured, and then her wretched cousin had come sniffing around Marswell . . .

She couldn't remain in Derbyshire.

And yet she'd had nowhere to go.

So in what was probably the only rash decision of her life, she'd packed up her house, buried the silver in the back garden, and booked passage from Liverpool to New York. When she arrived, however, Thomas was nowhere to be found.

She'd located his regiment, but no one had answers for her, and when she persisted with her questions, she was dismissed by the military brass like a pesky little fly. She'd been ignored, patronized, and probably lied to. She'd used up nearly all her funds, was getting by on one meal a day, and was living in a boardinghouse room directly next to a woman who might or might not have been a prostitute.

(That she was having relations was a certainty; the only question was whether she was being paid for them. And Cecilia had to say, she rather hoped she was, because whatever that woman was doing, it sounded like an awful lot of work.)

But then, after nearly a week of getting nowhere, Cecilia overheard one soldier telling another that a man had been brought to hospital a few days earlier. He'd had a blow to the head and was unconscious. His name was Rokesby.

Edward Rokesby. It had to be.

Cecilia had never actually laid eyes on the man, but he was her brother's closest friend, and she *felt* like she knew him. She knew, for example, that he was from Kent, that he was the second son of the Earl of Manston, and that he had a younger brother in the navy and another at Eton. His sister was married, but she had no children, and the thing he missed most of all from home was his cook's gooseberry fool.

His older brother was called George, and she had

been surprised when Edward had admitted that he did not envy him his position as heir. With an earldom came an appalling lack of freedom, he'd once written, and he knew that his place was in the army, fighting for King and Country.

Cecilia supposed that an outsider might have been shocked at the level of intimacy in their correspondence, but she'd learned that war made philosophers of men. And maybe it was for that reason that Edward Rokesby had begun adding little notes of his own at the end of Thomas's letters to her. There was something comforting about sharing one's thoughts with a stranger. It was easy to be brave with someone one would never face across a dining table or in a drawing room.

Or at least this was Cecilia's hypothesis. Maybe he was writing all the same things to his family and friends back in Kent. She'd heard from her brother that he was "practically engaged" to his neighbor. Surely Edward was penning letters to her, too.

And it wasn't as if Edward was *actually* writing to Cecilia. It had started with little snippets from Thomas: *Edward says such-and-such* or *I am compelled by Captain Rokesby to point out* . . .

The first few had been terribly amusing, and Cecilia, stuck at Marswell with mounting bills and a disinterested father, had welcomed the unexpected smile his words brought to her face. So she replied in kind, adding little bits and pieces to her own missives: *Please tell Captain Rokesby . . .* and later: *I cannot help but think that Captain Rokesby would enjoy . . .*

Then one day she saw that her brother's latest missive included a paragraph written by another hand. It was a short greeting, containing little more than a description of wildflowers, but it was from Edward. He'd signed it

> *Devotedly,*
> *Capt. Edward Rokesby*

Devotedly.

Devotedly.

A silly smile had erupted across her face, and then she'd felt the veriest fool. She was mooning over a man she'd never even met.

A man she probably never *would* meet.

But she couldn't help it. It didn't matter if the summer sun was shining brightly across the lakes— with her brother gone, life in Derbyshire always seemed so gray. Her days rolled from one to the next, with almost no variation. She took care of the house, checked the budget, and tended to her father, not that he ever noticed. There was the occasional local assembly, but over half the men her age had bought commissions or enlisted, and the dance floor always contained twice the number of ladies as gentlemen.

So when the son of an earl wrote to her of wild-flowers . . .

Her heart did a little flip.

Honestly, it was the closest she'd got to a flirtation in years.

But when she had made the decision to travel to New York, it had been her brother, and not Edward Rokesby, that she had been thinking about. When that messenger had arrived with news from Thomas's commanding officer . . .

It had been the worst day of her life.

The letter had been addressed to her father, of course. Cecilia had thanked the messenger and made sure he was given something to eat, never once mentioning that Walter Harcourt had died unexpectedly three days earlier. She'd taken the folded envelope to her room, closed and locked the door, and then stared at it for a long, shaky minute before summoning the courage to slide her finger under the wax seal.

Her first emotion had been one of relief. She'd been so sure it was going to tell her that Thomas was dead, that there was no one left in the world she truly loved. An injury seemed almost a blessing at that point.

But then Cousin Horace had arrived.

Cecilia hadn't been surprised that he had shown up for her father's funeral. It was what one did, after all, even if one didn't enjoy particularly close friendships with one's relations. But then Horace had *stayed*. And by God, he was annoying. He did not speak so much as pontificate, and Cecilia couldn't take two steps without him sidling up behind her, expressing his deep worry for her well-being.

Worse, he kept making comments about Thomas, and how dangerous it was for a soldier in the colonies. Wouldn't they all be so relieved when he returned to his rightful place as owner of Marswell.

The unspoken message being, of course, that if he didn't return, Horace would inherit it all.

Bloody, stupid entail. Cecilia knew she was supposed to honor her forebearers, but by God, if she could go back in time and find her great-great-grandfather, she would wring his neck. He'd bought the land and built the house, and in his delusions of dynastic grandeur he'd imposed a strict entail. Marswell went from father to son, and if not that, any male cousin would do. Never mind that Cecilia had lived there her entire life, that she knew every nook and cranny, that the servants trusted and respected her. If Thomas died, Cousin Horace would swoop in from Lancashire and take it all away.

Cecilia had tried to keep him in the dark about Thomas's injury, but news like that was impossible to keep under wraps. Some well-meaning neighbor must have said something, because Horace didn't wait even a full day after the funeral before declaring that as Cecilia's closest male relative, he must assume responsibility for her welfare.

Clearly, he said, they must marry.

No, Cecilia had thought in shocked silence. *No, they really must not.*

"You must face facts," he said, taking a step toward her. "You are alone. You cannot remain indefinitely at Marswell without a chaperone."

"I shall go to my great-aunt," she said.

"Sophie?" he said dismissively. "She's hardly capable."

"My other great-aunt. Dorcas."

His eyes narrowed. "I am not familiar with an aunt Dorcas."

"You wouldn't be," Cecilia said. "She's my mother's aunt."

"And where does she live?"

Considering that she was wholly a figment of Cecilia's imagination, nowhere, but her mother's mother had been Scottish, so Cecilia said, "Edinburgh."

"You would leave your home?"

If it meant avoiding marriage to Horace, yes.

"I will make you see reason," Horace growled, and then before she knew what he was about, he kissed her.

Cecilia drew one breath after he released her, and then she slapped him.

Horace slapped her back, and a week later, Cecilia left for New York.

The journey had taken five weeks—more than enough time for Cecilia to second- and third-guess her decision. But she truly did not know what else she could have done. She wasn't sure why Horace was so dead-set on marrying her when he had a good chance of inheriting Marswell anyway. She could only speculate that he was having financial troubles and needed someplace to live. If he married Cecilia he could move in right away and cross his fingers that Thomas would never come home.

Cecilia knew that marriage to her cousin was the sensible choice. If Thomas did die, she would be able to remain at her beloved childhood home. She could pass it along to her children.

But oh dear God, those children would also be Horace's children, and the thought of lying with that man . . . Nay, the thought of *living* with that man . . .

She couldn't do it. Marswell wasn't worth it.

Still, her situation was tenuous. Horace couldn't actually force her to accept his suit, but he could make her life very uncomfortable, and he was right about one thing—she couldn't remain at Marswell indefinitely without a chaperone. She was of age—barely, at twenty-two—and her friends and neighbors would give her some leeway given her circumstances, but a young woman on her own was an invitation for gossip. If Cecilia had a care for her reputation, she was going to have to leave.

The irony was enough to make her want to scream. She was preserving her good name by taking off by herself across an ocean. All she had to do was make sure no one in Derbyshire knew about it.

But Thomas was her older brother, her protector, her closest friend. For him she would make a journey that even she knew was reckless, possibly fruitless. Men died of infection far more often than they did of battlefield injury. She knew her brother might be gone by the time she reached New York.

She just hadn't expected him to be *literally* gone.

It was during this maelstrom of frustration and helplessness that she heard of Edward's injury. Driven by a burning need to help *some*one, she had marched herself to the hospital. If she could not tend to her brother, by

God, she would tend to her brother's best friend. This voyage to the New World would not be for nothing.

The hospital turned out to be a church that had been taken over by the British Army, which was strange enough, but when she asked to see Edward, she was told in no uncertain terms that she was not welcome. Captain Rokesby was an officer, a rather sharp-nosed sentry informed her. He was the son of an earl, and far too important for visitors of the plebian variety.

Cecilia was still trying to figure out what the devil he meant by *that* when he looked down his nose and told her that the only people allowed to see Captain Rokesby would be military personnel and family.

At which point Cecilia blurted out, "I am his wife!"

And once *that* had come out of her mouth, there was really no backing away from it.

In retrospect, it was amazing she'd got away with it. She'd probably have been thrown out on her ear if not for the presence of Edward's commanding officer. Colonel Stubbs was not the most affable of men, but he knew of Edward and Thomas's friendship, and he had not been surprised to hear that Edward had married his friend's sister.

Before Cecilia even had a chance to think, she was spinning a tale of a courtship in letters, and a proxy marriage on a ship.

Astoundingly, everyone believed her.

She could not regret her lies, however. There was no denying that Edward had improved under her care. She'd sponged his forehead when he'd grown feverish, and she'd shifted his weight as best she could to prevent bedsores. It was true that she'd seen more of his body than was appropriate for an unmarried lady, but surely the rules of society must be suspended in wartime.

And no one would know.

No one would know. This, she repeated to herself on an almost hourly basis. She was five thousand miles from Derbyshire. Everyone she knew thought she'd gone off to visit her maiden aunt. Furthermore, the Harcourts did not move in the same circles as the Rokesbys. She supposed that Edward might be considered a person of interest among society gossips, but she certainly wasn't, and it seemed impossible that tales of the Earl of Manston's second son might reach her tiny village of Matlock Bath.

As for what she would do when he finally woke up . . .

Well, in all honesty, she'd never quite figured that out. But as it happened, it didn't matter. She'd run through a hundred different scenarios in her mind, but not one of them had involved him *recognizing* her.

"Cecilia?" he said. He was blinking up at her, and

she was momentarily stunned, mesmerized by how blue his eyes were.

She ought to have known that.

Then she realized how ridiculous she was being. She had no reason to know the color of his eyes.

But still. Somehow . . .

It seemed like something she should have known.

"You're awake," she said dumbly. She tried to say more, but the sound twisted in her throat. She fought simply to breathe, overcome with emotion she had not even realized she felt. With a shaking hand, she leaned down and touched his forehead. Why, she did not know; he had not had a fever for nearly two days. But she was overwhelmed by a need to touch him, to feel with her hands what she saw with her eyes.

He was awake.

He was *alive*.

"Give him room," Colonel Stubbs ordered. "Go fetch the doctor."

"*You* fetch the doctor," Cecilia snapped, finally regaining some of her sense. "I'm his w—"

Her voice caught. She couldn't utter the lie. Not in front of Edward.

But Colonel Stubbs inferred what she did not actually say, and after muttering something unsavory under his breath, he stalked off in search of a doctor.

"Cecilia?" Edward said again. "What are you doing here?"

"I'll explain everything in a moment," she said in a rushed whisper. The colonel would be back soon, and she'd rather not make her explanations with an audience. Still, she couldn't have him giving her away, so she added, "For now, just—"

"Where am I?" he interrupted.

She grabbed an extra blanket. He needed another pillow, but these were in short supply, so a blanket would have to do. Helping him to sit up a little straighter, she tucked it behind him as she said, "You're in hospital."

He looked dubiously around the room. The architecture was clearly ecclesiastical. "With a stained glass window?"

"It's a church. Well, it *was* a church. It's a hospital now."

"But where?" he asked, a little too urgently.

Her hands stilled. Something wasn't right. She turned her head, just enough for her eyes to meet his. "We are in New York Town."

He frowned. "I thought I was . . ."

She waited, but he did not finish his thought. "You thought you were what?" she asked.

He stared vacantly for a moment, then said, "I don't know. I was . . ." His words trailed off, and his face twisted. It almost looked as if it hurt him to think so hard.

"I was supposed to go to Connecticut," he finally said.

Cecilia slowly straightened. "You did go to Connecticut."

His lips parted. "I did?"

"Yes. You were there for over a month."

"What?" Something flashed in his eyes. Cecilia thought it might be fear.

"Don't you remember?" she asked.

He began to blink far more rapidly than was normal. "Over a month, you say?"

"That's what they told me. I only just arrived."

"Over a month," he said again. He started shaking his head. "How could that . . ."

"You must not overtax yourself," Cecilia said, reaching out to take his hand in hers again. It seemed to calm him. It certainly calmed her.

"I don't remember . . . I was in Connecticut?" He looked up sharply, and his grip on her hand grew uncomfortably tight. "How did I come to be back in New York?"

She gave a helpless shrug. She didn't have the answers he sought. "I don't know. I was looking for

Thomas, and I heard you were here. You were found near Kip's Bay, bleeding from your head."

"You were looking for Thomas," he echoed, and she could practically see the wheels of his mind spinning frantically behind his eyes. "Why were you looking for Thomas?"

"I'd got word he was injured, but now he's missing, and—"

Edward's breathing grew labored. "When were we married?"

Cecilia's lips parted. She tried to answer, she really did, but she could only manage to stammer a few useless pronouns. Did he actually think they were married? He'd never even *seen* her before this day.

"I don't remember," he said.

Cecilia chose her words carefully. "You don't remember what?"

He looked up at her with haunted eyes. "I don't know."

Cecilia knew she should try to comfort him, but she could only stare. His eyes were hollow, and his skin, already pallid from his illness, seemed to go almost gray. He gripped the bed as if it were a lifeboat, and she had the insane urge to do the same. The room was spinning around them, shrinking into a tight little tunnel.

She could barely breathe.

And he looked like he might shatter.

She forced her eyes to meet his, and she asked the only question that remained.

"Do you remember anything?"

Chapter 2

The barracks here at Hampton Court Palace are tolerable, more than tolerable, I suppose, although nothing to the comforts of home. The officers are housed two to a two-room apartment, so we have a bit of privacy. I have been assigned to live with another lieutenant, a fellow named Rokesby. He is the son of an earl, if you can believe that . . .

—FROM THOMAS HARCOURT
TO HIS SISTER CECILIA

Edward fought to breathe. His heart felt as if it were trying to claw its way out of his chest, and all he could think was that he had to get off this cot. He had to figure out what was going on. He had to—

"Stop," Cecilia cried, throwing herself on him in an effort to keep him down. "You must calm yourself."

"Let me up," he argued, although some tiny rational part of his mind was trying to remind him that he didn't know where to go.

"Please," she begged, transferring her weight to her grip on each of his wrists. "Take a moment, catch your breath."

He looked up at her, chest heaving. "What is happening?"

She swallowed and glanced about. "I think we should wait for the doctor."

But he was far too agitated to listen. "What day is this?" he demanded.

She blinked, as if taken off guard. "Friday."

"The *date*," he bit off.

She didn't answer right away. When she did, her words were slow, careful. "It is the twenty-fifth day of June."

Edward's heart started pounding anew. "What?"

"If you will only wait for—"

"It cannot be." Edward shoved himself into a more upright position. "You are wrong."

She shook her head slowly. "I'm not wrong."

"No. No." He looked frantically about the room. "Colonel!" he yelled. "Doctor! Anyone!"

"Edward, stop!" she cried, moving to block him when he flung his legs over the side of the bed. "Please, wait for the doctor to see you!"

"You there!" he ordered, pointing a shaky arm toward a dark-skinned man sweeping the floor. "What day is it?"

The man looked to Cecilia with wide eyes, silently asking for guidance.

"What day is it?" Edward said again. "The month. Tell me the month."

Again, the man's eyes flicked to Cecilia's, but he answered, "It is June, sir. End of the month."

"No," Edward said, falling back to the bed. "No."

He closed his eyes, trying to force his thoughts through the pounding in his skull. There had to be a way to fix this. If he just concentrated hard enough, focused on the last thing he could remember . . .

He snapped his eyes back open and looked straight at Cecilia. "I don't remember you."

Her throat worked, and Edward knew he should be ashamed of himself for bringing her so close to tears. She was a lady. She was his *wife*. But surely she would forgive him. He had to know . . . he had to understand what was happening.

"You said my name," she whispered, "when you woke up."

"I know who you are," he said. "I just don't know *you*."

Her face trembled as she rose to her feet, and she tucked a lock of her hair behind her ear before clasping her hands together. She was nervous, that much was easy to see. And then the most disjointed thought popped into his head—she didn't look very much like that miniature her brother carried about. Her mouth was wide and full, nothing like that sweet, mysterious half moon in her portrait. And her hair wasn't golden either, at least not the heavenly shade rendered by the painter. It was more of a dark blond. Rather like Thomas's, actually, although not quite as shot through with brass.

He supposed she didn't spend as much time in the sun.

"You are Cecilia Harcourt, aren't you?" he asked. Because it had just occurred to him—she had never actually confirmed this fact.

She nodded. "Yes, of course."

"And you're here, in New York." He stared at her, searching her face. "Why?"

He saw her eyes flick toward the other side of the room, even as she gave her head a little shake. "It's complicated."

"But we're married." He wasn't sure whether he'd said it as a statement or a question.

He wasn't sure if he wanted it to be a statement or a question.

She sat warily on the bed. Edward didn't blame her for her hesitance. He'd been thrashing about like a trapped animal. She must be quite strong to have been able to subdue him.

Or else he'd become quite weak.

Cecilia swallowed, looking very much as if she were steeling herself for something difficult. "I need to tell you—"

"*What is going on?*"

She jerked back, and they both looked over at Colonel Stubbs, who was stalking across the chapel with the doctor in tow.

"Why are the blankets on the floor?" the colonel demanded.

Cecilia rose once again to her feet, moving aside so that the doctor could take her place at Edward's side. "He was struggling," she said. "He's confused."

"I'm not confused," Edward snapped.

The doctor looked at her. Edward wanted to grab him by the throat. Why was he looking at Cecilia? *He* was the patient.

"He seems to be missing . . ." Cecilia caught her lip between her teeth, her eyes flitting back and forth between Edward and the doctor. She didn't know what to say. Edward couldn't blame her.

"Mrs. Rokesby?" the doctor prodded.

There it was again. *Mrs. Rokesby.* He was married. How the hell was he married?

"Well," she said helplessly, trying to find the correct words for an impossible situation. "I think he doesn't remember, ehrm . . ."

"Spit it out, woman," Colonel Stubbs barked.

Edward was half out of the bed before he realized what he was about. "Your *tone*, Colonel," he growled.

"No, no," Cecilia said quickly. "It's all right. He means no disrespect. We are all frustrated."

Edward snorted and would have rolled his eyes except she chose that moment to lay a gentle hand on his shoulder. His shirt was thin, almost threadbare, and he could feel the soft ridges and contours of her fingers settling against him with cool, quiet strength.

It calmed him. His temper did not magically evaporate, but he was able to take a long, even breath—just enough to keep himself from going for the colonel's throat.

"He was not sure of the date," Cecilia said, her voice

gaining in certitude. "I believe he thought it was . . ." She looked over at Edward.

"Not June," he said sharply.

The doctor frowned and took Edward's wrist, nodding as he counted his pulse. When he was through he looked first into one of Edward's eyes and then the other.

"My eyes are fine," Edward muttered.

"What is the last thing you remember, Captain Rokesby?" the doctor asked.

Edward opened his mouth, fully intending to answer the question, but his mind stretched before him like an endless expanse of gray misty air. He was on the ocean, the steel blue water unnaturally calm. Not a ripple, not a wave.

Not a thought or memory.

He grabbed the bedsheets in frustration. How the hell was he supposed to recover his memory if he wasn't even sure what he *did* remember?

"Try, Rokesby," Colonel Stubbs said gruffly.

"I *am* trying," Edward snapped. Did they think he was an idiot? That he didn't care? They had no idea what was going on in his head, what it felt like to have a huge blank space where memories ought to be.

"I don't know," he finally said. He needed to get

ahold of himself. He was a soldier; he had been trained to be calm in the face of danger. "I think . . . maybe . . . I was supposed to go to Connecticut Colony."

"You did go to Connecticut Colony," Colonel Stubbs said. "Do you remember?"

Edward shook his head. He tried . . . he wanted to . . . but there was nothing. Just the vague idea that someone had asked him to go.

"It was an important journey," the colonel pressed. "There is much we need you to tell us."

"Well, that's not likely now, is it?" Edward said bitterly.

"Please, you must not put such pressure on him," Cecilia intervened. "He's only just woken up."

"Your concern does you credit," Colonel Stubbs said, "but these are matters of vital military importance, and they cannot be put aside for an aching head." He glanced over at a nearby soldier and jerked his head toward the door. "Escort Mrs. Rokesby outside. She may return once we finish questioning the captain."

Oh no. *That* was not happening. "My wife will remain by my side," Edward bit off.

"She cannot be party to such sensitive information."

"That's hardly an issue, since I have nothing to tell you."

Cecilia stepped between the colonel and the bed. "You must give him time to regain his memory."

"Mrs. Rokesby is correct," the doctor said. "Cases such as this are rare, but it is very likely he will regain most, if not all, of his memories."

"When?" Colonel Stubbs demanded.

"I cannot say. In the meantime, we must afford him all the peace and quiet that is possible under such difficult circumstances."

"No," Edward said, because peace and quiet was the last thing he needed. This had to be like everything else in his life. If you wanted to excel, you worked hard, you trained, you practiced.

You didn't lie in bed, hoping for a bit of peace and quiet.

He looked over at Cecilia. She knew him. He might not remember her face, but they had exchanged letters for over a year. *She knew him.* She knew that he could not lie about and do nothing.

"Cecilia," he said, "surely you must understand."

"I think the doctor must be correct," she said quietly. "If you would only rest . . ."

But Edward was already shaking his head. They were wrong, all of them. They didn't—

God*damn* it.

A searing pain shot through his skull.

"What is wrong?" Cecilia cried. Edward's last sight before squeezing his eyes shut was her looking frantically toward the doctor. "What is happening to him?"

"My head," Edward gasped. He must have shaken it too quickly. It felt as if his brain were slamming into his skull.

"Are you remembering something?" Colonel Stubbs asked.

"No, you bloody—" Edward cut himself off before he called him something unforgivable. "It just *hurts*."

"That's enough," Cecilia declared. "I will not permit you to question him any further."

"You will not *permit* me?" Colonel Stubbs countered. "I am his commanding officer."

It was a pity that Edward could not bring himself to open his eyes, because he would really have liked to have seen the colonel's face when Cecilia said, "You are not *my* commanding officer."

"If I might intervene," the doctor said.

Edward heard someone step aside, and then he felt the mattress dip as the doctor sat beside him.

"Can you open your eyes?"

Edward shook his head, slowly this time. It felt as if the only way to fight the pain was to keep his eyes tightly closed.

"It can be like this with a head injury," the doctor said gently. "They can take time to heal, and are often very painful in the process. I'm afraid it does no help to rush things."

"I understand," Edward said. He did not like it, but he understood.

"That's more than we physicians can claim," the doctor replied. His voice was a bit quieter, as if he'd turned to speak to someone else. "There is much we do not know about injuries to the brain. In fact, I'd wager what we don't know far outweighs that which we do."

Edward did not find this reassuring.

"Your wife has cared for you most diligently," the doctor said, patting Edward's arm. "I recommend that she continue to do so, if possible out of hospital."

"Out of hospital?" Cecilia echoed.

Edward still hadn't opened his eyes, but he heard a note of panic in her voice.

"He is no longer feverish," the doctor said to her, "and the wound on his head is healing well. I see no sign of infection."

Edward touched his head and winced.

"I wouldn't do that," the doctor said.

Edward finally pried his eyes open and looked down at his fingers. He'd half expected to see blood.

"I can't remove him from hospital," Cecilia said.

"You will be just fine," the doctor said reassuringly. "He cannot hope for better care than from his wife."

"No," she said, "you don't understand. I have no place to take him."

"Where are you staying now?" Edward asked. He was suddenly reminded that she was his wife, and he was responsible for her well-being and safety.

"I've rented a room. It's not far. But there is only the one bed."

For the first time since he'd woken up, Edward felt the beginnings of a smile.

"The one small bed," she clarified. "It hardly fits me. Your feet will hang over the side." And then, when no one said anything fast enough to stave off her palpable unease, she added, "It is a boardinghouse for women. He would not be allowed."

Edward turned to Colonel Stubbs with rising disbelief. "My wife has been staying in a boardinghouse?"

"We didn't know she was here," the colonel replied.

"You've obviously known for three days."

"She was already situated . . ."

A hard, cold fury began to rise within him. Edward knew the nature of the women's boardinghouses in New York Town. It didn't matter if he could not recall the wedding, Cecilia was his *wife*.

And the army let her stay in such questionable lodg-ings?

Edward had been raised a gentleman—a *Rokesby*—and there were some insults that could not be borne. He forgot the pain in his skull, forgot even that he'd lost his bloody memory. All he knew was that his wife, the woman he was sworn to cherish and protect, had been badly neglected by the very band of brothers to whom he had devoted the last three years.

His voice was diamond hard when he said, "You will find her alternate lodgings."

Stubbs's brows rose. They both knew who was the colonel and who was merely the captain.

But Edward was undeterred. He had spent most of his military career playing down his noble lineage, but in this, he had no such reservations.

"This woman," he said, "is the Honorable Mrs. Edward Rokesby."

Colonel Stubbs opened his mouth to speak, but Edward would not allow it. "She is my wife and the daughter-in-law of the Earl of Manston," he contin-ued, his voice icing over with generations of aristocratic breeding. "She does not belong in a boardinghouse."

Cecilia, obviously uncomfortable, tried to intervene. "I have been perfectly well," she said quickly. "I assure you."

"I am not assured," Edward responded, never taking his eyes off Colonel Stubbs.

"We will find her more suitable lodgings," Colonel Stubbs said grudgingly.

"Tonight," Edward clarified.

The look on the colonel's face said clearly that he found this to be an unreasonable request, but after a tense moment of silence he said, "We can put her in the Devil's Head."

Edward nodded. The Devil's Head Inn catered primarily to British officers and was considered the finest establishment of its kind in New York Town. This wasn't saying much, but short of installing Cecilia in a private home, Edward couldn't think of anyplace better. New York was desperately overcrowded, and it seemed that half the army's resources went to finding places for its men to sleep. The Devil's Head would not have been suitable for a lady traveling alone, but as the wife of an officer, Cecilia would be safe and respected.

"Montby leaves tomorrow," Colonel Stubbs said. "His room is big enough for you both."

"Move him in with another officer," Edward ordered. "She needs a room tonight."

"Tomorrow will be fine," Cecilia said.

Edward ignored her. "*Tonight.*"

Colonel Stubbs nodded. "I'll speak to Montby."

Edward gave another curt nod. He knew Captain Montby. He, like all the officers, would give up his room in a heartbeat if it meant the safety of a gentlewoman.

"In the meantime," the doctor said, "he must remain calm and sedate." He turned to Cecilia. "He must not be upset in any way."

"It is difficult to imagine being more upset than I am right now," Edward said.

The doctor smiled. "It is a very good sign that you retain your sense of humor."

Edward decided not to point out that he had not been making a joke.

"We shall have you out of here by tomorrow," Colonel Stubbs said briskly. He turned to Cecilia. "In the meantime, fill him in on all he has missed. Perhaps it will jog his memory."

"An excellent idea," the doctor said. "I am sure your husband will want to know how you came to be here in New York, Mrs. Rokesby."

Cecilia tried to smile. "Of course, sir."

"And remember, do not upset him." The doctor tipped an indulgent glance toward Edward and added, "Further."

Colonel Stubbs spoke briefly to Cecilia about her move to the Devil's Head, and then the two men departed, leaving Edward once again alone with his wife. Well, alone as one could be in a church full of sick soldiers.

He looked at Cecilia, standing awkwardly near his bed.

His wife. Bloody hell.

He still didn't understand how it had come to pass, but it must be true. Colonel Stubbs seemed to believe it, and he'd always been a by-the-book sort of man. Plus, this was Cecilia Harcourt, sister of his closest friend. If he was going to find himself married to a woman he didn't think he'd actually met, he supposed she would be the one.

Still, it seemed like the sort of thing he'd remember.

"When were we wed?" he asked.

She was staring off toward the far end of the transept. He wasn't sure if she was listening.

"Cecilia?"

"A few months ago," she said, turning back around to face him. "You should sleep."

"I'm not tired."

"No?" She gave a wobbly smile as she settled into the chair next to his bed. "I'm exhausted."

"I am sorry," he said instantly. He felt like he should rise. Give her his hand.

Be a gentleman.

"I did not think," he said.

"You have not had much opportunity to do so," she said in a dry voice.

His lips parted with surprise, and then he thought—*there* was the Cecilia Harcourt he knew so well. Or thought he knew so well. Truth be told, he could not recall ever having seen her face. But she sounded just like her letters, and he had held her words close to his heart during the worst of the war.

Sometimes he wondered if it was strange that he had looked forward to her letters to Thomas more than he did the ones coming to him from his own family.

"Forgive me," she said. "I have a most inappropriate sense of humor."

"I like it," he said.

She looked over at him, and he thought he saw something a little grateful in her eyes.

Such an interesting color, they were. A seafoam green so pale she would surely have been called fey in another era. Which seemed somehow wrong; she was as down-to-earth and reliable as any person he'd ever met.

Or thought he'd met.

She touched her cheek self-consciously. "Have I something on my face?"

"Just looking at you," he said.

"There is not much to see."

This made him smile. "I must disagree."

She flushed, and he realized he was flirting with his wife. Strange.

And yet possibly the least strange thing of the day.

"I wish I remembered . . ." he began.

She looked at him.

He wished he remembered meeting her for the first time. He wished he remembered their wedding.

He wished he remembered kissing her.

"Edward?" she said softly.

"Everything," he said, the word coming out with a little more edge than he'd intended. "I wish I remembered everything."

"I'm sure you will." She smiled tightly, but there was something wrong about it. It didn't reach her eyes, and then he realized that *she* hadn't met *his* eyes. He wondered what she wasn't telling him. Had someone told her more about his condition than she had shared with him? He didn't know when they could have done so; she had not left his side since he'd awakened.

"You look like Thomas," he said abruptly.

"Do you think so?" She gave him a puzzled look. "No one else seems to. Well, except for the hair." She touched it then, probably without even realizing she'd done so. It had been pulled back into an inexpertly pinned bun, and the bits that had fallen out hung limply against her cheek. He wondered how long it was, how it might look against her back.

"I favor our mother," she said. "Or so I've been told. I never knew her. Thomas is more like our father."

Edward shook his head. "It's not in the features. It is your expressions."

"I beg your pardon?"

"Yes, right there!" He grinned, feeling a bit more alive than he had just a moment earlier. "You make the same expressions. When you said, 'I beg your pardon,' you tilted your head exactly the same way he does."

She quirked a smile. "Does he beg your pardon so very often?"

"Not nearly as much as he should."

She burst out laughing at that. "Oh, thank you," she said, wiping her eyes. "I haven't laughed since . . ." She shook her head. "I can't remember when."

He reached out and took her hand. "You haven't had much to laugh about," he said quietly.

Her throat worked as she nodded, and for one awful moment Edward thought she might cry. But still, he knew he could not remain silent. "What happened to Thomas?" he asked.

She took a deep breath, then slowly exhaled. "I received word that he had been injured and was recuperating in New York Town. I was concerned—well, you can see for yourself," she said, waving a hand toward the rest of the room. "There are not enough people to nurse the wounded soldiers. I did not want my brother to be alone."

Edward considered this. "I am surprised your father allowed you to make the trip."

"My father has died."

Bloody hell. "I am sorry," he said. "It seems my tact has departed along with my memory." Although in truth, he could not have known. Her dress was pink, and she showed no signs of mourning.

She caught him eyeing the dusty rose fabric of her sleeve. "I know," she said with a sheepish pout to her lower lip. "I should be in blacks. But I only had the one dress, and it was wool bombazine. I should roast like a chicken if I wore it here."

"Our uniforms are rather uncomfortable in the summer months," Edward agreed.

"Indeed. Thomas had said as much in his letters. It was because of his descriptions of the summer temperatures that I knew not to bring it."

"I am sure you are more fetching in pink," Edward said.

She blinked at the compliment. He could not blame her. The sheer ordinariness of it seemed oddly out of place considering their location in a hospital.

In a church.

In the middle of a war.

Add in his lost memory and found wife, and truly, he did not see how his life might get any more bizarre.

"Thank you," Cecilia said, before clearing her throat and continuing with "But you asked about my father. You are correct. He would not have permitted me to travel to New York. He was not the most conscientious of parents, but even he would have put his foot down. Although . . ." She let out a little choke of uncomfortable laughter. "I'm not sure how quickly he would have noticed my absence."

"I assure you, anyone would notice your absence."

She gave him a sideways sort of look. "You haven't met my father. As long as the house is—excuse me, was—running smoothly, he wouldn't have noticed a thing."

Edward nodded slowly. Thomas had not said a lot about Walter Harcourt, but what he had seemed to confirm Cecilia's description. He'd complained more than once that their father was too content to let Cecilia molder away as his unpaid housekeeper. She needed to find someone to marry, Thomas had said. She needed to leave Marswell and make a life of her own.

Had Thomas been playing matchmaker? Edward hadn't thought so at the time.

"Was it an accident?" Edward asked.

"No, but it was a surprise. He was napping in his study." She gave a sad little shrug. "He didn't wake up."

"His heart?"

"The doctor said there was no way to know for certain. It doesn't matter, though, really, does it?" She looked over at him with an achingly wise expression, and Edward could have sworn he *felt* it. There was something about her eyes, the color, the clarity. When they met his, he felt as if the breath was sucked from his body.

Would it always be like this?

Was this why he'd married her?

"You look tired," she said, adding before he could interrupt, "I know you said you're not, but you *look* it."

But he didn't want to sleep. He couldn't bear the thought of allowing his mind to slip back into unconsciousness. He'd lost too much time already. He needed it back. Every moment. Every memory.

"You didn't say what happened to Thomas," he reminded her.

A wave of worry washed over her face. "I don't know," she said with a choke in her voice. "No one seems to know where he is."

"How is that possible?"

She gave a helpless shrug.

"You spoke to Colonel Stubbs?"

"Of course."

"General Garth?"

"They would not permit me to see him."

"What?" This was not to be borne. "As my wife—"

"I did not tell them I was your wife."

He stared at her. "Why the hell not?"

"I don't know." She jumped up from her seat, hugging her arms to her body. "I think I was just—well, I was there as Thomas's sister."

"But surely when you gave your name."

She caught her lower lip between her teeth before saying, "I don't think anyone made the connection."

"General Garth did not realize that Mrs. Edward Rokesby was my wife?"

"Well, I told you I didn't see him." She moved back to his side, busying herself with tucking his blankets around him. "You're getting too upset. We can talk about this tomorrow."

"We *will* talk about this tomorrow," he growled.

"Or the next day."

His eyes met hers.

"Depending on your health."

"Cecilia—"

"I will brook no argument," she cut in. "I may not be able to do anything for my brother just now, but I can help you. And if that means forcing you to hold your bloody horses . . ."

He stared at her, drinking her in. Her jaw was set, and she had one foot slightly forward, as if ready to charge. He could almost imagine her brandishing a sword, waving it above her head with a battle cry.

She was Joan of Arc. She was Boudicca. She was every woman who'd ever fought to protect her family.

"My fierce warrior," he murmured.

She gave him a look.

He didn't apologize.

"I should go," she said abruptly. "Colonel Stubbs is sending someone to collect me this evening. I need to pack my things."

He wasn't sure how many things she'd managed to collect since arriving in North America, but Edward knew better than to get between a woman and her traveling trunk.

"You will be all right without me?"

He nodded.

This made her frown. "You wouldn't tell me if you thought otherwise, would you?"

He gave her a quirk of a smile. "Of course not."

This made her roll her eyes. "I will be back in the morning."

"I look forward to it."

And he did. He couldn't remember the last time he looked forward to something more.

Of course, he couldn't remember anything.

But still.

Chapter 3

The son of an earl? La-di-da, how you have come up in the world, my brother. I hope he is not unbearable about it.

—FROM CECILIA HARCOURT TO

HER BROTHER THOMAS

Several hours later, as Cecilia followed the cheerful young lieutenant who had been dispatched to escort her to the Devil's Head, she wondered when her heart might finally stop pounding. Dear heavens, how many lies had she told this afternoon? She had tried to keep her answers as close to the truth as possible, both to ease her conscience and because she had no idea how else to keep track of it all.

She should have told Edward the truth. She'd been about to, honestly, but then Colonel Stubbs had returned with the doctor. There was no way she was going to make her confession with *that* audience. She would have been booted from the hospital for certain, and Edward still needed her.

She still needed him.

She was alone in a very strange land. She was almost out of funds. And now that her reason for holding herself together had woken up, she could finally admit to herself—she was scared out of her mind.

If Edward repudiated her she'd be soon in the streets. She'd have no choice but to go back to England, and she couldn't do that, not without discovering what had happened to her brother. She had sacrificed so much to make this journey. It had taken every ounce of her courage. She could not give up now.

But how could she continue to lie to him? Edward Rokesby was a good man. He did not deserve to be taken advantage of in such a brazen manner. Furthermore, he was Thomas's closest friend. The two men had met when they had first entered the army, and as officers in the same regiment, they'd been sent over to North America at the same time. As far as Cecilia knew, they had served together ever since.

She knew that Edward felt kindly toward her. If she told him the truth, surely he'd understand why she'd lied. He would want to help her. Wouldn't he?

But all this was neither here nor there. Or at the very least it could be put off until the following day. The Devil's Head was just down the street, and with it the promise of a warm bed and a filling meal. Surely she deserved that much.

Goal for today: Don't feel guilty. At least not for eating a proper meal.

"Almost there," the lieutenant said with a smile.

Cecilia gave him a nod. New York was such a strange place. According to the woman who'd run her boardinghouse, there were more than twenty thousand people crowded into what was not a very large area at the southern tip of Manhattan Island. Cecilia wasn't sure what the population had been before the war, but she'd been told that numbers had surged once the British had taken over the city as their headquarters. Scarlet-clad soldiers were everywhere, and every available building had been pressed into service to house them. Supporters of the Continental Congress had long since left town, but they had been replaced and more by a rush of Loyalist refugees who'd fled neighboring colonies in search of British protection.

But the strangest sight—to Cecilia, at least—were the Negroes. She had never seen people with such dark skin before, and she'd been startled by how many of them there were in the bustling port town.

"Escaped slaves," the lieutenant said, following Cecilia's gaze to the dark-skinned man coming out of the blacksmith's shop across the street.

"I beg your pardon?"

"They've been coming up here by the hundreds," the lieutenant said with a shrug. "General Clinton freed them all last month, but no one in Patriot territories is obeying the order, so their slaves have been running away to us." He frowned. "Not sure we've got room for them, to be honest. But you can't blame a man for wanting to be free."

"No," Cecilia murmured, glancing back over her shoulder. When she turned back to the lieutenant, he was already at the entrance to the Devil's Head Inn.

"Here we are," he said, holding the door for her.

"Thank you." She stepped in and then out of his way so that he might locate the innkeeper. Clutching her meager valise in front of her, Cecilia took in the main room of the inn and public house. It looked very much like its British counterparts—dimly lit, a bit too crowded, and with sticky bits on the floor that Cecilia chose to believe were ale. A buxom young woman moved swiftly between the tables, deftly setting down mugs with one hand as she cleared dishes with the other. Behind the bar a man with a bushy mustache fiddled with the tap on a barrel, cursing when it seemed to jam up.

It would have felt like home had not almost every seat been filled with scarlet-clad soldiers.

There were a few ladies among their ranks, and from their clothing and demeanor Cecilia assumed they were respectable. Officers' wives, maybe? She'd heard that some women had accompanied their husbands to the New World. She supposed she was one of them now, for at least one more day.

"Miss Harcourt!"

Startled, Cecilia turned toward a table in the middle of the room. One of the soldiers—a man of middling years with thinning brown hair—was rising to his feet. "Miss Harcourt," he repeated. "It is a surprise to see you here."

Her lips parted. She knew this man. She *detested* this man. He was the first person she'd sought out in her quest to find Thomas, and he'd been the most con-descending and unhelpful of the bunch.

"Major Wilkins," she said, bobbing a polite curtsy even as her mind was whirring with unease. More lies. She needed to come up with more lies, and quickly.

"Are you well?" he asked in his customary brusque voice.

"I am." She glanced over at the lieutenant, who was now conferring with another soldier. "Thank you for asking."

"I had assumed you would be planning your return to England."

She gave him a little smile and a shrug in lieu of a reply. Truly, she did not wish to speak with him. And she had never given him any indication that she planned to leave New York.

"Mrs. Rokesby! Ah, there you are."

Saved by the young lieutenant, Cecilia thought gratefully. He was making his way back to her side, a large brass key in his hand.

"I spoke to the innkeeper," he said, "and to—"

"Mrs. Rokesby?" Major Wilkins interjected.

The lieutenant snapped to attention when he saw the major. "Sir," he said.

Wilkins brushed him off. "Did he call you Mrs. Rokesby?"

"Is that not your name?" the lieutenant asked.

Cecilia fought against the fist that seemed to be closing around her heart. "I—"

The major turned back to her with a frown. "I thought you to be unmarried."

"I was," she blurted out. "I mean—" Damn it, that wasn't going to hold water. She couldn't have got herself married in the last three days. "I was. Some time ago. I was unmarried. We all were. I mean, if one is married now, one once was un—"

She didn't even bother to finish. Good God, she sounded the worst sort of ninny. She was giving women everywhere a bad name.

"Mrs. Rokesby is married to Captain Rokesby," the lieutenant said helpfully.

Major Wilkins turned to her with a thunderous expression. "Captain *Edward* Rokesby?"

Cecilia nodded. As far as she knew, there was no other Captain Rokesby, but as she was already tripping over her falsehoods, she deemed it best not to try to score a point with a snide comment.

"Why the h—" He cleared his throat. "I beg your pardon. Why did you not say so?"

Cecilia recalled her conversation with Edward. *Stick to the same lies,* she reminded herself. "I was inquiring about my brother," she explained. "It seemed the more important relationship."

The major looked at her as if she'd lost her mind. Cecilia knew very well what he was thinking. Edward Rokesby was the son of an earl. She'd have to be an idiot not to press *that* connection.

There was a heavy beat of silence while the major blinked his expression back into something approaching respectful, then he cleared his throat and said, "I was very glad to hear that your husband had returned to New York." His brows drew together with some suspicion. "He was missing for some time, was he not?"

The implication being: Why hadn't she been searching for her *husband*?

Cecilia injected a bit of steel into her spine. "I was already aware of his safe return when I came to you about Thomas." It wasn't true, but he didn't need to know that.

"I see." He had the grace to look at least a little ashamed. "I beg your pardon."

Cecilia gave him a regal nod, the sort, she thought, that might be employed by a countess. Or a countess's daughter-in-law.

Major Wilkins cleared his throat, then said, "I will make further inquiries about your brother's whereabouts."

"Further?" Cecilia echoed. She had not been under the impression that he had made *any* inquiries thus far.

He flushed. "Will your husband be out of hospital soon?"

"Tomorrow."

"Tomorrow, you say?"

"Yes," she said slowly, just barely resisting the urge to add, "As I just said."

"And will you be staying here at the Devil's Head?"

"Captain and Mrs. Rokesby are taking over Captain Montby's room," the lieutenant supplied helpfully.

"Ah, good of him. Good man, good man."

"I do hope we are not inconveniencing him," Cecilia said. She glanced toward the tables, wondering if the displaced Captain Montby was seated at one. "I should like to thank him if possible."

"He's happy to do it," Major Wilkins declared, even though there was no way he could have known this for certain.

"Well," Cecilia said, trying not to gaze longingly at the stairs she assumed led up to her bedchamber. "It was very nice to see you, but I have had a very long day."

"Of course," the major said. He bowed crisply. "I shall report back tomorrow."

"Report . . . back?"

"With news of your brother. Or if not that, then at least an accounting of our inquiries."

"Thank you," Cecilia said, startled by his newfound solicitude.

Major Wilkins turned to the lieutenant. "What time do you expect Captain Rokesby tomorrow?"

Really? He was asking the *lieutenant*? "Sometime in the afternoon," Cecilia said sharply, even though she had no idea what time she planned to fetch him. She waited for Major Wilkins to turn to her before adding, "The lieutenant is unlikely to have special knowledge of the matter."

"She's quite right," the lieutenant said cheerfully. "My orders were to escort Mrs. Rokesby to her new accommodations. Tomorrow I'm back up to Haarlem."

Cecilia gave Major Wilkins a bland smile.

"Of course," the major said gruffly. "Forgive me, Mrs. Rokesby."

"Think nothing of it," Cecilia said. Much as she'd like to box the major's ears, she knew she could not afford to alienate him. She was not certain of his precise job, but he seemed to be in charge of keeping track of the soldiers currently billeted nearby.

"Will you and Captain Rokesby be here at half five?" he asked.

She looked him squarely in the eye. "If you are coming with news of my brother, then yes, we will most definitely be here."

"Very well. Good evening, ma'am." He executed a sharp bow of his chin, and then said to her escort, "Lieutenant."

Major Wilkins returned to his table, leaving Cecilia

with the lieutenant, who let out a little *oh* before saying, "I almost forgot. Your key."

"Thank you," Cecilia said, taking it from him. She turned it over in her hand.

"Room twelve," the lieutenant said.

"Yes," Cecilia said, glancing down at the large "12" etched into the metal. "I will see myself up."

The lieutenant gave a grateful nod; he was young and clearly uncomfortable with the idea of escorting a lady to her bedchamber, even a married one such as she.

Married. Dear God. How was she going to extricate herself from this web of lies? And perhaps more importantly, *when*? It wouldn't be tomorrow. She might have claimed to be Edward's wife so that she could remain by his side and nurse him to health, but it was clear—appallingly so—that the wife of Captain Rokesby held far more sway with Major Wilkins than the humble Miss Harcourt.

Cecilia knew that she owed it to Edward to end this farce as soon as possible, but her brother's fate hung in the balance.

She would tell him the truth. Obviously.

Eventually.

She just couldn't do it tomorrow. Tomorrow she had to be Mrs. Rokesby. And after that . . .

Cecilia sighed as she slipped the key into the lock of

her room and turned. She feared she was going to have to be Mrs. Rokesby until she found her brother.

"Forgive me," she whispered.

It would have to be enough.

Edward had every intention of being upright, in uniform, and ready to depart when Cecilia arrived at the hospital the following day. Instead he was in bed, wearing the same shirt he'd been in for he-truly-did-not-know-how-long, and sleeping so soundly Cecilia apparently thought he'd slipped back into a coma.

"Edward?" he heard, her voice whispering at the edges of his consciousness. "Edward?"

He mumbled something. Or maybe he grumbled it. He wasn't sure what the difference was. Attitude, probably.

"Oh, thank God," she whispered, and he sensed, rather than heard, her settle back into the chair next to his bed.

He should probably wake up.

Maybe he would open his eyes and the whole world would be restored to him. It would be June, and it would make sense that it was June. He would be married, and that would make sense too, especially if he remembered what it felt like to kiss her.

Because he'd really like to kiss her. It was all he'd

thought about the night before. Or at least most. Half, at least. He was as randy as the next man, especially now that he was married to Cecilia Harcourt, but he also had a working sense of smell, and what he really wanted was to take a bath.

God help him, he stank.

He lay still for a few minutes, his mind resting serenely behind his closed eyelids. There was something rather pleasant about unmoving reflection. He didn't have to do anything but think. He could not recall the last time he'd enjoyed such a luxury.

And yes, he was well aware that he could not recall anything of the last three or so months. He was still quite certain he had not spent it sifting peacefully through his own thoughts, listening to the muffled sounds of his wife beside him. He was reminded of those moments the day before, the ones right before he'd opened his eyes. He'd heard her breathing then, too. It was different, though, now that he knew who she was. It sounded the same, but it was different.

It was strange, really. He would never have believed that he'd one day be content to lie in bed and listen to a woman breathe. She emitted more sighs than he would have liked, though. She was tired. Maybe worried. Probably both.

He should tell her he was awake. It was past time.

But then he heard her murmur, "What am I to do with you?"

Honestly, he couldn't resist. He opened his eyes. "With me?"

She shrieked, jumping so far out of her chair it was a wonder she didn't hit the ceiling.

Edward started to laugh. Big belly laughs that hurt his ribs and squeezed his lungs, and even as Cecilia glared at him, her hand over her obviously racing heart, he laughed and laughed.

And just like before, he knew that this was not something he'd done in a very long while.

"You're awake," his wife accused.

"I wasn't," he said, "but then someone started whispering my name."

"That was *ages* ago."

He shrugged, unrepentant.

"You look better today," she said.

He lifted his brows.

"A little less . . . gray."

He decided to be grateful no one had offered him a looking glass. "I need to shave," he said, rubbing his chin. How many days' growth was this? At least two weeks. Probably closer to three. He frowned.

"What is it?" she asked.

"Does anyone know how long I was unconscious?"

She shook her head. "I don't think so. No one knows how long you were unconscious before you were found, but I can't imagine it was very long. They said the wound on your head was fresh."

He winced. *Fresh* was the sort of word one liked when applied to strawberries, not skulls.

"So probably not more than eight days," she concluded. "Why?"

"My beard," he said. "It has been far more than a week since I last shaved."

She stared at him for a moment. "I'm not sure what that means," she finally said.

"Nor I," he admitted. "But it's worth taking note of it."

"Have you a valet?"

He gave her a look.

"Don't look at me that way. I know very well that many officers travel with a manservant."

"I do not."

A moment passed, then Cecilia said, "You must be very hungry. I got a bit of broth into you, but that's all."

Edward placed a hand on his midsection. His hipbones were definitely more prominent than they'd been since childhood. "I seem to have lost some weight."

"Did you eat after I left yesterday?"

"Not much. I was famished, but then I started to feel ill."

She nodded, glancing down at her hands before saying, "I did not have the opportunity to tell you yesterday, but I took the liberty of writing to your family."

His family. Holy God above. He had not even thought of them.

His eyes met hers.

"They had been informed that you had gone missing," she explained. "General Garth wrote to them several months ago."

Edward put a hand to his face, covering his eyes. He could only imagine his mother. She would not have taken it well.

"I wrote that you had been injured, but I did not go into detail," she said. "I thought it most important that they know you had been found."

"Found," Edward echoed. The word was apt. He had not been returned, nor had he escaped. Instead he had been found near Kip's Bay. The devil only knew how he'd got there.

"When did you arrive in New York?" he asked abruptly. Better to ask questions about what he did not know than to agonize over what he did not remember.

"Almost a fortnight ago," she said.

"You came looking for me?"

"No," she admitted. "I didn't—that is to say, I would not be so foolish to cross an ocean to look for a man who was missing."

"And yet you are here."

"Thomas was injured," she reminded him. "He needed me."

"So you came for your brother," he said.

She regarded him with a frank, open stare, as if she was wondering if this was an interrogation. "I was led to believe I would find him in hospital."

"As opposed to me."

Her lower lip caught between her teeth. "Well, yes. I did not—that is to say, I did not know you were missing."

"General Garth did not write to *you*?"

She shook her head. "I don't believe he had been made aware of the marriage."

"So . . . wait." He squeezed his eyes shut, then opened them. He felt very twitchy, but something didn't make sense. The timeline was off. "Did we marry here? No, we couldn't have done. Not if I was missing."

"It—it was a proxy marriage." Her face flushed, and she looked almost embarrassed to admit it.

"I married you by proxy?" he asked, dumbfounded.

"Thomas wanted it," she mumbled.

"Is that even legal?"

Her eyes grew very wide, and he instantly felt like a heel. This woman had cared for him for three days while he was in a coma, and here he was implying that they might not even be married. She did not deserve such disrespect. "Forget I asked," he said quickly. "We can sort all that out later."

She nodded gratefully, then yawned.

"Did you rest yesterday?" he asked.

Her lips curved into the tiniest—and the tiredest—of smiles. "I believe that is my line."

He returned the wry expression. "From what I understand, I have done nothing *but* rest these past few days."

She tilted her head, a silent *touché*.

"You did not answer my question," he reminded her. "Did you rest?"

"Some. I rather think I'm out of practice. And it was a strange room." A lock of hair fell from her coiffure, and she frowned before tucking it back behind her ear. "I always find it difficult to sleep the first night in new surroundings."

"I'd wager you have not slept well in weeks, then."

At that she smiled. "Actually, I slept very well on the ship. The rocking motion agreed with me."

"I'm jealous. I spent most of my crossing puking up my guts."

She smothered a laugh. "I'm sorry."

"Just be grateful you weren't there. I would not have seemed such a matrimonial catch." He considered this. "Then again, I'm no prize right now."

"Oh, don't be—"

"Unwashed, unshaved . . ."

"Edward . . ."

"Malodorous." He waited. "I notice you do not contradict me there."

"You do have a certain, ah, *fragrance*."

"And do not forget that I am missing a small corner of my mind."

She instantly stiffened. "You should not say such things."

His tone was light but his eyes were straight and direct on hers as he said, "If I don't find something to mock in this, I shall have to cry."

She went very still.

"Figuratively," he said, taking pity on her. "You needn't worry. I shan't break down in tears."

"If you did," she said haltingly, "I shouldn't think the less of you. I—I would—"

"Care for me? Tend to my wounds? Dry the salty rivers of my tears?"

Her lips parted, but he did not think she was

shocked, merely perplexed. "I did not realize you were such a devotee of sarcasm," she said.

He shrugged. "I'm not sure I am."

She went a bit straight as she considered this, her brow puckering until three lines formed in the center of her forehead. She did not move for several seconds, and only when a little whoosh of air crossed her lips did he realize she had been holding her breath. It came out with a bit of her voice, resulting in a pensive noise.

"You seem to be analyzing me," he said.

She did not deny it. "It is very interesting," she said, "what you do and do not recall."

"It is difficult for me to view it as an academic pursuit," he said without rancor, "but by all means, you should do so. Any breakthroughs will be much appreciated."

She shifted in her seat. "Have you remembered anything new?"

"Since yesterday?"

She nodded.

"No. At least I don't think so. It's difficult to tell when I don't remember what I don't remember. I'm not even certain where the memory gap begins."

"I'm told you left for Connecticut in early March." Her head tilted to the side, and that mischievous lock of hair fell out of place again. "Do you remember that?"

He thought about this for a moment. "No," he said. "I vaguely recall being told to go, or rather that I *was* going to be told to go . . ." He scrubbed the heel of his hand against one of his eyes. What did that even *mean*? He looked up at Cecilia. "I don't know why, though."

"It will come back to you eventually," she said. "The doctor said that when the head is concussed, the brain needs time to recover."

He frowned.

"Before you woke up," she clarified.

"Ah."

They sat in silence for a few moments, and then, with an awkward motion toward his injury, she asked, "Does it hurt?"

"Like the very devil."

She moved to stand. "I can get you laudanum."

"No," he said quickly. "Thank you. I would rather keep a clear head." Then he realized what a ridiculous statement that was, all things considered. "Or at least clear enough to recall the events of the last day."

Her lips twitched.

"Go ahead," he said. "Laugh."

"I really shouldn't." But she did. Just a little.

And the sound was lovely.

Then she yawned.

"Sleep," he urged.

"Oh, I couldn't. I just got here."

"I won't tell."

She gave him a look. "Who would you tell?"

"Fair point," he conceded. "But still, you obviously need to sleep."

"I can sleep tonight." She wiggled a little in her chair, trying to get comfortable. "I'm just going to rest my eyes for a moment."

He snickered.

"Don't mock me," she warned.

"Or you'll what? You'd never even see me coming."

She opened one eye. "I have outstanding reflexes."

Edward chuckled at that, watching as she returned to her expression of repose. She yawned again, this time not even trying to cover it.

Was that what it meant to be married? That one could yawn with impunity? If so, Edward supposed that the institution had much to recommend it.

He watched her as she "rested her eyes." She really was lovely. Thomas had said his sister was pretty, but in that offhand, brotherly sort of way. He saw what Edward supposed he saw in his own sister Mary: a nice face with all the pieces in the right spots. Thomas would never have noticed, for example, that Cecilia's eyelashes were a few shades darker than her hair, or that when her eyes were closed, they formed two delicate arcs, almost like slivers of a waxing moon.

Her lips were full, although not in that rosebud way the poets seemed wild for. When she slept, they didn't quite touch, and he could imagine the whisper of her breath passing between them.

"Do you think you will be able to leave for the Devil's Head this afternoon?" she asked.

"I thought you were asleep."

"I told you, I'm just resting my eyes."

In this she was not lying. She did not so much as lift a lash as she spoke.

"I should do," he said. "The doctor wishes to see me once more before I go. I trust the room is acceptable?"

She nodded, eyes still closed. "You might find it small."

"But you don't?"

"I don't require grand surroundings."

"Neither do I."

She opened her eyes. "I'm sorry. I did not mean to imply that you did."

"I have spent many a night sleeping rough. Any room with a bed will be a luxury. Well, except this one, I suppose," he said, looking about the makeshift ward. The church pews had been moved against the walls, and the men were lying in a motley collection of cots and beds. A few were on the floor.

"It's depressing," she said quietly.

He nodded. He should be grateful. He was whole of limb and body. Weak, perhaps, but he would heal. Some of the other men in the room were not so lucky.

But still, he wanted out.

"I *am* hungry," he suddenly declared.

She looked up, and he found he rather enjoyed the startled look in her amazing eyes.

"If the doctor wishes to see me, he can bl—" Edward cleared his throat. "He can find me at the Devil's Head."

"Are you sure?" She gave him a concerned look. "I shouldn't want—"

He cut her off by pointing toward a pile of fabric— scarlet and tan—on a nearby pew. "I think that's my uniform over there. Would you be so kind as to fetch it?"

"But the doctor—"

"Or I'll do it myself, and I'm warning you, I'm bare-arsed under this shirt."

Her cheeks burned scarlet—not quite as deep a hue as his coat, but impressively close—and suddenly it occurred to him:

A proxy marriage.

Him: Several months in Connecticut.

Her: Two weeks in New York.

No wonder he had not recognized her face. He'd never seen her before.

Their marriage?

It had never been consummated.

Chapter 4

Lieutenant Rokesby isn't unbearable at all. In fact, he's quite a decent fellow. I think you'd like him. He is from Kent and is practically engaged to his neighbor.

I showed him your miniature. He said you were very pretty.

—FROM THOMAS HARCOURT
TO HIS SISTER CECILIA

E dward had insisted upon dressing himself, so Cecilia took this time to head outside to find them something to eat. She had spent the better part of a week in this neighborhood and knew every shop and storefront on the street. The most economical option—

and thus her usual choice—was currant buns from Mr. Mather's cart. They were tolerably tasty, although she suspected their low price was made possible by the inclusion of no more than three currants per bun.

Mr. Lowell, a bit farther down the street, sold actual Chelsea buns, with spiraled dough and cinnamon spice. Cecilia had never counted their currants; she'd eaten only one, bought day-old, and she'd devoured it far too quickly to do anything but moan with pleasure at the sticky-sweet sugar glaze as it dissolved on her tongue.

But around the corner—that was where one found the shop of Mr. Rooijakkers, the Dutch baker. Cecilia had gone in only once; that was all it had taken to see that (a) she could not afford his treats and (b) if she could, she'd be fat as a house in no time.

If there was ever a time for extravagance, though, surely this was the day, with Edward having awakened and in goodish health. Cecilia had two coins in her pocket, enough for a fine treat, and she no longer had to worry about paying for her boardinghouse room. She supposed she should be saving her pennies—the Lord only knew where she'd find herself in the weeks to come—but she could not bring herself to scrimp. Not today.

She pushed open the door, smiling at the tinkle of the bell above, and then sighing with delight at the heavenly smells wafting toward her from the kitchen in the back.

"May I help you?" asked the ginger-haired woman standing behind the counter. She was perhaps a few years older than Cecilia and spoke with a very slight accent, one Cecilia would not have been able to place had she not already known that the proprietors hailed from Holland.

"Yes, thank you, I'll have a round bread loaf, please," Cecilia said, motioning toward a row of three sitting plump and pretty on the shelf, with a mottled golden crust that looked different from anything she'd seen back home. "Are they all the same price?"

The woman cocked her head to the side. "They were, but now that you mention it, the one on the right does look a bit small. You can have it for a ha'penny less."

Cecilia was already calculating where she might go to purchase butter or cheese to eat with the bread, but then she just had to ask, "What is that delicious smell?"

The woman beamed. "*Speculaas.* Freshly baked. Have you never tried one?"

Cecilia shook her head. She was so hungry. She'd finally had a proper meal the night before, but it had only seemed to remind her belly how badly she had been mistreating it. And while the steak and kidney pie at the Devil's Head had been good, Cecilia was positively salivating at the thought of something sweet.

"I broke one taking them off the tray," the woman said. "You can have it for free."

"Oh no, I couldn't—"

The woman waved this off. "You've never had one. I can't charge you for trying."

"Actually, you could," Cecilia said with a smile, "but I'll not argue with you further."

"I haven't seen you in the shop before." The woman said this over her shoulder as she scooted into the kitchen.

"I came in once," Cecilia said, declining to mention that she had not made a purchase. "Last week. There was an older gentleman here."

"My father," the woman confirmed.

"Then you are Miss Rooey—ehrm, Roojak—" Good heavens, how did one pronounce it?

"Rooijakkers," the woman said with a grin as she came back through the doorway. "But actually I'm Mrs. Leverett."

"Thank heavens," Cecilia said with a relieved smile. "I know you just said your name, but I don't think I could reproduce it."

"I have often told my husband it is why I married him," Mrs. Leverett joked.

Cecilia laughed until she realized that she too was holding on to a husband for his name. In her case, however, it was so that Major Wilkins would do his bloody job.

"Dutch is not an easy language," Mrs. Leverett said, "but if you plan to be in New York Town for some time, you might find it worthwhile to learn a few phrases."

"I don't know how long I will be here," Cecilia said honestly. Hopefully not too long. She just wanted to find her brother.

And make sure Edward regained his strength. She couldn't possibly leave until she was assured of his welfare.

"Your English is excellent," she said to the baker.

"I was born here. My parents too, but we speak Dutch in the home. Here"—she held out two pieces of flat, caramel-brown biscuit—"try it."

Cecilia thanked her again, fitting the pieces together into their original oblong shape before lifting the smaller one to her mouth and taking a nibble. "Oh my goodness! This is divine."

"You like it, then?" Mrs. Leverett's eyes went wide with delight.

"How could I not?" It tasted of cardamom and clove and slightly burnt sugar. It was completely foreign and yet somehow made her homesick. Perhaps it was the mere act of sharing a biscuit over conversation. Cecilia had been too busy to realize that she had also been lonely.

"Some of the officers say they are too thin and crumbly," Mrs. Leverett said.

"They are mad," Cecilia replied through her somewhat full mouth. "Although I must say, these would be excellent with tea."

"Not easy to come by, I'm afraid."

"No," Cecilia said regretfully. She'd known enough to bring some with her, but she had not packed nearly enough, and she'd run out two-thirds of the way across the Atlantic. By the final week she was reusing her leaves and cutting her rations in half for each pot.

"I should not complain," Mrs. Leverett said. "We are still able to get sugar, and that is far more important for a bakery."

Cecilia nodded, taking a nibble of the second half of her biscuit. She needed to make this one last a little longer.

"The officers have tea," Mrs. Leverett continued. "Not a lot, but more than anyone else."

Edward was an officer. Cecilia did not wish to take advantage of his wealth, but if he could procure some tea . . .

She thought she might offer up a very small portion of her soul for a good cup.

"You did not say your name," Mrs. Leverett said.

"Oh, I'm so sorry. I'm quite in a fog today. I am Miss Har—I'm sorry. Mrs. Rokesby."

The other woman smiled knowingly. "Newly married?"

"Quite." How *quite*, Cecilia could not possibly explain. "My husband"—she tried not to stumble over the word—"is an officer. A captain."

"I had suspected as much," Mrs. Leverett remarked. "No other reason you'd be here in New York Town in the middle of a war."

"It's strange," Cecilia mused. "It doesn't feel like a war. If I didn't see the wounded soldiers . . ." She stopped, reconsidering her words. She might not be witness to actual fighting in this British outpost, but signs of struggle and deprivation were everywhere. The harbor was filled with prison ships, and indeed, when Cecilia's ship had sailed in, she had been warned to stay below as they passed.

The smell, she'd heard, was too much to bear.

"I beg your pardon," she said to the other woman. "I spoke most callously. There is much more to war than the front of a battlefield."

Mrs. Leverett smiled, but it was a sad smile. Tired. "There is no need to apologize. It has been relatively quiet here for two years. Pray God it remains so."

"Indeed," Cecilia murmured. She glanced out the window—why, she wasn't sure. "I suppose I must go soon. But first, please do wrap up a half dozen *speculaas*." She frowned, doing a little arithmetic in her head. She had just enough money in her pocket. "No, make that a dozen."

"A full dozen?" Mrs. Leverett gave her a cheeky grin. "I hope you find that tea."

"I hope so too. I'm celebrating. My husband"—there was that word again—"is leaving hospital today."

"Oh, I'm so sorry. I did not realize. But I assume this means he is recovered."

"Almost." Cecilia thought of Edward, still so thin and pale. She had not even seen him out of bed yet. "He still needs time to rest and regain his strength."

"How lucky he is to have his wife at his side."

Cecilia nodded, but her throat felt tight. She wished she could say it was because the *speculaas* had made her thirsty, but she was fairly certain it was her own conscience.

"You know," Mrs. Leverett said, "there is much to enjoy here in New York, even with the war so close. The upper crust still hosts parties. I do not attend, of course, but I see the ladies in their finery from time to time."

"Really?" Cecilia's brows rose.

"Oh yes. And I believe there will be a performance of *Macbeth* next week at the John Street Theatre."

"You're joking."

Mrs. Leverett held up a hand. "On my father's ovens, I swear it."

Cecilia could not help but laugh at that. "Perhaps I shall try to attend. It has been some time since I went to the theater."

"I cannot vouch for the quality of the production," Mrs. Leverett said. "I believe that most of the roles are being played by British officers."

Cecilia tried to imagine Colonel Stubbs or Major Wilkins treading the boards. It was not a pretty image.

"My sister went when they did *Othello*," Mrs. Leverett continued. "She said the scenery was very prettily painted."

If that wasn't damning with faint praise, Cecilia didn't know what was. But beggars couldn't be choosers, and truly, she didn't often get to see Shakespeare in Derbyshire. Maybe she would try to go.

If Edward was up to it.

If they were still "married."

Cecilia sighed.

"Did you say something?"

Cecilia shook her head, but it must have been a rhetorical question because Mrs. Leverett was already wrapping the *speculaas* in a cloth. "I'm afraid we haven't paper," the baker said with an apologetic expression. "Like tea, it is in short supply."

"It means I shall have to come back to return your cloth," Cecilia said. And when she realized how happy that made her—just the thought of sharing a greeting with a woman her own age—she said, "I'm Cecilia."

"Beatrix," said the other woman.

"I'm very glad to have met you," Cecilia said. "And thank you for—no, wait. How do I say *thank you* in Dutch?"

Beatrix smiled broadly. "*Dank u.*"

Cecilia blinked in surprise. "Really? That's it?"

"You picked an easy one," Beatrix said with a shrug. "If you wanted to learn *please* . . ."

"Oh, don't tell me," Cecilia said, knowing that she would, regardless.

"*Alstublieft,*" Beatrix said with a grin. "And don't say it sounds like a sneeze."

Cecilia chuckled. "I'll stick to *dank u.* At least for now."

"Go on," Beatrix said. "Get back to your husband."

That word again. Cecilia smiled her farewell, but it

felt hollow. What would Beatrix Leverett think if she knew Cecilia was nothing but a fraud?

She got out of the store before her tears could prick their way out of her eyes.

"I hope you have a sweet tooth, because I bought—oh."

Edward looked up. His wife had returned with a small cloth bundle and a determined smile.

Not determined enough, though. It wobbled and fell when she saw him sitting with slumped shoulders at the end of his bed.

"Are you all right?" she asked.

Not really. He'd managed to dress himself, but that was only because she'd placed his uniform on the bed before she left. Honestly, he didn't know if he would have been able to make it across the room on his own. He'd known he was weak, but he had not realized just how much until he had swung his legs over the side of his cot and tried to stand.

He was pathetic.

"I'm fine," he muttered.

"Of course," she murmured unconvincingly. "I . . . ah . . . Would you care for a biscuit?"

He watched her slim hands as she unwrapped her bundle.

"*Speculaas*," he said, recognizing them instantly.

"You've had them before? Oh, of course you have. I forget, you've been here for years."

"Not years," he said, taking one of the thin biscuits. "I was in Massachusetts for nearly a year. Then Rhode Island." He took a bite. God, they were good. He looked up. "And apparently Connecticut too, not that I remember it."

Cecilia sat on the end of the bed. Well, more like a perch. She had that look of someone who didn't want to get too comfortable. "Did the Dutch settle all over the colonies?"

"Just here." He finished off the biscuit and reached for another. "It hasn't been New Amsterdam for over a century, but most of the Dutch stayed when the island traded ownership." He frowned. Actually, he had no idea if most had stayed, but walking around town, it felt like they had. Dutch influence was all over the island, from the distinctive zigzag façades on the buildings to the *speculaas* biscuits and crunch bread at the bakery.

"I learned how to say *thank you*," she said.

He felt himself smile. "Very ambitious of you."

She gave him a look. "I take it you know the phrase, then."

He took another biscuit. "*Dank u.*"

"You're quite welcome," she said with a little flick of

her eyes, "but perhaps you should slow down. I don't think it's a good idea to eat too much at once."

"Probably not," he agreed, but he ate it, anyway.

She waited patiently while he finished, then she waited patiently while he sat on the edge of the cot, trying to summon his strength.

She was a patient woman, his wife. She'd have to be, sitting three days at his boring bedside. Not much to do with an unconscious husband.

He thought about her journey across the Atlantic. To get word of her brother and then decide to go help him, all the time knowing it would take months . . .

That too bore the hallmark of a patient individual.

He wondered if she sometimes wanted to scream in frustration.

She was going to have to be patient for a bit longer, he thought grimly. His legs were like jelly. He could barely walk. Hell, even just standing was a chore, and as for making their marriage legal in every way . . .

That was going to have to wait.

More was the pity.

Although it did occur to him that they could still get out of this union if they so chose. Annulment on account of nonconsummation was a tricky legal maneuver, but then again, so was a proxy marriage. If he did not want to be married, he was fairly certain he did not have to be.

"Edward?"

Her voice tickled at the edge of his mind, but he was too lost in his thoughts to respond. *Did* he wish to be married to her? If not, he damned well couldn't accompany her to the Devil's Head. He might not possess the strength to take her properly to bed, but if they shared a room, even for one night, she would be thoroughly compromised.

"Edward?"

He turned, slowly, forcing himself to focus. She was looking at him with concern, but even that could not cloud the startling clarity of her eyes.

She laid a hand over his. "Are you certain you are well enough to leave today? Should I find the doctor?"

He searched her face. "Do you want to be married to me?"

"What?" Something close to alarm raced over her features. "I don't understand."

"You don't have to be married to me," he said carefully. "We have not consummated the marriage."

Her lips parted, and oddly enough, he could see that she was not breathing. "I thought you didn't remember," she whispered.

"I don't have to remember. It's simple logic. I was in

Connecticut when you arrived. We had never been in a room together before you came to the hospital."

She swallowed, and his eyes fell to her throat, to the delicate arc of it, to the pulse quivering under her skin.

God, he wanted to kiss her.

"What do you want, Cecilia?"

Say you want me.

The thought burst through his brain. He did not want her to leave him. He could barely stand on his own. It would be weeks before he'd regain even half his strength. He needed her.

And he wanted her.

But most of all, he wanted her to want him.

Cecilia did not speak for several seconds. Her hand left his, and she hugged her arms to her body. She seemed to be looking at a soldier on the other side of the church as she asked, "Are you offering to release me?"

"If that is what you want."

Slowly, her eyes met his. "What do *you* want?"

"That is not the question."

"I rather think it is."

"I am a gentleman," he said stiffly. "I will bow to your wishes in this matter."

"I . . ." She caught her lower lip between her teeth. "I . . . don't want you to feel trapped."

"I don't feel trapped."

"You don't?" She sounded honestly surprised.

He shrugged. "I have to marry eventually."

If she found this unromantic, it did not show on her face.

"I obviously agreed to the marriage," he said. He loved Thomas Harcourt like a brother, but Edward could not imagine what might have made him consent to a marriage he did not want. If he was married to Cecilia, he had damned well wanted to be.

He looked closely at her.

Her gaze slipped to the floor.

Was she assessing her options? Trying to decide if she truly wished to be the wife of a man whose brain was not whole? He might remain this way for the rest of his life. For all they knew the damage went deeper than his memory. What if he awakened one day and could no longer speak? Or move properly? She might find herself being forced to care for him as she would a child.

It could happen. There was no way to know.

"What do you want, Cecilia?" he asked, aware that a note of impatience had entered his voice.

"I . . ." She swallowed, and when she spoke again, her voice was a little more certain. "I think we should go to the Devil's Head. This is not a conversation I wish to have here."

"Nothing is going to change in the next half hour."

"Nevertheless, you could do with a meal not made of flour and sugar. And a bath. And a shave." She stood, but not so fast that he missed the pink flush of her cheeks. "I shall offer you privacy for the latter two."

"Very generous of you."

She did not comment upon his dry tone. Instead she reached for his coat, which lay draped like a slash of scarlet across the foot of his bed. She held it out. "We have a meeting this afternoon. With Major Wilkins."

"Why?"

"He brings news of Thomas. Or at least I hope he does. I saw him at the inn last night. He said he would make inquiries."

"He has not already done so?"

She looked slightly uncomfortable as she said, "I took your advice and informed him of our marriage."

Ah. Now it became clear. She needed him too. Edward forced a smile around his gritted teeth. It was not the first time a lady had found his name the most attractive thing about him. At least this lady had unselfish motives.

She held out his coat. With some effort, he stood and allowed her to help him don it.

"You'll be warm," she warned him.

"It is, as you say, June."

"Not like June in Derbyshire," she muttered.

He permitted himself a smile at that. The summer air in the colonies had an unpleasant solid quality to it. Rather like fog, if one heated it to the temperature of one's body.

He looked toward the door, took a breath. "I . . . I will need help."

"We all need help," she said quietly. She took his arm, and then slowly, without a word, they made their way out to the street, where a carriage awaited to take them the short distance to the Devil's Head.

Chapter 5

You showed him my miniature? How terribly em-
barrassing. Thomas, whatever were you thinking?
Of course he must call me pretty. He could hardly
do otherwise. You are my brother. He can't very
well comment on my freakishly large nose.

—FROM CECILIA HARCOURT TO
HER BROTHER THOMAS

One hour later, Cecilia was seated in the front
room of the Devil's Head, methodically finishing her lunch while Edward perused a recent copy of
the *Royal Gazette*. She had also started her meal with
a newspaper in her hand, but she had been so startled
by the paragraph advertising the sale of "One Negro
Man, a good Cook and not a Seasick," that she'd put it

down and instead set her eyes on her plate of pork and potatoes.

Edward, on the other hand, read the newssheet from front to back, and then, after asking the innkeeper to locate an issue from the previous week, repeated the process with that. He hadn't bothered to explain, but it was clear to Cecilia that he was trying to fill the gaps in his memory. She wasn't sure that it would help; she rather doubted he was going to find clues about his time in Connecticut in a public newspaper. But it certainly wouldn't hurt, and anyway, he seemed like the sort of man who would want to keep abreast of the news of the day. He was like Thomas that way. Her brother never excused himself from the breakfast table without finishing the entire *London Times*. It was several days old by the time it reached them in Matlock Bath, but that never seemed to bother him. Better to be delayed in the news than ignorant altogether, he'd often said, and besides, there was nothing they could do about it.

Change what you can, he'd once told her, *and accept what you can't*. She wondered what Thomas would think of her recent behavior. She had a feeling he would have placed his injury and subsequent disappearance firmly in the "accept what you can't" category.

She let out a little snort. It was a bit too late for that now.

"Did you say something?" Edward asked.

She shook her head. "Just thinking of Thomas," she said, since she was actively trying *not* to lie whenever possible.

"We will find him," Edward said. "Or we'll get news. One way or another."

Cecilia swallowed, trying to push down the lump in her throat as she gave him a grateful nod. She was not alone in this anymore. She was still scared, and anxious, and full of self-doubt, but she wasn't alone.

It was staggering what a difference that made.

Edward started to say something more, but they were interrupted by the young woman who had brought their food earlier. Like everyone in New York, Cecilia thought, she looked tired and overworked.

And hot. Honestly, Cecilia didn't know how people lived through these summers. The air at home was never this thick with moisture unless it was actually raining.

She'd heard the winters were equally extreme. She prayed she was not still here when the first snow fell. One of the soldiers in hospital had told her that the ground froze through like a rock, and the wind was enough to nip your ears off.

"Sir," the young lady said with a quick curtsy, "your bath is ready."

"You need it even more now," Cecilia said, motioning to his ink-smudged fingers. It went without saying that no one at the Devil's Head had the time or inclination to seal the ink with a hot iron.

"It does make one long for the comforts of home," he murmured, glancing idly at his fingertips.

She arched a brow. "Really? This is what you miss most? A well-ironed newspaper?"

He shot her a bit of a look, but she rather thought he liked when she teased him. He was not the sort of man who would wish to be treated like an invalid, with people tiptoeing around him and watching their words. Still, when he set down the newspaper and glanced toward the exit, Cecilia stopped herself from asking if he would like assistance up the stairs and instead stood and silently held out her arm. She had seen what it cost him to ask for her help back in the hospital.

Some things were best done without words.

She was grateful, actually, that he'd ignored her in favor of the *Gazette* throughout their meal. She was still unnerved by his offer to release her from their marriage. She had never—*never*—expected him to do that. In retrospect, she counted herself fortunate that her knees hadn't buckled beneath her. She had been just standing there with a pile of Dutch biscuits and all of a sudden he offered to set her free.

As if *he* had been the one to trap *her*.

She should have done it. She tried to lie to herself and say that she would have done it except . . .

The expression on his face.

He'd not moved a muscle. But it wasn't as if he'd frozen. He was just . . . still.

She'd thought he might have been holding his breath.

She'd thought he might not even have realized he was holding his breath.

He did not want her to go.

Cecilia did not know why she was so certain of this; there was no reason for her to know his expressions, to be able to interpret the emotions held deep and tight behind his sapphire eyes. She'd only truly known him—face-to-face—for one day.

She couldn't imagine why he wanted her to stay, save for the fact that he needed a nursemaid and she was convenient, but he seemed to want to remain married to her.

The irony just grew and grew.

But, she reminded herself, she could not risk revealing the truth before their meeting with Major Wilkins. She had a feeling that Captain Edward Rokesby was a paragon of honesty, and she did not know if he would, or even could, bring himself to lie to his military superior. He might feel honor bound to inform him that while he did wish to aid Miss Cecilia Harcourt in her search for her brother, he was not, as a point of fact, her husband.

Cecilia could not even imagine the outcome of *that* conversation.

No, if she confessed her duplicity to Edward, it would have to be after they saw the major.

She told herself this was acceptable.

She told herself lots of things.

And then she tried not to think about it.

"The treads on the stairs are narrow," she said to Edward as they approached the stairs, "and the risers are steep."

He grunted his thanks for the warning, and with her hand supporting his arm, they made their way up. She could not imagine what this did to him, to be so dependent on others. She had never seen him in full health, but he was tall, probably almost a full six feet, and his shoulders looked as if they would be broad and strong when he had a bit more muscle on his bones.

This was not a man used to needing help up a flight of stairs.

"We're just down the hall," she said, tipping her head to the left when they reached their floor. "Number twelve."

He nodded, and when they approached their door,

she let go of his arm and handed him the key. It was not much, but it was something he could do for her, and she knew it would make him feel a little better, even if he did not realize why.

But then, in the last second before he slid the key into place, he said, "This is your last chance."

"I—I beg your pardon?"

The key turned in the lock, the click echoing loudly in the hall.

"If you wish to annul our union," he said in a voice that did not waver, "you must tell me now."

Cecilia tried to say something, truly she did, but her heart was slamming toward her throat, and her fingers and toes almost felt as if they were fizzing with nerves. She did not think she had ever been so startled. Or panicked.

"I will say this only once," Edward said, his steadiness a clear contrast to the pandemonium erupting inside her. "Once you enter the room, our marriage is final."

Nervous laughter bubbled through her throat. "Don't be silly. You're hardly going to ravish me this afternoon." Then it occurred to her that she might have just insulted his manhood. "Er, at least not before your bath."

"You know as well as I that it does not matter *when*

I take you to bed," he said, his eyes burning down on hers. "Once we enter that room together, as a married couple, you will be compromised."

"You can't compromise your wife," she tried to joke.

He swore, the single word emerging in a low, frustrated growl. The blasphemy was utterly out of character, and enough to startle Cecilia into taking a step back.

"This is nothing to make light of," he said. Again, he seemed to be holding himself scrupulously still, but this time he was betrayed by the pulse beating furiously in his throat. "I am offering you the opportunity to leave."

She felt her head shaking. "But why?"

He looked up and down the hall before hissing, "Because I'm bloody well damaged."

It would have been a shout if they were not in so public a place, of that Cecilia was sure. The intensity of his voice would be seared on her mind for an eternity.

And it broke her heart.

"No, Edward," she tried to reassure him. "You must not think that way. You are—"

"I am missing a piece of my mind," he cut in.

"No. No." It was all she could seem to say.

He grabbed her shoulders, his fingers biting her

skin. "You need to understand this, Cecilia. I am not whole."

She shook her head. She wanted to tell him that he was perfect, and that she was a fraud. And that she was so so sorry for taking advantage of his condition.

She would never be able to make this up to him.

He let go of her abruptly. "I am not the man you married."

"I'm probably not the woman you married either," she mumbled.

He stared at her. He stared at her for so long that her skin began to tingle. "But I think . . ." she whispered, only just figuring it out as the words left her lips. "I think you might need me."

"Jesus God, Cecilia, you have no idea."

And then, right in the middle of the corridor, he hauled her into his arms and kissed her.

He hadn't planned to do it. For Christ's sake, he'd been *trying* to do the right thing. But she'd been staring up at him with those seafoam eyes, and when she'd whispered that he needed her . . .

The only thing that could have made him harder was if she'd said *she* needed *him.*

He had no strength. He'd lost at least a stone and

could not even make it up the stairs on his own, but by God he could kiss his wife.

"Edward," she gasped.

He tugged her through the door. "We're staying married."

"Oh God."

He had no idea what she meant by that, but he didn't think he cared.

The room was small, with a bed that took up nearly half the floor, so it wasn't difficult for him to find his way to the edge of the mattress and sit, pulling her along with him.

"Edward, I—"

"Shhh," he commanded, taking her face in his hands. "I want to look at you."

"Why?"

He smiled. "Because you're mine."

Her lips parted into a delectable oval, and he took that as a sign from above and kissed her again. She did not respond at first, but she did not push him away. Rather, he had the sense that she was holding herself very still, holding her very breath, waiting to see if the moment was real.

And then, just when he thought he must pull himself away, he felt it—a tiny movement of her lips, the sound of her voice through his skin as she made a small moan.

"Cecilia," he whispered. He did not know what he had done these last few months, but he had a feeling it had not been something to be proud of. It had not been pure, and lovely, and everything he saw when he looked in her eyes.

When he kissed her, he tasted the promise of re-demption.

He brushed his mouth over hers, softly, like a whis-per. But it wasn't quite enough, and when she let out a little mewl of desire, he nipped her, his teeth scraping gently along the soft skin of her inner lip.

He wanted to do this all afternoon. Just lie next to her on the bed and worship her like the goddess she was. It would be just a kiss; he was hardly capable of anything more. But it would be an endless kiss—soft, slow, and deep, each caress melting into the next.

It was so strange—desire without urgency. He de-cided he liked it—for now. When he was strong, when he once again felt like himself, he would make love to her with every piece of his soul, and he knew enough of himself—and of her—that the experience would take him to the edge.

And then push him right over.

"You are beautiful," he murmured, and then, be-cause it seemed so important that she knew he saw the beauty she held within, he said, "and so good."

She stiffened. It was the tiniest motion, but his every sense was so attuned to her he would have known it if she had breathed differently.

"We must stop," she said, and although he heard regret in her voice, he did not hear a lack of resolve.

He sighed. He wanted her. He felt it inside like a growing plume, but he could not make love to her in this state—unwashed, exhausted. She deserved far more, and frankly, so did he.

"Your water will grow cold," she said.

He glanced over at the tub. It was not large, but it would do, and he knew that the steam rising from the surface would not last long.

"I should go downstairs," she said, awkwardly coming to her feet. The dress she was wearing was a soft, dusty pink, and her hand seemed to melt into it as she clutched at the skirts, twisting the material between her fingers.

She looked utterly mortified, and he could not help but find it adorable.

"You should not feel embarrassed," he reminded her. "I am your husband."

"Not yet," she mumbled. "Not that way."

He felt a smile rising inside.

"I really should go," she said without actually taking a step.

The smile spread into a fully fledged grin. "Do not

leave on my account. I believe in medieval times, bathing one's husband was considered an important wifely duty."

At that she rolled her eyes, and a warm happiness began to roll out within him. She was amusing when she was embarrassed, but he liked it better when she was holding her own against him.

"I could drown, you know," he said.

"Oh please."

"I could. I'm very tired. What if I fell asleep in the tub?"

She paused, and for a few seconds he thought she might actually believe him. "You're not going to fall asleep in the tub," she finally said.

He gave a dramatic sigh, as if to say—*You never know*, but he took pity on her and said, "Come back in ten minutes."

"Only ten?"

"Is that a comment on my general level of filth?"

"Yes," she said quite plainly.

He laughed aloud. "You are very entertaining, did you know that, Cecilia Rokesby?"

She rolled her eyes again, handing him the towel that had been left folded neatly at the end of the bed.

He feigned a sigh. "I would say it was why I married you, but we both know that isn't true."

She turned to look at him, her face oddly without expression. "What did you say?"

He shrugged as he pulled off his coat. "I obviously don't remember why I married you."

"Oh. I thought you meant . . ."

He regarded her with raised brows.

"Never mind."

"No, tell me."

But her face had already gone quite red. "I thought perhaps you were referring to . . ."

He waited. She didn't finish. "The kiss?" he supplied.

He had not thought her skin could reach an even deeper hue, but it did. He took the two steps that lay between them and touched her chin with just enough pressure to raise her gaze to his.

"If I had kissed you before our wedding," he said softly, "there would be no doubt right now as to the permanence of our marriage."

Her brow wrinkled in adorable confusion.

He brushed his lips against hers and then said against her cheek, "If I had known what it meant to kiss you, I should not have allowed the army to send me away."

"You're just saying that," she said, her words a mumble near his ear.

He drew back with an amused smile.

"You would not refuse a direct order," she said.

"From you? Never."

"Stop," she said, batting him playfully away. "You know that's not what I meant."

He took her hand and dropped a courtly kiss on her knuckles. Damn if he wasn't feeling ridiculously romantic. "I assure you, Mrs. Rokesby, I would have found time for a wedding night."

"You need to take your bath."

"Ouch."

"Unless you like cold water."

He was beginning to think he might *need* cold water. "Point taken. But if I might add one more thing to the conversation . . ."

"Why do I think I will be blushing like a fiend a few seconds from now?"

"You're already blushing," he took great joy in telling her, "and I was merely going to say—"

"I'll be downstairs!" she called, making a dash for the door.

Edward smiled from the top of his head to the tips of his toes, even when all that was left for him to look at was the inside of his bedroom door.

"I was merely going to say," he said aloud, his happiness coloring each word warm and pink, "that it would have been spectacular."

It will *be spectacular,* he thought as he stripped off the rest of his clothing and lowered himself into the tub.

Soon, if he had anything to do with it.

Chapter 6

What the devil are you talking about? You don't have a freakishly large nose.

—FROM THOMAS HARCOURT

TO HIS SISTER CECILIA

Edward had said he needed ten minutes, but Cecilia waited a solid twenty-five before venturing back to room twelve. She had been planning to remain downstairs for half an hour, but then she started thinking—he was still terribly weak. What if he was having difficulty getting out of the tub?

The water would be cold by now. He could be catching a chill. He deserved his privacy, and she certainly wanted to give it to him, but not at the expense of his health.

It was true that she had seen him in a most improper state when she was caring for him back in hospital, but she'd not seen *all* of him. She'd learned to be very creative with the bedsheet. She'd draped it this way and that, always managing to preserve his dignity.

And her modesty.

All of New York might think her a married woman, but she was still very much an innocent, even if one kiss from Captain Edward Rokesby had left her breathless.

Breathless?

Brainless.

It really ought to be illegal for a man to have eyes that color. Somewhere between aquamarine and sapphire, they could mesmerize a girl with a glance. And yes, her eyes had been closed when he was kissing her, but that mattered little when all she could picture was that last moment before his lips touched hers, when she'd thought she might drown in the deep blue of his gaze.

Cecilia had always liked her own eyes, taking pride in the pale green color that set her apart from the crowd. But Edward . . .

He was a beautiful man, there was no getting around that.

But he also might be freezing to death, she thought.

Or rather, freezing until he was chilled, and heaven knew that could kill him.

She headed up the stairs.

"Edward?" she called out, knocking softly on the door. Then she thought—why was she being quiet?

She knocked harder. "Edward?"

No response.

A little frisson of apprehension skidded up her arm, and she grabbed the door handle and turned.

She said his name again as the door swung open, and she stepped in, eyes averted. When he did not reply to that, she finally turned toward the tub.

"You did fall asleep!" The words popped right out of her mouth before it could occur to her that she might not wish to wake him up in such a vigorous manner.

"Gah!" Edward came awake with a yelp and a splash, water flying through the air as Cecilia dashed across the room for no reason she could figure.

But she couldn't just stand there in front of him. He was *naked.*

"You said you wouldn't fall asleep," she accused, her back firmly to the bathtub.

"No, *you* said I wouldn't fall asleep," he countered.

He was right, drat it all.

"Well," she said, in that tone that clearly said she

hadn't a clue how to conduct herself. "I expect your water has gone cold."

There was a beat of silence, followed by "It's tolerable."

She shifted her weight from foot to foot, then gave up and crossed her arms tightly over her chest. She wasn't angry; rather, she didn't seem to know what to do with her body. "I shouldn't want you to catch a chill," she said to her feet.

"No."

No? That was all he was going to say? *No?*

"Er, Cecilia?"

She made a little sound of acknowledgment.

"Do you think you might close the door?"

"*OhmygoodnessI'msorry.*" She ran back across the room—which was not a terribly graceful endeavor given the close confines—and slammed the door shut with considerably more effort than was warranted.

"Are you still here?" Edward asked. Cecilia belatedly realized that he could not see her. His back was mostly to the door, and the tub was far too small for him to comfortably twist around.

"Er, yes?" It came out like a question. She had no idea why.

There was a short pause, during which he was probably pondering how to best reply to such a ridiculous response. In the end, however, he just asked, "Do you think you might hand me the towel?"

"Oh. Yes. Of course." Fastidiously keeping her back to the tub, she edged over to the bed and grabbed the towel. From there she only had to reach her arm back to hand it to him.

He took it, then said, "I do not say this to embarrass you—"

Which meant she was going to be mortified.

"—and I do appreciate your efforts to preserve my modesty, but did you not see, ah, *me* when you were caring for me earlier this week?"

"Not like this," she mumbled.

Again, a little pause, and this time she could picture his brow coming together in a furrow as he considered her answer.

"I kept you covered with the sheet," she finally said.

"At all times?"

"I was highly motivated."

He let out a chuckle at that.

"I think I'll go back downstairs," she said, edging her way back to the door. "I had only wanted to make sure you weren't catching a chill."

"In June?"

"You've been ill," she said primly.

He sighed. "I still am."

Cecilia pressed her lips together, summoning her courage. He was right, and his health was more important than her tender sensibilities. She took a breath. "Do you need assistance getting out of the tub?"

"No," he said quietly. "At least I hope not."

"Perhaps I should stay." She moved a little closer to the door. "Just while you get out. In case you need me."

She hoped he didn't. It was not a large towel.

A moment later she heard a heave of exertion, followed by the sound of water sloshing against the side of the tub.

"Are you—"

"I'm fine," he bit off.

"I'm sorry." She shouldn't have asked. He was proud. But she had been nursing him for days; it was difficult to stop, even if she was desperately trying to keep her eyes to herself.

"It's not your fault."

She nodded, even though she had no idea if he was looking at her.

"You can turn around now."

"Are you sure?"

"I'm covered," he said, sounding perhaps just a bit fed up with her prudishness.

"Thank you." She turned around. Slowly, though. She wasn't sure how he defined *covered*.

He was on the bed, propped up against the pillows with the blankets pulled over his lap. His chest was bare. It was no more than she'd seen when she'd sponged down his fever in hospital, but it seemed very different when his eyes were open and alert.

"You look better," she said. It was true. He'd washed his hair, and his skin had a healthier glow.

He gave a tired smile, and touched his beard. "I did not shave."

"That's all right," she assured him. "There is no rush."

"I don't think I'll feel properly clean until I do."

"Oh. Well . . ." Cecilia knew she should offer to shave him. It was clearly the one task she could perform for him that would make the greatest difference to his comfort, but it was such an intimate gesture. The only man she had ever shaved was her father. He'd not had a valet, and when his hands had grown arthritic she had taken over the task.

"You don't have to," Edward said.

"No, no, I can do it." She was being silly and missish. She'd crossed the Atlantic Ocean by herself. She'd stood toe-to-toe with Colonel Zachary Stubbs of His Majesty's Army and lied to his face in order to save a man's life. Surely she could shave that man's beard.

"I should probably inquire if you have ever shaved a man before," Edward murmured.

She stifled a smile as she glanced around the room for the razor and brush. "It does seem like a prudent question before allowing me to take a knife to your throat."

He chuckled. "There is a small leather box in my trunk. You will find what you need there."

Right. His trunk. Edward's belongings had been kept safe for him while he was missing; Colonel Stubbs had arranged to have them sent over to the Devil's Head earlier that day.

Cecilia peered into the trunk, at the neatly folded clothing, the books, the papers. It seemed terribly intimate to be going through his belongings. What did a man bring with him to a strange land? She supposed it should not seem such an odd question to her. After all, she had also packed for a voyage across the ocean. But unlike Edward, she had never intended to stay long. She had brought only the barest of essentials; memories of home had not been a priority. In fact, the sole memento she had packed was a miniature of her brother, and that was only because she thought it might help to locate him once she reached North America.

She huffed to herself. She had thought she might

need help finding Thomas within a hospital. Little did she know she'd be searching an entire colony.

"Do you see it?" Edward asked.

"Ehrm, no," she murmured, setting aside a soft white linen shirt. It was well-worn and had clearly been washed many times, but she knew enough of stitchery to see that it had been exceedingly well-made. Thomas had not had such fine shirts. Had his held up as well as Edward's? She tried to picture her brother mending his clothes and failed miserably. She had always done such things for him. She'd complained, but she'd done it.

What she wouldn't give to do such things again.

"Cecilia?"

"I'm sorry." She spied the corner of a leather box and wrapped her hand around it. "My mind was wandering."

"Somewhere interesting, I hope."

She turned to face him. "I was thinking of my brother."

Edward's face grew solemn. "Of course. I'm sorry."

"I should have liked to have helped him pack his trunk," she said. She glanced over her shoulder at Edward. He did not reply, but he gave a little nod, the sort that said he understood.

"He did not come home before he left for North

America," Cecilia continued. "I don't know that he had anyone to help him." She looked up. "Did you?"

"My mother," Edward confirmed. "She insisted. But I was able to make a visit home before I sailed. Crake House is not far from the coast. The journey is under two hours on a swift mount."

Cecilia nodded sadly. Edward and Thomas's regiment had departed for the New World from the bustling port of Chatham, in Kent. It had been much too far from Derbyshire for Thomas to consider a trip home.

"Thomas came home with me a few times," Edward said.

"He did?" Cecilia was surprised by how happy this made her. Thomas's accounts of his barracks were somewhat grim. She was glad that he'd had the chance to spend some time in a proper home, with a proper family. She glanced over at Edward and with a little smile and a shake of her head said, "He never mentioned it."

"And here I thought the two of you told each other everything."

"Not everything," Cecilia said, mostly to herself. She certainly had not written to Thomas about how much she enjoyed hearing from Edward in his letters to her. If she had had the chance to sit with her brother, to talk with him face-to-face, would she have told him that she was a little bit in love with his best friend?

She thought not. Some things were private, even from one's favorite brother.

She swallowed the lump forming in her throat. Thomas always liked to say that he was her favorite brother, to which she always replied that he was her *only* brother. And then their father, who'd never really had much of a sense of humor, would grumble that he'd heard this before, and honestly, couldn't the two of them work this out?

"What are you thinking about?" Edward asked.

"Sorry. Thomas again." She scrunched up one side of her mouth. "Did I look sad?"

"No. Rather happy, actually."

"Oh." She blinked a few times. "I suppose I was."

Edward nodded toward the open trunk. "You said you would have liked to help him pack?"

She thought for a moment, her eyes growing wistful. "I think so. It would have been nice to have been able to picture him with his things."

Edward nodded.

"Not necessary, of course," she said briskly, turning so that he would not see her blinking back her tears. "But it would have been nice."

"I didn't really need my mother's help," Edward said quietly.

Cecilia turned slowly to look at him, staring at the face that had become so dear to her in such a short time. She did not know what his mother looked like, but somehow she could still picture the scene: Edward, tall and strong and capable, feigning a touch of incompetence so that his mother could fuss over him.

She met his eyes with solemn respect. "You are a good man, Edward Rokesby."

For a moment he looked almost surprised by the compliment, and then he blushed, although it was mostly obscured by his beard. She dipped her chin to hide her smile. He'd not be able to hide behind his whiskers for long.

"She's my mother," Edward mumbled.

Cecilia flipped open one of the buckles on the shaving kit. "Like I said, a good man."

He blushed again. She couldn't see it—she'd already turned away—but she would have sworn that she could feel it, rippling through the still air of the room.

She loved that he blushed.

She loved that she'd caused it.

Still smiling to herself, she looked back down at the trunk, trailing her fingers along its edge. Like all his things, it was well-made, of fine wood and iron, with

Edward's initials formed by a pattern of nails at the top. "What is the *G* for?"

"*G?*"

"Your initials. *EGR.*"

"Ah. George."

She nodded. "Of course."

"Why do you say *of course?*"

She glanced over at him. "What else would it be?"

He rolled his eyes. "Gregory. Geoffrey."

"No," she said with the beginnings of a sly smile. "*Gawain.*"

She rolled her eyes. "Please. You're a George."

"My brother is a George," he corrected.

"So are you, apparently."

He shrugged. "It's a family name." He watched as she opened the leather bag and took out his straight razor. "What is yours?"

"My middle name? Esmerelda."

His eyes widened. "Really?"

She laughed. "No. Not really. I'm hardly so exotic. It's Anne. After my mother."

"Cecilia Anne. It's lovely."

Her cheeks grew warm, which struck her as bizarre, given how many other, far more blush-worthy things had happened to her that day.

"How did you shave while you were in Connecticut?" she asked. His straight razor had obviously been packed away with the rest of his belongings. He had not had it with him when he'd reappeared in Kip's Bay.

He blinked a few times. "I don't know."

"Oh, I'm so sorry." What an idiot she was. Of course he did not know.

"But," he said, in a clear attempt to put a halt to her embarrassment, "I do own two razors. The one in your hand is from my grandfather. The other was purchased right before I left. I generally take that one when I am traveling rough." He frowned. "I wonder what happened to it."

"I don't recall seeing it with your things at the hospital."

"Did I *have* things at the hospital?"

She frowned. "Now that you ask, no. Just the clothes on your back, I'm told. And whatever was in your pockets. I wasn't there when you were brought in."

"Well." He scratched his chin. "I suppose that is why I don't take my good razor."

"It's very fine," Cecilia murmured. The handle was ivory, beautifully carved and warm in her hand. The blade, the finest Sheffield steel.

"I'm named for him," Edward said. "My grandfather. His initials are in the handle. It's why he gave it to me."

Cecilia looked down. Sure enough, *EGR* had been etched delicately at the tip of the ivory. "My father's razor was similar," she said, moving over to the washbasin. It was empty, so she dipped it in the tub. "The handle isn't as fine, but the steel is the same."

"You are a connoisseur of steel blades?"

She gave him an arch look. "Are you afraid?"

"I think I should be."

She chuckled. "Anyone living so close to Sheffield knows their steel. Several of the men in the village have left in the last few years to go work at the crucible furnaces."

"Not a pleasant occupation, I should think."

"No." Cecilia thought of her neighbors—her former neighbors, she supposed. They were all young men, mostly the sons of tenant farmers. But none of them looked young after a year or two at the furnaces. "I'm told the pay is considerably better than working in the fields," she said. "I certainly hope that's true."

He nodded as she added a little soap to a dish and worked it into a lather with the brush she'd found alongside the razor. She brought it over to his bedside and frowned.

"What?"

"Your beard is quite long."

"I'm not as scruffy as that."

"It's longer than my father's ever was."

"Is that where you honed your skills?"

"Every day for the last few years of his life." She tilted her head to the side, like an artist examining her canvas. "It would be best if we could trim it first."

"Alas, I have no shears."

Cecilia had a sudden vision of the gardener going after his face with the hedge trimmers and had to stifle a snort of laughter.

"What?" Edward demanded.

"Oh, you don't want to know." She picked up the brush. "Let's give this a go."

Edward lifted his chin, allowing her to coat the left side of his face with the soapy lather. It wasn't as thick as she'd want, but it would do. She worked carefully, using one hand to stretch his skin while the other scraped the blade down from cheek to chin. With each pass she rinsed the blade in the washtub, watching as the water grew thick with his whiskers.

"You have quite a lot of red in your beard," she observed. "Does one of your parents have red hair?"

He started to shake his head.

"Don't move!"

He looked at her sideways. "Don't ask me questions."

"Touché."

"My mother's hair is blond," Edward said the next

time she rinsed the razor. "My father's is brown. Same as mine. Or rather, it used to be. He's going gray. Or silver, as he prefers to call it." He frowned, and his eyes clouded with something that looked an awful lot like regret. "I imagine he'll have quite a bit more when I see him again."

"Gray hair?" she asked, keeping her voice carefully light.

"Indeed." He tipped his chin up as she went to work on his throat. "Thank you again for writing to them."

"Of course. I only wish there was some way to get word to them faster." She'd managed to get the letter to the Rokesbys out on the very next ship, but still, it would be at least three weeks before it reached England. And then another five before they might expect a response.

They fell into silence as Cecilia continued her work. She was finding it much more difficult to do a proper job than when she'd shaved her father. Edward's whiskers had to be at least a half inch long—much different than the single day's growth she was used to.

To say nothing of the fact that this was Edward. And he had just kissed her.

And she'd liked it. Very much.

When she leaned toward him, the air seemed to change around her, swirling with awareness. It was almost electric, stealing her breath and prickling at her skin. And then when she finally did draw air, it was as if she was breathing in *him*. He smelled delicious, which made no sense, since he smelled like soap. And man.

And heat.

Dear God, she was going mad. You couldn't smell heat. And soap wasn't delicious. But nothing seemed to make sense when she was standing this close to Edward Rokesby. He addled her brain, and her lungs felt tight . . . or light . . . or something.

Honestly, it was a miracle she was able to keep her hand steady.

"Can you turn your head just a bit?" she asked. "I need to get that spot by your ear."

He complied, and she leaned even closer. She needed to angle the razor just so to avoid nicking him. She was so close now she could see her breath ruffling his hair. It would be so easy just to sigh, to let herself melt into him, to feel her body against his.

"Cecilia?"

She heard his voice, but she couldn't seem to do anything about it. She felt almost suspended, as if the air was thick enough to hold her in place. And then, as if her brain had needed an extra moment to get through to the rest of her body, she pulled herself back, blinking away what she could only assume was the fog of desire.

"Sorry," she said, the word seeming to come more from her throat than her lips. "Lost in my thoughts."

It wasn't a lie.

"It need not be perfect," he said, his voice strained. "As long as you get the bulk of it off, I can do a closer shave tomorrow."

"Of course," she answered, taking an unsteady step back. "I . . . ah . . . that will take much less time. And you're tired."

"Right," he agreed.

"You'll want . . . ehrm . . ." She blinked a few times. His bare torso was most distracting. "Do you want to don a shirt?"

"Perhaps after we finish. So it doesn't get wet."

"Of course," she said. Again. She looked down at his chest. A small blob of lather clung to the light sprinkling of hair, just above his nipple. She reached out to wipe it away, but the moment she touched his skin, his hand wrapped around her wrist.

"No," he said.

It was a warning.

He wanted her.

Maybe even more than she wanted him.

She licked her lips, which had gone unaccountably dry.

"Don't do that," he choked out.

Her eyes flew to his, and she was electrified, gripped by the intensity of his piercing blue gaze. She felt it in her chest, a pounding, pulsing thing, and for a moment she could not speak. His hand was hot against her skin, his touch unexpectedly tender.

"I can't leave you like this," she said.

He stared at her, uncomprehending. Or maybe like he thought he must have misheard.

She motioned to his beard, full on the right side, completely absent on the left. "You look rather half-baked."

He touched his chin, right at the spot where whiskers met skin, and let out a little puff of amusement.

"You look ridiculous," she said.

He stroked one side of his face, then the other.

Cecilia held up the razor and brush. "Perhaps I should finish."

His right brow rose into a perfect arch. "You don't think I should meet with Major Wilkins like this?"

"I think I might pay good money to see that." She scooted around to the other side of the bed, relieved that the tension seemed to have been broken. "If I had money."

Edward moved across the mattress so that he was closer to the edge, then held still while she soaped him up. "You are short of funds?" he asked.

Cecilia paused, wondering just how much she should tell him. She settled on: "This has proven a more expensive journey than I had anticipated."

"Such is true for most journeys, I imagine."

"So I'm told." She rinsed the razor in the tub. "This is the first I've ventured more than twenty miles out of Derbyshire."

"Really?"

"Don't move," she admonished. She'd had the blade right at his throat when he'd startled.

"Sorry, but really? The first time?"

She shrugged, rinsing the blade again. "Where would I have gone?"

"London?"

"No reason to go." The Harcourts were respectable, to be sure, but hardly the sort to send a daughter to the capital for a Season. Plus, her father hated cities. He made a fuss when he had to go to Sheffield. The one time he'd been forced to attend to business in Manchester, he'd complained for days. "No one to take me either," Cecilia added.

"I will take you."

Her hand stilled. He thought they were married.

Of course he'd think he might someday take her to London.

"That is, if you wish," he added, misunderstanding her hesitation.

She forced a smile. "That would be lovely."

"We'll go to the theater," he said with a yawn. "Or maybe the opera. Do you like the opera?"

Suddenly she was desperate to end the conversation. Her mind was filled with visions of a future that included the both of them, a future where her last name really was Rokesby, and she lived in a darling house in Kent with three little children, all with their father's arrestingly blue eyes.

It was a lovely future. It just wasn't hers.

"Cecilia?"

"We're all done," she said, a little too loudly.

"Already?" His brow furrowed into a quizzical vee as he touched his right cheek. "You did this side much faster than the other."

She shrugged. "Easier as I went along, I suppose." She hadn't done quite as careful a job on the right side, but it wasn't noticeable unless one got right up next to him. And at any rate, he'd said he was going to do it again tomorrow.

"I should let you rest. You're tired, and we have that meeting later."

"You don't have to leave."

She did. For her own sake. "I'll bother you," she said.

"Not if I'm sleeping." He yawned again, then smiled, and Cecilia was nearly thrown back by the force of his beauty.

"What?" he asked. He touched his face. "Did you miss a spot?"

"You look different clean-shaven," she said. Or did she whisper it?

He gave her a loopy smile. "More handsome, I trust."

Much more. She wouldn't have thought that possible.

"I should go. We'll need someone to take care of the water and—"

"Stay," he said simply. "I like having you here."

And as Cecilia gingerly sat on the far side of the bed, it seemed impossible that he could not hear the sound of her heart breaking.

Chapter 7

*Oh for heaven's sake, I know I don't have a freak-
ishly large nose. I was merely making a point. You
cannot expect honesty from Mr. Rokesby when the
subject of conversation is your sister. He must be
complimentary. I think it is an unwritten dictum
among men, is it not?*

What does Lieutenant Rokesby look like?

—FROM CECILIA HARCOURT TO
HER BROTHER THOMAS

When they went downstairs at half five that evening, Major Wilkins was already waiting for
them in the dining room, seated near the wall with a
mug of ale and a plate of bread and cheese. Edward gave

him a crisp shoulder bow when he stood to greet them. He'd not served alongside Wilkins, but their paths had crossed often enough. The major served as a sort of administrator for the British garrison in New York and was certainly the correct place to begin in any search for a missing soldier.

Edward had always found him somewhat pompous, but with that came a rigid adherence to rules and order, which he supposed was a necessary trait in a military administrator. And truth be told, *he* wouldn't have wanted the man's job.

Cecilia wasted no time once they were seated. "Have you any news of my brother?"

Major Wilkins gave her what even Edward could recognize as a condescending look, then said, "It is a large theater of war, my dear. We cannot expect to find one man so quickly." He motioned to the plate at the center of the table. "Cheese?"

Cecilia was momentarily flummoxed by the change of subject, but she seemed to regain her purpose quickly. "This is the army," she protested. "The British Army. Are we not the most advanced, the most well-organized force in the world?"

"Of course, but—"

"How could we lose a man?"

Edward laid a gentle hand on her arm. "The chaos of war can test even the most well-run of militaries. I myself went missing for months."

"But he wasn't missing when he went missing!" she cried.

Wilkins chortled with amusement at her malapropism, and Edward nearly groaned at his insensitivity.

"Oh, now that's a good one," the major said, cutting off a thick slice of cheddar. "Wasn't missing when he went missing. Heh heh. The colonel will love that one."

"I misspoke," Cecilia said tightly.

Edward watched her carefully. He'd thought to intervene on her behalf, but she seemed to be in good control of the situation. Or if not the situation, at least of herself.

"What I meant," she continued, her eyes icing over in a way that ought to have frightened Major Wilkins, "was that Thomas was here in New York. In hospital. And then he wasn't. It's not as if he was on a battlefield or off scouting behind enemy lines."

Scouting behind enemy lines. Edward frowned as the words rolled around between his ears. Was that what he'd been doing in Connecticut? It seemed the most likely scenario. But why? He didn't recall ever having done so before.

"Well, that's just the thing," Major Wilkins said. "I

can find no record of your brother having been in hospital."

"What?" Cecilia's head jerked as she looked to Edward and then back again at the major. "That's impossible."

Wilkins shrugged unapologetically. "I had my man go through the records. The name and rank of every soldier who is brought to hospital is recorded in a ledger. We make note of the date of arrival and the date of, ehrm, departure."

"Departure?" Cecilia echoed.

"Or death." Wilkins had the grace to look at least a little uncomfortable upon raising this possibility. "Regardless, we could not find record of your brother."

"But he was injured," Cecilia protested. "We received notice." She turned back to Edward, visibly agitated. "My father received a letter from General Garth. He wrote that Thomas had been injured, but that it wasn't a mortal wound and he was recovering in hospital. Is there another hospital?"

Edward looked to Major Wilkins.

"Not on this part of the island."

"Not on *this part*?" Cecilia said, leaping onto his choice of words.

"There is something of an infirmary up in Haarlem," Wilkins answered with the sort of sigh that said he wished he hadn't brought it up. "I wouldn't call it a hospital." He glanced over at Edward with a meaningful look in his eye. "Wouldn't want to stay there myself, if you know what I mean."

Cecilia blanched.

"For God's sake," Edward snapped, "you're talking about the lady's brother."

The major turned to Cecilia with a contrite expression. "My apologies, ma'am."

She nodded, a tense little motion made heartbreaking by the convulsive swallow in her throat.

"The infirmary in Haarlem is rudimentary at best," Major Wilkins said to Cecilia. "Your brother is an officer. He would not have been brought to such a place."

"But if it was the closest facility . . ."

"His wound was not life-threatening. He would have been moved."

Edward did not like the idea of enlisted men being forced to convalesce in subpar conditions merely on account of their rank, but there were only so many beds in the hospital here at the southern end of Manhattan Island. "He's right," he said to Cecilia. The army would always move the officers first.

"Perhaps Thomas would have had reason to refuse a transfer," Cecilia suggested. "If he was with his men he might not have wished to leave them."

"This would have been months ago," Edward said, hating that he had to pierce her hopes this way. "Even if he had stayed to be with his men, surely he would have moved down here by now."

"Oh, of a certain," Major Wilkins said matter-of-factly. "There's simply no way he'd be up in Haarlem."

"You can hardly even call it a town," Edward said to Cecilia. "There's the Morris Mansion, but beyond that, it's more of a collection of abandoned colonial camps."

"But don't we have men there?"

"Merely to keep it from falling back into enemy hands," Major Wilkins said. "Good farmland up there too. We've got some crops almost ready for harvest."

"We?" Edward could not help but inquire.

"The Haarlem farmers are loyal to the king," the major said firmly.

Edward wasn't so sure about that, but this hardly seemed the time for a discussion on the local political leanings.

"We went through six months of records at the hospital," Major Wilkins said, bringing the conversation back to its purpose. He reached out to fix himself another piece of bread and cheese, scowling when the cheddar crumbled on the knife. "We could not find any mention of your brother. Honestly, it's as if he never existed."

Edward fought a groan. By God, the man had no tact.

"But you will continue to make inquiries?" Cecilia asked.

"Of course, of course." The major looked to Edward. "It is the least I can do."

"The very least," Edward muttered.

Major Wilkins drew back. "I beg your pardon?"

"Why did you not give my wife this information when you spoke to her last week?" Edward asked.

The major went still, his food mere inches from his mouth. "I didn't know she was your wife."

Edward could have cheerfully strangled him. "How does that make a difference?"

Major Wilkins just stared.

"She was still Captain Harcourt's sister. She deserved your respect and consideration regardless of her marital status."

"We are not used to fielding questions from family members," the major said in a stiff voice.

Edward had about six different replies to that, but he decided there was nothing to be gained in further antagonizing the major. Instead he turned to Cecilia. "Do you have that letter from General Garth with you?"

"Of course." She reached into her skirt pocket. "I carry it with me at all times."

Edward took it from her slender hand and unfolded the paper. He read it silently, then held it out toward Major Wilkins.

"What?" Cecilia asked. "What is wrong?"

The major's bushy brows came together, and he didn't look up from the letter as he said, "This doesn't sound like General Garth."

"What do you mean?" Cecilia turned frantically toward Edward. "What does he mean?"

"There's something wrong with it," Edward said. "I can't put my finger on it."

"But why would someone send me such a thing?"

"I don't know." He pressed his fingers to his temple, which had begun to ache.

Cecilia caught the motion immediately. "Are you all right?"

"I'm fine."

"Because we can—"

"We are here about Thomas," he said sharply. "Not me." He took a breath. He could get through this meeting. He might have to go right back to bed when they were through, he might even take that dose of laudanum she'd been threatening him with, but he could make it through one goddamned meeting with Major Wilkins.

He was not so damaged as that.

He looked up to realize that both Cecilia and the major were watching him with expressions of wary concern.

"I trust your injury does not bother you overmuch," Wilkins said gruffly.

"It hurts like the devil," Edward said through gritted teeth, "but I'm alive, so I'm trying to be grateful for that."

Cecilia looked at him with sharp surprise. He supposed he could not blame her. He was not normally so caustic.

Wilkins cleared his throat. "Right, well. Regardless, I was most relieved to hear of your safe return."

Edward sighed. "My apologies," he said. "My temper grows short when my head hurts more than normal."

Cecilia leaned in and said in a quiet voice, "Shall I take you back upstairs?"

"It is not necessary," Edward muttered. His breath caught as the pain in his temple intensified. "Not yet, anyway." He looked back over at Wilkins, who was frowning as he reread the letter from the general.

"What is it?" Edward asked.

The major scratched his chin. "Why would Garth . . . ?" He shook his head. "Never mind."

"No," Cecilia said quickly. "Tell me."

Major Wilkins hesitated, as if he was trying to figure out the best way to express his thoughts. "I find this an odd collection of information," he finally said.

"What do you mean?" Cecilia asked.

"It's not what one would normally write in a letter to a soldier's family," the major said. He looked to Edward for confirmation.

"I suppose," Edward replied, still rubbing his temple. It wasn't doing much good, but he couldn't seem to stop. "I've not written such a missive myself."

"But you said something was wrong with the letter," Cecilia reminded him.

"Nothing so specific," Edward told her. "It just feels off. I know General Garth. I can't put my finger on why, but it doesn't sound like something he would write."

"I *have* written such missives," Major Wilkins said. "Many of them."

"And . . . ?" Cecilia prodded.

He took a long breath. "And I would never write that a man was injured but it was not life-threatening. There is no way to know that. It takes a month for word to get home. Anything could happen in that time."

While Cecilia nodded, the major went on. "I have seen far more men succumb to infection than to the trauma of their original wounds. I lost a man last month because of a blister." He looked to Edward with an expression of disbelief. "A blister."

Edward shot a quick glance at Cecilia. She was holding herself still, the very model of upright British stoicism. But her eyes were haunted, and he had the awful sensation that if he touched her—just one finger to her arm—she would shatter.

And yet he was desperate to hold her. He wanted to hold her so tightly that she could not break apart. To hold her so long that her worries and fears melted from her body and seeped into his own.

He wanted to absorb her pain.

He wanted to be her strength.

He would be, he vowed. He would recover. He would heal. He would be the husband she deserved.

The husband he deserved to be.

"It was on his foot," the major was saying, oblivious to Cecilia's distress. "His stockings must have rubbed him the wrong way. He'd been marching through swamp. It's impossible to keep your feet dry, you know."

Cecilia, to her great credit, managed a sympathetic nod.

Major Wilkins put his hand on his mug of ale, but he did not pick it up. He seemed to sag a little, as if the memory still had the ability to puncture him. "The cursed thing must have broken open because within a day it was infected and within a week he was dead."

Cecilia swallowed. "I'm very sorry for your loss." She looked down at her hands, clasped together on the table, and Edward had the distinct sensation that she was trying to keep them from trembling. As if the only way to do that was to keep her eyes on her fingers, watching them for signs of weakness.

She was so strong, his wife. He wondered if she realized it.

The major blinked as if surprised by her condolences. "Thank you," he said awkwardly. "It was . . . Well, it was a loss."

"They all are," Edward said in a quiet voice, and for a moment he and the major, with whom he had so little in common, were brothers in arms.

Several seconds passed before anyone spoke. Finally Major Wilkins cleared his throat and said, "May I keep this?" He held up the letter from General Garth.

Cecilia barely moved, but Edward saw the turmoil she held tightly behind her pale green eyes. Her chin drew back—just the tiniest hint of movement—and her lower lip trembled before she caught it between her teeth. The letter from the general was her only connection to her brother, and she was clearly loath to part with it.

"Let him take it," he said to her when she looked to him for guidance. Wilkins could be a boor, but he was a good soldier, and he needed the letter if he was going to get any further in their search for Thomas.

"I will treat it with great care," Wilkins assured her. He tucked the folded missive in an inside coat pocket and patted it. "I give you my word."

"Thank you," Cecilia said. "I apologize if I seem ungrateful. I do appreciate your help."

A most gracious sentiment, Edward thought, especially considering the major's complete lack of cooperation up to this point.

"Right, well. I'll be on my way." Major Wilkins stood, giving Cecilia a polite bow of his head before turning to Edward. "I do hope your injury improves."

Edward acknowledged this with a nod. "You will forgive me if I do not rise." He felt rather queasy all of a sudden, and he had a horrendous premonition that he might empty the contents of his belly if he tried to stand.

"Of course, of course," the major said in his usual gruff manner. "Think nothing of it."

"Wait!" Cecilia called out, scrambling to her feet as Wilkins turned to leave.

He tilted his head toward her. "Ma'am?"

"Will you take me to Haarlem tomorrow?"

"What?" Sour stomach be damned, Edward hauled himself upright for that.

"I would like to visit that infirmary," Cecilia said to the major.

"I will take you," Edward cut in.

"I don't think you are in any condition—"

"*I* will take you."

Wilkins looked from Edward to Cecilia and back with only slightly concealed amusement before offering her a little shrug. "I cannot countermand a husband's wishes."

"But I need to go," Cecilia protested. "Thomas could be—"

"We have already determined that it is highly un-likely that he is in Haarlem," Edward said. He clutched the edge of the table, hoping that he wasn't being too obvious about it. A touch of vertigo had descended upon him with his sudden rise to his feet.

"But he could have been there," Cecilia said. "And if that's the case, someone will remember him."

"I will take you," Edward said again. Haarlem was only about ten miles away, but ever since the British had lost (and then regained) the territory in 1776, it had felt like more of a wild outpost than the former Dutch village it was. It was no place for a lady alone, and while he did not doubt Major Wilkins's ability to watch over

Cecilia, he could not help but think that it was his duty as her husband to see to her safety.

"If you will allow me to take my leave," Major Wilkins said, bowing again to Cecilia.

She gave a curt nod. Edward was fairly certain, however, that her ire was not directed at the major. Indeed, the moment Wilkins departed, she turned to Edward and, with jutted chin, said, "I must go to that infirmary."

"And you will go." He lowered himself back into his seat. "Just not tomorrow."

"But—"

"Nothing will change in a day," he cut in, far too exhausted to argue with her on this matter. "Wilkins is making inquiries. He will gain far more information from General Garth's attaché than we will from a journey up the island."

"Surely it would be better if we pursued both avenues of inquiry," she said, sitting back down beside him.

"I do not argue with you on that point," he said. He closed his eyes briefly, fighting the wave of fatigue that had fallen over him like a blanket. With a sigh, he continued, "Nothing will be lost if we wait a day or two. I promise."

"How can you promise?"

God, she was like a dog with a bone. Edward would

admire her tenacity if he weren't so goddamned ill. "Fine," he snapped. "I can't promise. For all I know the Continental Army could arrive tomorrow and we will all die before we get the chance to investigate the infirmary. But I can promise that given everything I know—which admittedly isn't much, but it's more than you do—a few days will not make a difference."

She stared at him in shock. It occurred to him that perhaps he ought not to have married a woman with such extraordinary eyes. Because when she stared, it took every ounce of his fortitude not to squirm in his seat.

If he were a metaphysical man, he'd think she could see straight to his soul.

"Major Wilkins could have taken me," she said with soft defiance.

He fought the urge to groan. "Do you really wish to spend the day with Major Wilkins?"

"Of course not, but—"

"What if you are forced to spend the night? Did you consider that possibility?"

"I made it across the Atlantic on my own, Edward. I'm sure I can tolerate a night in Haarlem."

"But you shouldn't have to," he ground out. "You married me, Cecilia. For God's sake, let me protect you."

"But you can't."

Edward reeled in his seat. Her words had been soft, but if she had pulled back her fist and slammed it into his neck she could not have landed a better punch.

"I'm sorry," she said quickly. "I'm so sorry. I didn't mean—"

"I know what you meant."

"No, I don't think you do."

His temper, which had been simmering at the surface, started to spit and sizzle. "You're right," he said in a harsh voice. "I don't know. Do you know why? Because I don't know *you*. I'm married to you, or so I'm told—"

She flinched.

"—and while I can imagine all sorts of reasons why such a union would have come to pass, I can't remember a single one of them."

She said nothing, made no movement save for a tiny tremble passing over her lips.

"You *are* my wife, aren't you?" he asked, but his tone was so unkind that he rescinded the question immediately. "Forgive me," he muttered. "That was uncalled for."

She regarded him for a few more seconds, her face revealing nothing of her thoughts. But she was pale, unsettlingly so as she said, "I think you should rest."

"I know I should rest," he said irritably. "Do you

think I don't feel what is going on in my head? It's as if someone is taking a hammer to my skull. From the inside out."

She reached across the table and placed her hand atop his.

"I don't feel well," he said. Four little words, yet so hard for a man to say. But still, he felt so much better for having done so.

No, not better. Relieved. Which he supposed was a form of better.

"You are doing remarkably well," she said. "You must not forget that it has been only a day since you woke up."

He eyed her with a narrowed stare. "Don't say that Rome wasn't built in a day."

"I would never," she promised, and he could hear the smile in her voice.

"I felt better this afternoon," he said. His voice was small, almost childlike to his ears.

"Better? Or improved?"

"Improved," he admitted. "Although when I kissed you . . ."

He smiled. When he kissed her, he'd almost felt whole.

Cecilia stood and gently took his arm. "Let's go upstairs."

He did not have the energy to argue.

"I shall have supper brought to the room," she said as they made their way to the stairs.

"Not much," he said. "My stomach . . . I don't know what I could keep down."

She looked at him intently. Probably measuring how green his skin had become.

"Broth," she said. "You must have something. Otherwise you will never regain your strength."

He nodded. Broth sounded possible.

"Perhaps some laudanum," she said quietly.

"A small amount."

"Very small, I promise."

When they arrived at the top of the stairs, he reached into his coat pocket and took out the key. Wordlessly, he handed it to her and leaned against the wall while she unlocked the door.

"I'll help you with your boots," she said, and he saw that she had led him inside and sat him down on the bed without him even realizing it.

"I would remind you that you should not overexert yourself," she said as she pulled off one boot, "but I am aware that your exertions today were for Thomas."

"And for you," he said.

Her hands stilled, but only for a moment. He might

not have noticed it if he weren't so exquisitely aware of her touch.

"Thank you," she said. She reached behind his heel and gripped his other boot, giving it a sharp tug before sliding it off. Edward crawled under the blankets while she meticulously put them in the corner. "I'll prepare the laudanum," she said.

He closed his eyes. He wasn't sleepy, but his head felt better when his eyes were closed.

"I wonder if you should have remained in hospital for another day." Her voice was closer now, and he heard her shaking liquid in a bottle.

"No," he said. "I would rather be here with you."

Again, she stilled. He didn't need to see her to know it.

"The hospital was unbearable," he said. "Some of the men . . ." He didn't know how much to tell her, how much she already knew. Had she spent the night by his side while he was unconscious? Did she know what it meant to try to sleep while across the room, a man moaned in agony, crying out for his mother?

"I agree with you," she said, nudging him to scoot into a more upright position. "This is a much more pleasant place to recuperate. But the doctor is at the hospital."

"Do you think so?" he said with a hint of a smile. "I'd wager he's downstairs having a pint. Or maybe over at the Fraunces. Better ale there, I think."

"Speaking of drinks," Cecilia said, her voice a delightful blend of no-nonsense and good humor, "here is your laudanum."

"Considerably more potent than a pint," Edward said, opening his eyes. It wasn't so bright any longer; Cecilia had pulled the curtains shut.

She held the cup to his lips, but he gave her a little shake and said, "I can do it myself."

"It's a very small dose," she promised.

"The doctor gave you instructions?"

"Yes, and I have some experience with the medicine. My father sometimes had megrims."

"I did not realize," he murmured.

"They were not frequent."

He drank the drug, wincing at the bitter taste of it.

"It's foul, I know," she said, but she did not sound especially sympathetic.

"You'd think the alcohol would make it tolerable."

She smiled a little at that. "I think the only thing that makes it tolerable is the promise of relief."

He rubbed his temple. "It hurts, Cecilia."

"I know."

"I just want to feel like myself again."

Her lips quivered. "We all want that."

He yawned, even though logically it was still too soon for the opiate to have taken effect. "You still need to tell me," he said, sliding back down under the covers.

"Tell you what?"

"Hmmm"—he made a funny little high-pitched noise as he thought about that—"everything."

"Everything, eh? That might be a touch ambitious."

"We have time."

"We do?" Now she sounded amused.

He nodded, and he realized that the drug must have taken hold because he had the oddest feeling—he was too tired to yawn. But he was still able to get a few words out.

"We're married," he said. "We have the rest of our lives."

Chapter 8

Edward Rokesby looks like a man, that's what he looks like. Really, Cecilia, you should know better than to ask me to describe another man. His hair is brown. What more can I say?

Furthermore, if you must know, I show your miniature to everyone. I know I am not as frequently sentimental as you might like, but I do love you, dear sister, and I am proud to call you mine. Also, you are a far more prolific letter writer than any other of the men here enjoy, and I do enjoy basking in their jealousy.

Edward, in particular, suffers from the green-eyed monster whenever the mail is brought forth. He has three brothers and one sister, and in terms

*of correspondence, you outdo all of them put to-
gether.*

—FROM THOMAS HARCOURT
TO HIS SISTER CECILIA

Three hours later, Cecilia was still haunted by his words.

We're married.

We have the rest of our lives.

Sitting at the small table tucked into the corner of their room at the Devil's Head Inn, she let her forehead drop into her hands. She had to tell him the truth. She had to tell him everything.

But how?

And more to the immediate point, when?

She'd told herself that she had to wait until after their meeting with Major Wilkins. Well, that had happened, but now Edward seemed to have taken a turn for the worse. She could not upset him now. He still needed her.

Oh, stop lying to yourself, she almost said aloud. He didn't need her. She might be making his recovery more pleasant, and maybe even more speedy, but if she were to suddenly disappear from his life, he would be just fine.

He'd needed her while he was unconscious. Now that he was awake she was not nearly so essential.

She looked over at him, sleeping peacefully in the bed. His dark hair had fallen forward over his brow. He needed a trim, but she found she liked it messy and untamed. It gave him a slightly rakish air, which was delightfully at odds with his upright character. His unruly locks reminded her that this honorable man still had a wicked and wry sense of humor, that he too could fall prey to frustration and anger.

He was not perfect.

He was *real*.

And somehow this made her feel even worse.

I will make this up to you, she vowed.

She would earn his forgiveness.

But it was becoming more and more difficult to imagine how that might be possible. Edward's ironclad sense of honor—the very thing that had convinced her that she could not reveal her lie before they met with Major Wilkins—meant that she was caught in a new dilemma.

In his eyes, he had compromised her.

They might not be sharing a bed, but they were sharing a bedroom. Once Edward learned that she was not actually his wife, he would insist upon marrying her. He was above all a gentleman, and his gentleman's honor would never allow him to do otherwise.

And while Cecilia could not stop herself from dreaming—just a little bit—about a life as Mrs. Edward Rokesby, how could she live with herself if she trapped him into marriage in truth?

He would resent her. No, he would hate her.

No, he wouldn't hate her, but he would never forgive her.

She sighed. He was never going to forgive her, regardless.

"Cecilia?"

She startled. "You're awake."

Edward gave her a sleepy smile. "Barely."

Cecilia stood and crossed the short distance to the bed. Edward had fallen asleep fully clothed, but about an hour into his nap she'd thought he looked uncomfortable and had removed his cravat. It was a testament to the laudanum that he'd barely stirred when she'd done so.

"How are you feeling?" she asked.

He frowned, and Cecilia thought it a good sign that he had to think about it. "Better," he said, then corrected himself with a little twist of his lips. "Improved."

"Are you hungry?"

He had to think about that one too. "Yes, although I'm not sure if food would sit well in my stomach."

"Try some broth," she said. She stood and picked up the small tureen she'd fetched from the kitchen ten minutes earlier. "It's still warm."

He pushed himself up into a sitting position. "Did I sleep long?"

"About three hours. The laudanum worked quickly."

"Three hours," he murmured, sounding surprised. His brow furrowed as he blinked a few times.

"Are you trying to decide if your head still hurts?" Cecilia asked with a smile.

"No," he answered plainly. "It definitely still hurts."

"Oh." She wasn't really sure what to say to that, so she just added, "I'm sorry."

"It's different, though."

She set the tureen on the table next to the bed and sat beside him. "Different?"

"Less piercing, I think. More of a dull ache."

"Surely that must be an improvement."

He touched his temple lightly and murmured, "I think so."

"Do you need assistance?" Cecilia asked, motioning to the soup.

He gave her a hint of a smile. "I can manage, although a spoon might be helpful."

"Oh!" She jumped to her feet. "I'm so sorry. Do you know, I think they forgot to give me one."

"No matter. I can just drink it." He raised the tureen to his lips and took a sip.

"Good?" Cecilia asked when he let out a satisfied sigh.

"Quite. Thank you for getting it."

She waited for him to take a few more sips, then said, "You really do look better than you did at the meeting with Major Wilkins." Then it occurred to her that he might think she was trying to talk him into taking her to Haarlem sooner rather than later, so she added, "Not well enough to head north tomorrow, though."

He seemed to find that amusing. "Maybe the next day."

"Probably not then, either," she admitted. She let out a breath. "I have had time to reflect upon our meeting with Major Wilkins. He said that he would make inquiries at the Haarlem infirmary. I still wish to visit myself, but for now, that is enough." She swallowed, and she wasn't sure which of them she was trying to reassure when she said, "I will be patient."

What other choice did she have?

He set the soup on the table and took her hand. "I want to find Thomas as much as you do."

"I know." Cecilia looked down at their entwined fingers. It was odd how well they seemed to fit together. His hands were large and square, his skin tanned and rough from work. And hers—well, they were no longer so white and delicate, but she took pride in her new-found calluses. They seemed to say that she was capable, that she could take control of her own destiny. She saw strength in her hands, strength she had not known she possessed.

"We will find him," Edward said.

She looked up. "We might not."

His eyes, almost navy blue in the fading light, settled on hers.

"I must be realistic," she said.

"Realistic, yes," he said, "but not fatalistic."

"No." She managed a little smile. "I'm not that."

Not yet, anyway.

They did not speak for a few moments, and the silence, which began as something companionable, grew heavy and awkward as Cecilia realized that Edward was trying to figure out the best way to broach an uncomfortable topic. Finally, after clearing his throat several times, he said, "I would like to know more about our marriage."

Her heart stopped. She'd known this was coming, but still, for a brief moment she could not breathe.

"I do not question your word," he said. "You are

Thomas's sister, and I hope you will not judge me as too forward if I tell you that I have long felt that I know you from your letters to him."

She had to look away.

"But I would like to know how it all came about."

Cecilia swallowed. She'd had several days to come up with a story, but thinking about a lie wasn't the same as saying it out loud. "It was Thomas's wish," she told him. This much was true, or at least she assumed it was. Surely her brother would want to see his dearest friend marry his sister. "He was worried about me," she added.

"Because of your father's death?"

"He does not know of that," Cecilia answered honestly. "But I know that he has long been concerned about my future."

"He had said as much to me," Edward confirmed.

She looked up in surprise. "He did?"

"Forgive me. I do not wish to speak ill of the dead, but Thomas had intimated that your father was less concerned with your future than he was with his present."

Cecilia swallowed. Her father had been a good man, but also a fundamentally selfish one. Still, she'd loved him. And she'd known that he'd loved her to the best of his ability. "I brought comfort to my father's life," she said, picking her words as if walking through a field of flowers. There had been good times too, and these were what she wished to gather into a bouquet. "And he gave me purpose."

Edward had been watching her closely as she spoke, and when she chanced a look in his eyes she saw something she thought was pride. Mixed for certain with skepticism. He saw through her words, but he admired her for saying them.

"Anyway," she said, trying to lighten her tone, "Thomas knew that my father was ailing."

Edward's head tipped to the side. "I thought you said it was sudden."

"It was," she said hastily. "I mean, I think it's often like that. Very slow, and then quite quick."

He didn't say anything.

"Or maybe it's not," she said. Dear God, she sounded like an idiot, but she couldn't seem to shut her mouth. "I haven't much experience with the dying. None, actually, except for my father."

"Nor I," Edward said. "Not with natural death, at least."

Cecilia looked at him. His eyes had gone dark.

"I do not count the battlefield as natural," he said quietly.

"No, of course not." Cecilia didn't even want to think about what he had seen. The death of a young man in his prime was far different than the passing of a man her father's age.

Edward took another sip of his soup, and Cecilia took this to be a signal that she should continue with her tale. "Then my cousin asked for my hand," she said.

"I take it from your tone that this was not a welcome proposal."

Her mouth grew tight. "No."

"Your father did not rebuff him? Wait"—Edward's hand rose a few inches, his forefinger flexed the way one did before raising a point in a conversation—"was this before or after he died?"

"Before," Cecilia replied. Her heart sank an inch. This was where the lies began. Horace had not become a menace until after her father had died, and Thomas had never known that he had begun to pressure Cecilia to marry him.

"Of course. It would have to have been because . . ." Edward frowned, pulling his hand from hers and rubbing his chin. "Maybe it's my head slowing me down, but I can't keep the timeline straight. I might need you to write this down for me."

"Of course," Cecilia said, but her guilt beat inside her like a drum. She could not believe she was letting him think *he* was the reason the story was so difficult to follow. She tried for a smile, but she wasn't sure she managed more than a twitch of her lips. "I can hardly believe it either."

"I'm sorry?"

She should have known she would have to explain that comment. "Just that I can't quite believe I'm here. In New York."

"With me."

She looked at him, at this honorable and generous man she did not deserve. "With you."

He took her hand and brought it to his lips. Cecilia's heart melted a little, even as her conscience sobbed. Why did this man have to be so bloody nice?

She took a breath. "Marswell is entailed, and Horace will inherit if something should happen to Thomas."

"Is that why he proposed?"

She gave him a look. "You don't think he was overwhelmed by my natural charm and beauty?"

"No, that would be why *I* proposed." Edward started to grin, but it quickly fell to a grimace. "I did propose, didn't I?"

"Sort of. Ah . . ." She felt her face burn. "It was more of, ah . . ." She leapt upon the only possible answer. "Actually, Thomas took care of most of the arrangements."

Edward did not appear happy with this turn of events.

"It could hardly have happened any other way," Cecilia pointed out.

"Where was the ceremony?"

She'd thought of that one. "On the ship," she said.

"Really?" He looked frankly baffled by the whole thing. "Then how did I . . . ?"

"I'm not sure," Cecilia said.

"But if you were on the ship, *when* did I . . . ?"

"Just before you left for Connecticut," Cecilia lied.

"I went through the ceremony three months before you did?"

"They don't have to take place at the same time," Cecilia said, aware that she was digging herself in ever deeper. She had more excuses prepared—that the vicar in her village refused to perform a proxy marriage, or that she had not wanted to say her vows until it became absolutely necessary so that Edward might withdraw from the marriage if he changed his mind. But before she could bring herself to utter another falsehood, she realized that he was stroking her finger, right where a ring ought to be.

"You don't even have a ring," he said.

"I don't need one," she said quickly.

His brow drew into a firm line. "You need one."

"It can wait, though."

Then, with a movement so sudden she wouldn't

have thought him capable of it in his current condition, he pushed himself upright and touched her chin. "Kiss me," he said.

"What?" she practically yelped.

"Kiss me."

"You're mad."

"It's possible," he said agreeably, "but I think any man would be quite sane to want to kiss you."

"Any man," she echoed, still trying to make sense of the moment.

"Perhaps not." He pretended to consider this. "I think I might be the jealous sort. So it would probably be quite foolish on their part."

She shook her head. Then rolled her eyes. Then did both. "You need to rest."

"A kiss first."

"*Edward.*"

He mocked her tone to perfection. "*Cecilia.*"

Her mouth fell open. "Are you making puppy eyes at me?"

"Is it working?"

Yes.

"No."

He hmmphed. "You're not a very accomplished liar, are you?"

Oh, he had no idea.

"Finish your broth," she ordered, trying—and failing—to sound stern.

"Do you mean to imply I don't have the strength to kiss you?"

"Oh my goodness, you're insufferable!"

One of his brows rose into a perfectly arrogant arch. "Because I'll have you know I take that as a dare."

She pressed her lips together in a futile attempt to hold back a smile. "What has got into you?"

He shrugged. "Happiness."

Just one word, and it knocked the breath right out of her. Underneath his honorable exterior, Edward Rokesby had a streak of playfulness a mile wide. She supposed she shouldn't have been so surprised. She'd seen hints of it in his letters.

All he'd needed to unlock it was a spot of joy.

"Kiss me," he said again.

"You need to rest."

"I just napped for three hours. I'm ridiculously awake now."

"One kiss," she heard herself saying, even as her mind was warning her not to do it.

"Just one," he agreed, then added, "I'm lying, of course."

"I'm not sure it counts as a lie if you confess to it in the same breath."

He tapped his cheek, reminding her.

Cecilia caught her lower lip between her teeth. Surely one kiss wouldn't hurt. And on the cheek, even. She leaned in.

He moved his head. Her lips touched his.

"You tricked me!"

His hand came to the back of her head. "Did I?"

"You know you did."

"Did you realize," he murmured, his breath hot and seductive against the corner of her mouth, "that when you speak against my lips it feels like a kiss?"

She nearly groaned. She did not have the strength to resist him. Not when he was like this—funny and endearing and so obviously delighted to have woken up to find himself married to her.

And now his lips were moving against hers, brushing slowly back and forth in a kiss that should have seemed chaste. But there was nothing innocent in the way her body arched toward his, eager for more. She'd been half in love with this man before they'd even met, and now her body recognized what her mind did not wish to admit—she wanted him, desperately, and in every way.

If he were not ill, if he were not still so weak, heaven only knew what would happen. Because she was not sure she would have the strength to stop them from consummating a marriage that did not even exist.

"*You* are the best medicine," Edward murmured against her skin.

"Don't discount the laudanum," she tried to joke. She needed to lighten the moment.

"I don't," he said, pulling back just far enough to look into her eyes. "Thank you for insisting that I take it. I do think it was a help."

"You're welcome," Cecilia said a little hesitantly. The change of topic was somewhat disorienting.

He stroked her cheek. "It's part of the reason I said that you are the best medicine. I spoke with the people at the hospital, you know. Yesterday, after you left."

She shook her head. She wasn't sure where he was going with this.

"They told me how well you cared for me. They told me that you insisted upon a higher standard of care than I might have received otherwise."

"Of—of course," she stammered. This had nothing to do with her being his wife. She would have done this regardless.

"One of them even said he did not think I would have awakened if not for you."

"I'm sure that's not true," she said, because she

could not take credit for that. And she could not let him think he owed her for it.

"It's funny," he murmured. "I can't recall thinking very much about getting married. I certainly don't recall thinking about *being* married. But I think I like it."

Tears began to pool in Cecilia's eyes. He reached out and brushed them away.

"Don't cry," he whispered.

"I'm not," she said, even though she was.

He smiled indulgently. "I think this might be the first time I've kissed a girl and made her cry."

"Georgie Porgie," she whispered, grateful for the distraction.

This seemed to amuse him. "It is my middle name."

She drew back, needing to put a little distance between them. But his hand slipped from her cheek to her shoulder and then down her arm to her hand. He would not let go, and she knew that deep in her heart, she did not want him to.

"It's getting late," he said.

She glanced toward the window. She'd long since pulled the curtains shut, but she could see around the edges that the day had fallen past dusk and was now somewhere close to night.

"Will you sleep tonight?" he said.

She knew what he was asking. Would she sleep in this bed?

"You need not feel uncomfortable," he said. "Much as I wish it were otherwise, I am not in any condition to make love to you."

Her face burned. She couldn't help it. "I thought you said you weren't tired," she mumbled.

"I'm not. But you are."

He was right. She was exhausted. She would have slept when he did, except that she'd felt she needed to watch over him. He'd looked so awful when she'd put him to bed earlier that evening. Worse, almost, than when he'd been in hospital.

If something happened to him, after all that had transpired . . .

She could not bear to consider it.

"Have you eaten?" he asked.

She nodded. She'd had a light meal when she'd gone down to get the broth.

"Good. We do not want the nurse to become the patient. I assure you, I would not be nearly so proficient in the role as you are." His face grew serious. "You must rest."

She knew this. She just didn't see how it was possible.

"I'm sure you still wish for modesty," he said, his own face taking on a slightly discomfited hue. Cecilia felt a little better knowing that he too saw the irregularity in their current situation.

"I give you my word that I will turn the other way," he said.

She just stared at him.

"While you change into your bedclothes," he explained.

"Oh, of course." God, she was an idiot.

"I'll even pull the covers over my head."

She rose to shaky feet. "That won't be necessary."

There was a pregnant pause, and then he said in a voice turned ever so hoarse, "It might."

Cecilia let out a little gasp of surprise at his admission, then rushed over to the wardrobe where she'd unpacked her meager supply of clothing. She'd brought one nightgown, a serviceable dress of white cotton devoid of lace or frills. Not the sort of thing a lady might tuck into her trousseau trunk.

"I'll just go over to the corner," she said.

"I'm already under the covers."

Indeed he was. While she'd been fetching her nightgown, he'd slid down until he was supine and had pulled the blanket over his face.

She would have laughed if she were not so utterly mortified herself.

With quick and efficient motions, Cecilia stripped off her clothing and jammed herself into her nightgown. It covered her from head to toe, just as much as any of her day frocks, and certainly more than an evening gown would, but still, she felt indecently exposed.

She normally gave her hair fifty strokes with a brush before bed, but this seemed excessive, especially while he had a blanket over his head, so instead she braided it into a sleeping plait. As for her teeth . . . She looked down at the toothbrush and powder she'd brought with her from England, then back over at the bed. Edward had not moved.

"I'll skip my teeth for tonight," she said. Maybe it would make him less likely to want to kiss her the following morning.

She set the toothbrush back in the wardrobe and hurried over to the far side of the bed. Carefully, so as to disturb as little of the bedclothes as possible, she lifted the blanket and crawled in.

"You can open your eyes now," she said.

He uncovered his face. "You're very far away," he said.

Cecilia pulled her right leg, which was half hanging

off the side, back onto the bed. "I think it's best," she said. She leaned over and blew out the candle, allowing darkness to wash over the room.

It didn't make her any less aware of the man lying next to her.

"Good night, Cecilia," he said.

"Good night." She shifted her position, rolling awkwardly onto her side with her back to him. This was how she generally slept, on her right side with her hands tucked under her cheek like a prayer. But it didn't feel comfortable tonight, and it certainly didn't feel natural.

She'd never fall asleep. Never.

And yet, somehow, she did.

Chapter 9

Do offer my greetings to Lieutenant Rokesby and assure him that if his siblings do not write as often as I, it can only be because they lead far more exciting lives. Derbyshire is nothing but dull this time of year. Oh, what am I saying? Derbyshire is always nothing but dull. It is a good thing, then, that I prefer an uneventful life.

—FROM CECILIA HARCOURT TO HER BROTHER THOMAS

Edward woke slowly the following morning, his mind reluctant to pull itself out of what was an exceedingly delightful dream. He was in a bed, which was noteworthy in itself—he was fairly sure he had not slept in a proper bed in months. And he was warm.

Toasty and lovely, but not too hot, the way one got during these oppressive New York summers.

Funny how nothing seemed to be actually happening in this dream; it was all about the feel of it. The cloud-like comfort of it all. Even his own body seemed eager to bask in the happy sensations. He'd woken up stiff, as he often did, but without the accompanying frustration of knowing nothing could come of it. Because in his dream he was curled up against a very delightful bottom, warm and plump, with a tantalizing little cleft that cradled him in a cozy, feminine embrace.

His hand stole down to cup one of her cheeks.

He sighed. Perfection.

He'd always liked women, liked the soft curves of their bodies, the way their skin lay pale and tender against his. He'd never been a rogue, nor had he been indiscriminate. Years ago his father had pulled him aside and put the fear of God and pox in him. And so while Edward had visited brothels with his friends, he'd never partaken of the goods. It was far safer, and in his opinion probably a great deal more pleasurable, to lie with a woman one actually knew. Discreet widows, mostly. The occasional opera singer.

But discreet widows and opera singers were not thick on the ground in the American colonies, and it had been a long time since he'd found himself so bliss-fully entwined with a set of female limbs.

He did love the feel of a warm woman next to him. Under him.

Surrounding him.

He drew her closer, this perfect lady of his dreams, and then . . .

He woke up.

For real.

Christ.

This was no dreamlike mystery woman in his arms, it was Cecilia, and her nightgown had ridden up in the night to reveal her very bare, very delightful backside.

He was still mostly dressed, having fallen asleep twice in his clothing, but his cock was protesting its confines mightily, and he really couldn't blame it, pressed up as it was against Cecilia's bottom.

Surely no man had ever found himself in such an ex-quisitely frustrating situation. She was his *wife.* Surely he had every right to draw her closer, to roll her over and begin kissing her until she was insensible with desire. He'd start at her mouth, then he'd move down the ele-gant length of her throat to the hollow of her collarbone.

From there it would be an easy slide to her breasts, which he still had not seen but was quite certain were perfectly sized and shaped for his hands. He wasn't sure how he knew this, except that everything else about her had proved perfect, so why not this?

And he had a feeling that at some point during the night before, he'd had one of those breasts cradled in his hand. His soul seemed to remember it, even if his mind did not.

But he had promised her that he would not take advantage of this forced proximity. He had promised himself that he would give her a proper wedding night, not something fumbled and rushed with a man operating at only half strength and stamina.

When he made love to her, she would have all the romance she deserved.

So now he needed to figure out how to extricate himself without waking her. Even though every masculine fiber of his being disagreed.

Some fibers disagreeing more than others.

First things first, he told himself. *Move the hand.*

He groaned. He really didn't want to move his hand.

But then Cecilia made a little noise like she might be waking up, and that seemed to jolt him out of his inaction. With a slow and careful motion, he pulled his hand away, letting his palm rest on his hip.

She mumbled something in her sleep, something

that sounded remarkably like "salmon mushie," then let out a sigh as she nestled into the pillows.

Disaster averted. Edward let himself breathe again.

Now he needed to get his arm out from underneath her. No easy task as she seemed to be using his hand as some sort of childlike lovey, pressing it up against her cheek like a favorite blanket or stuffed doll.

He gave it a little tug. She didn't budge.

He pulled with a bit more force, only to freeze when she let out a sound of sleepy irritation and burrowed harder against his hand.

Sleepy irritation. Who knew there even was such a thing?

Very well, he told himself, it was time to get serious. With an awkward shifting of his weight, he pressed his entire arm down into the mattress, creating enough of a depression for him to slide his limb out from under her without disturbing her position.

Unentangled at last. Edward started backing away, inch by inch by . . . scratch that, he didn't make it past the first two inches. It turned out that he had not been the one to cross the bed in the night, it had been Cecilia. And she apparently did not do things in half measures, because he was teetering right at the edge of the mattress.

There was nothing for it. He was going to have to get up and greet the day.

The day? He glanced toward the window. The dawn was probably more like it. Unsurprising, he supposed, since they'd fallen asleep relatively early the night before.

With one final look at Cecilia to make sure she was still sleeping soundly, Edward swung his legs over the side of the bed and stood. He didn't feel as weak as the day before, which made sense. He might have eaten nothing but broth the previous night, but he'd managed a proper meal when they'd first arrived at the Devil's Head. It was remarkable what a bit of meat and potatoes could do for a man.

His head felt somewhat better too, although some inner sense was warning him not to make any sudden, jerky movements. Which certainly ruled out a ten-mile ride up to Haarlem, but at least Cecilia had acquiesced on that score. He honestly didn't think they would find news of Thomas up at the northern outpost, but he would take her there as soon as he was able. And in the meantime, they would continue their investigation here.

He would not rest until they learned what had happened to Thomas. Edward owed this much to his friend.

And now to Cecilia, as well.

Still moving slowly, he crossed the short distance to the window and pulled the curtains back a few inches. The sun was rising over the New World, painting the sky with wide streaks of orange and pink. He thought about his family back in England. The day would have already started for them. Would they be eating their midday meal? Was the weather warm enough for a ride through the extensive grounds of Crake House? Or was spring still clinging to England, tickling the air with its chill and wind?

He missed his home, missed the deep greens of the lawns and hedges, the cool mist of the morning. He missed his mother's rosebushes, even though he'd never liked the cloying scent of them. Had he been home-sick before? He hadn't thought so, although maybe this ache had risen within him during the months that had gone missing from his memory.

Or perhaps it was something new. He had a wife now, and God willing, children would follow. He'd never thought to have a family here in the colonies. He'd always pictured himself back in Kent, settling into a property of his own, not too far from the rest of the Rokesbys.

Not that he'd ever pictured a specific woman in these hazy imaginings. He'd never courted anyone seriously, although everyone seemed to think he'd eventually marry his neighbor, Billie Bridgerton. He'd never bothered to disabuse people of this notion, and neither had Billie, but they would be a disaster as husband and wife. They were far too much like siblings to even think of marrying.

He chuckled, thinking of her. They'd run wild as children, he and Billie, along with his brother Andrew and sister Mary. It was a wonder they'd all reached adulthood in good health. He'd dislocated a shoulder and had a milk tooth knocked out before his eighth birthday. Andrew was always getting into some scrape or another. Only Mary had been immune to the constant injuries, although that was almost certainly less due to chance than to her superior sensibility.

And George, of course. George had never tested their mother's patience with breaks and bruises. But then again, he was several years older than the rest. He'd had far more important things to do than scamper about with his younger siblings.

Would Cecilia like his family? He rather thought she would, and he knew they would like her. He hoped she would not miss Derbyshire overmuch, but it didn't sound as if she had much left to tie her there, anyway. Thomas had expressed no great affection for their village; Edward would not be surprised if he remained in the army and rented Marswell out now that he was the owner.

Of course they had to find him first.

Privately, Edward was not optimistic. He had been putting on a brave front for Cecilia, but there was too much about Thomas's disappearance that made no sense for this tale to have a happy ending.

But then again, his own tale was filled with the improbable and bizarre—a lost memory, a found wife. Who was to say that Thomas would not be as lucky?

The warm hues of the sky were beginning to melt away, and Thomas let the curtain drop. He ought to get dressed—or rather redressed—before Cecilia woke up. He probably wouldn't bother with new breeches, but a fresh shirt was in order. His trunk had been set near the wardrobe, so he moved quietly across the room and opened it, pleased to see that his belongings appeared intact. He'd brought mostly clothing and equipment, but there were a few personal items mixed within. A slim volume of poetry he'd always enjoyed, a funny little wooden rabbit he and Andrew had carved when they were young.

He smiled to himself, suddenly wanting to see it again. They'd each decided to carve half, and the result had been the most misshapen, lopsided rodent ever to grace this earth. Billie had declared that if rabbits actually looked like that, they would have been predators if only because all the other animals would faint with shock.

"Then," she announced with the great drama she always employed, "they'd go in for the kill with their vicious little teeth . . ."

It was at that point that Edward's mother stumbled onto the conversation and put a halt to it, declaring that rabbits were "God's gentle creatures," and Billie should—

It was at *that* point that Edward had thrust the wooden rabbit in front of his mother's face, resulting in a shriek of such magnitude and pitch that the children were imitating it for weeks.

No one got it right, though. Not even Mary, and she could scream. (With so many brothers, she'd learned young.)

Edward dug down through his things, past the shirts and breeches, past the stockings he'd learned to mend himself. He felt around for the uneven edge of the rabbit, but his hand brushed first against a small bundle of paper, tied neatly with a piece of twine.

Letters. He'd saved all of the letters he'd received from home, not that his stack was anything compared to Thomas's. But this small pile represented everyone who was dear to him—his mother, with her tall, elegant script, his father, who never wrote much, but somehow managed to convey what he felt anyway. There was just one letter from Andrew. Edward supposed he could be forgiven; his younger brother was in the navy, and as hard as it could be for mail to reach Edward in New York, it had to be even harder for it to leave from wherever Andrew was posted.

With a nostalgic smile he continued riffling through the pile. Billie was a terrible correspondent, but she'd managed a few notes. His sister Mary was much better, and she had included a few scribblings from their youngest brother Nicholas, whom Edward was ashamed to say he barely knew. The age difference was great, and with such busy lives, they never seemed to be in the same place at the same time.

But it was at the bottom of the pile, hidden between two letters from his mother, where Edward found the most treasured piece of his collection.

Cecilia.

She had never written to him directly; they both knew that would have been highly improper. But she included a note to him at the bottom of most of her letters to her brother, and Edward had come to look forward to these embedded missives with a longing so deep he would never have admitted to it.

Thomas would say, "Ah, a letter has arrived from my sister," and Edward wouldn't even look up as he replied, "Oh, that's very nice, I hope she's well." But inside his heart beat a little harder, his lungs felt a little tighter, and as Thomas idly skimmed through Cecilia's words, Edward watched him out of the corner of his eye, trying not to scream, "Just read the bloody bit that's for me!"

No, it really would not have done to confess just how much he looked forward to Cecilia's letters.

And then one day, while Thomas was out, and Edward was resting in the room they shared, he found himself thinking of her. There was nothing abnormal about this. He thought about his best friend's sister far more than would be expected given that they had never actually met. But it had been more than a month since her last letter—an uncommonly lengthy break— and Edward was beginning to worry about her, even though he knew that the delay was almost certainly the fault of ocean winds and currents. The transatlantic post was far from dependable.

But as he lay on his bed, he realized that he could not remember precisely what she'd written in that last letter, and for some reason it became imperative that he do so. Had she described the village busybody as overbearing or overwrought? He could not recall, and it was important. It changed the meaning, and—

Before he knew it, he was in Thomas's things, fishing out Cecilia's letters just so he could reread the four sentences she had included for him.

It did not occur to him until he was done just how gravely he'd abused his friend's privacy.

That he was pathetic, he had realized all along.

Once he started he couldn't stop. Edward found himself sneaking peeks at Cecilia's letters whenever Thomas was away. It was his guilty, stealthy secret, and when he had learned that he was being sent to Connecticut, he'd filched two of her stationery sheets for himself, carefully taking only the ones where the final sheet of paper was almost entirely directed to him. Thomas would lose very little of his sister's words, and Edward would gain . . .

Well, he thought he would gain a little bit of sanity, to be frank. Maybe some hope.

In the end, he'd taken only one of her letters with him to Connecticut, opting to leave the other safely in his trunk. This seemed to have been a prudent plan. According to the people at the hospital, he had not had any papers or property when he'd been found at Kip's Bay. Heaven only knew where Cecilia's letter was now.

At the bottom of a lake, probably, or maybe kindling for a fire. Edward hoped it had been found by an enterprising bird, torn apart to cushion a nest.

Cecilia would probably like that, he thought.

He did too. It almost took the sting out of the loss.

He'd thought he'd kept it safe, always in his coat pocket. It was strange that—

Edward froze. This was the most he'd remembered since he'd awakened. Nothing of what he'd done or said, just that he'd carried a letter from his wife in his coat pocket.

Or had she even been his wife then? When *was* the date of their marriage? He'd asked her about it the day before, but they'd veered off the topic, and then—honestly, it was his own fault—he'd demanded that she kiss him.

If he hadn't got any answers, he had only himself to blame.

This letter, however—the one in his hands—was the one that was most dear to him. It was the first time she'd written expressly to him. There had been nothing terribly personal; it was as if she'd instinctively known that what he needed most was normalcy. She'd filled her page with the mundane, made delightful by her wry perspective.

Edward peeked over his shoulder to make sure that Cecilia was still sleeping, then he carefully unfolded the letter.

Dear Captain Rokesby,

Your description of the wildflowers in the colonies has made me long for spring, which is losing its fierce battle with winter here in Derbyshire. No, I lie. The battle is not fierce. Winter has crushed spring like a bug. We do not even have the pleasure of a fresh, powdery snow. Whatever precipitation we have gleaned has long since melted into a dirty, unpleasant slush, and I fear I have ruined two shoes this season. Not two pair, mind you, two shoes. The left of my slippers and the right of my boots. My frugal soul wants me to cobble together a pair from what remains, but I fear I am too vain for the resulting fashion, not to mention far too poor of balance. The heel of my boot is an inch higher than that of my slippers, and I am quite sure I shall trip over everything, fall down the stairs, and perhaps crash a window. Ask Thomas about the time I stumbled over the rug in our drawing room. 'Twas a sad cascade of maladies that followed.

Do keep yourself safe and Thomas as well, and I

will beseech of him to do the same. I shall think of
you often and keep you in my prayers.
       Your friend,
       Cecilia Harcourt

Edward stared at the elegant script for several seconds after he'd read all the words, his forefinger lightly
tracing the swirls of her name. *Your friend,* she'd written. Indeed, that was what she had been, even before
he'd known her.

His friend.

And now his wife.

Behind him, he heard the unmistakable sounds of
Cecilia waking up. He hastily refolded the letter, tucking it back into the pile from his family.

"Edward?" he heard her say. Her voice was still
thick and sleepy, as if at any moment she might slide
into an unexpected yawn.

"Good morning," he said, turning around.

"What were you reading?"

His hand tapped against his thigh. "Just a letter
from home."

"Oh." She was quiet for a moment, then softly said,
"You must miss your family dreadfully."

"I . . . yes," he said. And in that single moment
he felt like a green boy again, faced with the beauti-

ful girl across the room, the one no one had the courage to speak to. It was ridiculous, utterly mad. He was a grown man, and there had not been a woman who frightened him into silence for over a decade. But he felt as if he'd been caught red-handed.

If she found out that he'd stolen her letters . . .

He was mortified just thinking about it.

"Is something wrong?" she asked.

"No, no, of course not." He shoved the entire pile of letters back into his trunk. "Just . . . you know . . . thinking of home."

She nodded as she pushed herself upright, tucking the bedclothes primly around her.

"I haven't seen them in—ow!" Edward let out a stream of invective as his big toe slammed into the side of his trunk. He'd been so eager to hide the evidence of his lovesick foolishness that he had not been paying attention to where he was going.

"Are you all right?" she asked, sounding frankly surprised by his reaction.

Edward swore again, then immediately begged her pardon. It had been so long since he'd been in the presence of a lady. His manners were rusty.

"Do not apologize," she said. "There is nothing so awful as a stubbed toe. I only wish I could say the same when I stub mine."

"Billie does," he said.

"Who?"

"Oh, sorry. Billie Bridgerton. My neighbor." She was still in his thoughts, it seemed. Probably because he'd been looking through those letters from home.

"Oh yes. You've mentioned her."

"Have I?" he asked absently. He and Billie were the best of friends—truly, they'd grown up together. A bigger tomboy had never walked this earth, though, and he wasn't sure he'd even realized she was a girl until he was eight.

He chuckled at the memory.

Cecilia looked away.

"I can't imagine why I would have written to you about her," Edward said.

"You didn't," she explained. "Thomas did."

"Thomas?" That seemed odd.

She gave an unconcerned shrug. "You must have talked to him about her."

"I suppose." He reached back into the trunk to pull out a clean shirt. It was why he'd opened the bloody thing in the first place. "If you'll excuse me," he said before whipping his shirt over his head and pulling on the fresh one.

"Oh!" Cecilia exclaimed. "You have a scar."

He glanced back at her over his shoulder. "What?"

"There is a scar on your back. I never noticed it before." She frowned. "I suppose I wouldn't have done. While I was caring for you I never . . . Well, never mind." A moment passed and then she asked, "How did you get it?"

He reached around and pointed toward his left scapula. "This one?"

"Yes."

"I fell out of a tree."

"Recently?"

He gave her a look. Honestly. "I was nine."

This seemed to interest her, and she shifted position, sitting cross-legged under the covers. "What happened?"

"I fell out of a tree."

She groaned. "Surely there is more to the story than that."

"Not really," he said with a shrug. "For about two years I lied and said my brother pushed me, but in truth I just lost my balance. I hit a branch on the way down. Tore right through my shirt."

She chuckled at that. "You must have been the bane of your mother's existence."

"My mother and whoever was doing the mending. Although I imagine that shirt was irredeemable."

"Better a shirt than an arm or a leg."

"Oh, we ruined those as well."

"Good heavens!"

He grinned at her. "Billie broke both of her arms."

Cecilia's eyes bugged out. "At the same time?"

"Thankfully not, but Andrew and I had great fun imagining what it would have been like if she had. When she broke the second one, we tied the good one up in a sling, just to see how she managed."

"And she let you?"

"Let us? She was the one who suggested it."

"She sounds most singular," Cecilia said politely.

"Billie?" He shook his head. "There's no one else like her, that is for certain."

Cecilia looked down at the bed, picking idly at the covers. She seemed to be making some sort of pattern in her mind. "What is she doing now?" she asked.

"I have no idea," he said regretfully. It pained him that he was so cut off from his family. He'd had no news of them in over four months. And they likely thought he was dead.

"I'm sorry," Cecilia said. "I shouldn't have asked. I didn't think."

"It's all right," he replied. It certainly wasn't her fault. "Although I do wonder—might I have received correspondence during my absence? It seems likely that my family would have written to me before receiving notice that I'd gone missing."

"I don't know. We can certainly inquire."

Edward saw to his cuffs, fastening first the left and then right.

"Did they write to you often?" She smiled, but it looked forced. Or maybe she was just tired.

"My family?"

She nodded. "And your friends."

"None so often as you wrote to Thomas," he said ruefully. "I was forever jealous of that. We all were."

"Really?" Her smile lit her eyes this time.

"Really," he confirmed. "Thomas received more mail than I did, and you were his only correspondent."

"That can't be true."

"I assure you it is. Well, perhaps not if I count my mother," he admitted. "But that hardly seems fair."

She laughed at that. "What do you mean?"

"Mothers *have* to write to their sons, don't you think? But siblings and friends . . . well, they hardly need be so diligent."

"Our father never wrote to Thomas," Cecilia said. "Sometimes he asked me to pass along his greetings, but that is all." She didn't sound upset by this, or even resigned. Edward had a sudden recollection of his friend, idly whittling a stick at one of their shared camps. Thomas often spouted aphorisms, and one of his favorites had been: "Change what you can and accept what you can't."

That seemed to sum up Thomas's sister quite well.

He looked over at her, studying her for a moment. She was a woman of remarkable strength and grace. He wondered if she realized that.

He went back to fussing with his cuffs, even though they were fully fastened and straight. The urge to keep looking at her was too strong. He would embarrass her, or more likely, himself. But he wanted to watch her. He wanted to *learn* her. He wanted all of her secrets and desires, and he wanted her mundane stories, the little bits of her past that had fit into her like pieces of a puzzle.

How odd it was to want to *know* another person, inside and out. He could not recall ever wanting to do so before.

"I told you about my childhood," he said. He reached into his trunk for a fresh cravat and got to work tying it. "Tell me about yours."

"What do you wish to know?" she asked. She sounded vaguely surprised, perhaps a little amused.

"Did you play outside a great deal?"

"I did not break any arms, if that's what you're asking."

"It wasn't, but I'm relieved to hear it."

"We can't all be Billies," she quipped.

He felt his chin draw back and he turned to her, certain he'd misheard. "What did you say?"

"Nothing," she said, giving her head a little shake that said it wasn't worth talking about. "I was being silly. And no, I did not play outside a great deal. Not like you, at least. I much preferred to sit inside and read."

"Poetry? Prose?"

"Anything I could get my hands on. Thomas liked to call me a bookworm."

"More of a book dragon, I should think."

She laughed. "Why would you say that?"

"You are far too fierce to be a lowly worm."

Her eyes flicked up to the ceiling and she looked vaguely embarrassed. And perhaps a little proud as well. "I am quite sure you are the only person who has ever judged me to be fierce."

"You crossed an ocean to save your brother. That seems the very definition of fierceness to me."

"Perhaps." But the spark had left her voice.

He regarded her curiously. "Why so somber all of a sudden?"

"Just that . . ." She thought for a moment and sighed. "When I made for Liverpool—that was where I sailed from—I don't know that it was my love for Thomas that spurred me into action."

Edward walked to the bed and sat down on the edge, offering his silent support.

"I think . . . I think it was desperation." She tipped her face toward his, and he knew he would be forever haunted by the look in her eyes. It was not sorrow, nor was it fear. It was something much worse—resignation, as if she'd looked within herself and found something hollow. "I felt very alone," she admitted. "And scared. I don't know if . . ."

She did not finish her sentence right away. Edward held still, allowing his silence to be his encouragement.

"I don't know if I would have come if I had not felt so alone," she finally finished. "I'd like to think that I was thinking only of Thomas, and how much he needed my help, but I wonder if *I* needed to leave even more."

"There is no shame in that."

She looked up. "Isn't there?"

"No," he said fervently, taking hold of both her hands. "You are brave, and you have a true and beautiful heart. There is no shame in having fears and worries."

But her eyes would not meet his.

"And you are not alone," he vowed. "I promise. You will never be alone."

He waited for her to say something, to acknowledge the depth of his statement, but she did not. He could see that she was working to regain her composure. Her breathing slowly took on a more regular tenor, and she delicately pulled one of her hands from his to wipe away the moisture that clung to her lashes.

Then she said, "I would like to get dressed."

It was clearly a request for him to leave.

"Of course," he said, trying to ignore the pang of disappointment that bounced against his heart.

She gave a little nod and murmured her gratitude as he stood and walked to the door.

"Edward," she called out.

He turned, a ridiculous flare of hope rising within him.

"Your boots," she reminded him.

He looked down. He was still in his stockinged feet. He gave a curt nod—not that that would camouflage the deep flush racing up his neck—and grabbed his boots before heading out into the hall.

He could put on the damned things on the stairs.

Chapter 10

An uneventful life sounds marvelous just now. Our date of departure looms, and I do not look forward to the crossing. Did you know that it will take at least five weeks to reach North America? I'm told the journey is shorter coming home—the winds blow predominantly west to east and thus push the ships along. This is small comfort, though. We are not given an anticipated date of return.

Edward bids me to say hello and not to tell you that he is a miserable sailor.

—FROM THOMAS HARCOURT
TO HIS SISTER CECILIA

B y the time Cecilia found Edward in the main dining room of the Devil's Head, he was eating breakfast. And wearing his boots.

"Oh, do not rise," she said, when he pushed his chair back to stand. "Please."

He went still for the barest of moments, then gave a nod. It cost him, she realized, to forsake his manners as a gentleman. But he was ill. Mending, but ill. Surely he had the right to conserve his energy wherever possible.

And she had a duty to make sure that he did. It was her debt to pay. He might not realize that she owed it, but she did. She was taking advantage of his good nature and his good name. The very least she could do was restore his good health.

She sat across from him, pleased to see that he seemed to be eating more than he had the day before. She was convinced that his lingering weakness was due less to his head injury than it was to his not having eaten for a week.

Goal for today: Make sure that Edward ate properly.

Certainly easier than the previous day's goal, which was to stop lying so much.

"Are you enjoying your meal?" she asked politely. She did not know him well enough to know his moods, but he'd left their room in a strange rush, without even having put on his boots. Granted, she'd told him she wished to get dressed—which she supposed implied that she hoped for privacy—but surely that had not been an unreasonable request.

He folded the newspaper he'd been perusing, pushed a plate of bacon and eggs toward her, and said, "It's quite good, thank you."

"Is there tea?" Cecilia asked hopefully.

"Not this morning, I'm afraid. But"—he tilted his head toward a piece of paper near his plate—"we did receive an invitation."

It took Cecilia a few moments to understand what should have been a simple statement. "An invitation?" she echoed. "To what?"

And more to the point, from whom? As far as she was aware, the only people who knew she and Edward were married were a few army officers, the doctor, and the man who swept the floor in the church-hospital.

Or rather, they were the only people who *thought* they knew.

She tried to feign a smile. Her web was growing more tangled by the moment.

"Are you unwell?" Edward asked.

"No," she said, her voice emerging too suddenly from her throat. "I'm fine. Why do you ask?"

"You have a very odd expression on your face," he explained.

She cleared her throat. "Just hungry, I expect." Dear heavens, she was a terrible liar.

"It is from Governor Tryon," Edward said, sliding the invitation across the table. "He is hosting a ball."

"A ball. Now?" Cecilia shook her head in wonder. The lady at the bakery had said that there was still a bustling social scene in New York, but it seemed bizarre, what with battles being fought so close by.

"His daughter turns eighteen. I'm told he refused to allow the occasion to go unmarked."

Cecilia picked up the vellum—good heavens, where did one get vellum in New York?—and finally took the time to read the words. Sure enough, Captain the Honorable and Mrs. Rokesby had been invited to a celebration in three days' time.

She said the first thing that came into her mind: "I have nothing to wear."

Edward shrugged. "We'll find something."

She rolled her eyes. He was *such* a man. "In three days?"

"There is no shortage of seamstresses in need of coin."

"Which I don't have."

He looked up at her as if a small chunk of her brain had just flown out her ear. "But I do. And hence, so do you."

There was no way Cecilia could argue with that, no matter how mercenary it made her feel inside, so instead she mumbled, "You'd think they might have given us more notice."

Edward's head tipped thoughtfully to the side. "I imagine the invitations went out some time ago. I've only recently come back from the missing."

"Of course," she said hastily. Oh dear heavens, what was she to do about *this*? She could not go to a ball hosted by the Royal Governor of New York. She had told herself that the only reason she could get away with this charade was because no one would ever know.

She bit down hard on the inside of her cheek. No one but the governor, his wife, and every other leading Loyalist in the city.

Who might eventually return to England.

Where they might see Edward's family.

And ask them about his bride.

Good God.

"What is it?" Edward asked.

She looked up.

"You're frowning."

"Am I?" She was frankly surprised she had not burst into hysterical laughter.

He gave no reply in the affirmative, but his overly patient expression said quite clearly: *Yes, you are.*

Cecilia traced the elegant script of the invitation with her finger. "You don't find it surprising that I am included on the invitation?"

One of his hands flipped over in a what-on-earth-are-you-talking-about motion. "You are my wife."

"Yes, but how would the governor know?"

Edward cut a small piece of his slab of bacon. "I expect he's known for months."

She stared at him blankly.

He stared right back. "Is there any reason I wouldn't have told him we are married?"

"You know the governor?" she said, really wishing her voice had not squeaked on the third-to-last syllable.

He popped his bacon into his mouth and chewed before answering, "My mother is friends with his wife."

"Your mother," she repeated dumbly.

"I believe they made their bows in London together," he said. He frowned for a moment. "She was an extraordinary heiress."

"Your mother?"

"Mrs. Tryon."

"Oh."

"My mother as well, actually, but nothing so close to Aunt Margaret."

Cecilia froze. "*Aunt . . .* Margaret?"

He made a little wave with his hand, as if *that* would reassure her. "She is my godmother."

Cecilia realized that she had been holding a serving spoon full of eggs aloft for several seconds. Her wrist wobbled, and the yellow lump plopped onto her plate.

"The governor's wife is your godmother?" she eked out.

He nodded. "My sister's as well. She's not really our aunt, but we've called her that for as long as I can remember."

Cecilia's head bobbed in something resembling a nod, and although she realized that her lips were somewhat ajar, she could not seem to close them.

"Is something wrong?" he asked, clueless man that he was.

She took a moment to piece a sentence together. "You did not think to tell me that your godmother is married to the Royal Governor of New York?"

"It did not really come up in conversation."

"Good God." Cecilia sank back into her chair. That tangled web of hers? It was growing more wretchedly complex by the second. And if there was one thing she was certain of, she could not go to that ball and meet Edward's godmother. A godmother knew things. She would know, for example, that Edward had been "almost" engaged, and not to Cecilia.

She might even know the fiancée. And she would certainly want to know why Edward had forfeited an alliance with the Bridgerton family to marry a nobody like Cecilia.

"The governor," Cecilia repeated, just barely resisting the urge to let her head fall in her hands.

"He's just a man," Edward said unhelpfully.

"Says the son of an earl."

"What a snob you are," he said with a good-natured chuckle.

She drew back in affront. She was not perfect, and these days she was not even honest, but she was not a snob. "What do you mean by that?"

"Holding his position against him," he said with a continued grin.

"I'm *not*. Good heavens, no. It's quite the opposite. I'm holding my position against *me*."

He reached for more food. "Don't be silly."

"I'm a nobody."

"That," Edward said firmly, "is categorically untrue."

"Edward . . ."

"You're my wife."

That was categorically untrue. Cecilia had to slap a hand over her mouth to keep from laughing. Or crying.

Or both.

"Even if we were not married, you would be a cherished guest at the festivities."

"As the governor would have no knowledge of my existence, I would not *be* invited to the festivities."

"I expect he would know who you are. He's fiendishly good with names, and I'm sure at some point Thomas mentioned that he had a sister."

Cecilia nearly choked on her eggs. "Thomas knows the governor?"

"He dined with me there a few times," Edward said offhandedly.

"Of course," Cecilia said. Because . . . of course.

She had to put a stop to this. It was spiraling out of control. It was . . . It was . . .

"Actually," Edward mused, "he might be of help."

"I beg your pardon?"

"I don't know why I didn't think of it before." He looked up, his brow coming together over his blue, blue eyes. "We should apply to Governor Tryon for help in locating Thomas."

"Do you think he will know anything?"

"Almost assuredly not, but he knows how to apply pressure on the correct people."

Cecilia swallowed, trying to hold back tears of frustration. There it was again. That simple, inescapable truth. When it came to the search for her brother, all that really mattered was that one knew the correct people.

Her unease must have shown on her face, because Edward reached out and gave her hand a reassuring pat. "You should not feel uncomfortable," he told her. "You are a gentleman's daughter and now the daughter-in-law of the Earl of Manston. You have every right to attend that ball."

"It's not that," Cecilia said, although it was, a little. She had no experience hobnobbing with high-ranking officials. Then again, she had no experience hobnobbing with sons of earls either, but she seemed to be fake-married to one.

"Can you dance?" Edward asked.

"Of course I can dance," she practically snapped.

"Then you'll be fine."

She stared at him. "You have no clue, do you?"

He sat back in his chair, his left cheek bulging out as he pressed his tongue against the inside of it. He did that a fair bit, she realized. She wasn't quite sure yet what it meant.

"There are a lot of things about which I have no clue," he said in a voice that was far too patient to ever be mistaken for benign. "The events of the last three months, for example. How I came to have a lump the size of a robin's egg on my head. How I came to be married to *you*."

Cecilia stopped breathing.

"But what I *do* know," he went on, "is that it will give me great pleasure to buy you a pretty gown and attend a frivolous entertainment with you on my arm." He leaned forward, his eyes glittering with a strange, indecipherable ferocity. "It will be blessedly, inoffensively normal. Do you have any idea how much I crave the blessed, the inoffensive, and the normal?"

Cecilia didn't say a word.

"I thought not," he murmured. "So let's buy you a dress, shall we?"

She nodded. What else could she do?

As it turned out, it was not so easy to have an evening gown made for a woman in three days. One seamstress actually wept when she heard the amount of money Edward was willing to spend. She couldn't do it, she'd tearfully told him. Not without forty more pairs of hands.

"Will you take her measurements?" Edward asked.

"To what purpose?" an exasperated Cecilia demanded.

"Humor me," he said, and then he deposited her back at the Devil's Head while he paid a call upon his godmother. She had always enjoyed pretty things, for both herself and her daughter, and Edward was quite certain that she could be persuaded to share.

The governor and Mrs. Tryon lived with their daughter in a rented home at the edge of the town and had done—with the exception of a visit back to England—since the governor's mansion had burned to the ground in 1773. Edward had not been in New York at the time, but he'd heard all about it from his mother, who had heard all about it from Margaret Tryon. They'd lost everything they owned, and had very nearly lost their daughter too. Little Margaret—generally called May to differentiate from her mother—had survived only due to the quick thinking of her governess, who had thrown her from a second-story window into a snowbank.

Edward took a deep breath as the butler admitted him into the hall. He would have to keep his wits about him. Margaret Tryon was nobody's fool, and there was no point even trying to pretend he was in hale and hearty health. Indeed, the first words out of her mouth upon his entry into her sitting room were:

"You look terrible."

"Candid as always, Aunt Margaret," he said.

She gave him her signature one-shoulder shrug—
a throwback from her days among the French, she'd
always told him, although he wasn't sure when, exactly,
she'd been among the French—then presented her
cheek for a kiss, which he dutifully gave.

She drew back, assessing him with shrewd eyes. "I
would be remiss as your godmother if I did not point
out that your pallor is gray, your eyes are hollow, and
you've lost at least a stone."

He took a moment to digest this, then said, "You
look lovely."

This made her smile. "You always were a charming
boy."

Edward declined to point out that he was well into
his third decade of life. He was fairly certain that god-
mothers were legally permitted to refer to their charges
as boys and girls until they toddled off into the grave.

Margaret rang for tea, then leveled a frank stare in
his direction and said, "I am terribly cross with you."

He quirked a brow as he took a seat across from her.

"I have been waiting for you to visit. You returned
to New York over a week ago, did you not?"

"I spent the first eight or so days unconscious," he
said mildly.

"Ah." Her lips pressed together as she swallowed
her emotions. "I had not realized."

"I would imagine it is responsible for my terrible appearance, as you so termed it."

She regarded him for a long moment, then said, "When I next write to your mama, I shall not offer a detailed description of your countenance. Or at least not an accurate one."

"I appreciate that," Edward said honestly.

"Well," Margaret said. She tapped her fingers against the arm of her chair, something she often did when she was uncomfortable with her own displays of emotion. "How do you feel?"

"Better than yesterday." Which he supposed was something for which to be grateful.

His godmother, however, was not satisfied with this answer. "That could mean anything."

Edward considered the current state of his health. The dull ache in his head had become so constant that he could almost ignore it. Far more troublesome was his lack of stamina. He'd had to pause for what felt like a full minute after climbing the half flight of stairs to his godmother's front door. It wasn't even just to catch his breath. He'd needed time just to muster the energy to make his legs work. And the trip to the dressmaker with Cecilia had left him utterly wrecked. He'd paid the carriage driver double to take the (very) long way from the Devil's Head to the Tryons' home, just so he could close his eyes and not move a muscle for the duration.

But Aunt Margaret didn't need to know any of this. He gave her a light smile and said, "I'm walking unassisted, so that's an improvement."

Her brows rose.

"I'm still exhausted," he admitted, "and my head hurts. But I'm improving, and I'm alive, so I'm trying not to complain."

She nodded slowly. "Very stoic of you. I approve."

But before he could do so much as nod an acknowledgment, she changed the subject by saying, "You did not tell me you'd got married."

"I told very few people."

Her eyes narrowed. "Define very few."

"Well, about that . . ." Edward exhaled as he tried to figure out how best to explain his current situation to one of the few people in North America who had known him before his arrival on the continent. Also the only person who knew his mother, which was probably a far more pertinent fact.

Margaret Tryon waited with ten seconds of overt patience, then said, "Spit it."

Edward cracked a smile at that. His godmother was well-known for her frank speech. "I seem to have lost a bit of my memory."

Her lips parted, and she actually leaned forward. Edward would have congratulated himself on having cracked her unflappable veneer if his own injury weren't the unfortunate cause of the fissure.

"Fascinating," she said, eyes shining with what could only be described as academic interest. "I've never heard of such a thing. Well, no, I beg your pardon, of course I've heard of it. But it's always been one of those tales—someone knows someone else who thought they heard that another person once said they met some-one . . . You know what I mean."

Edward stared at her for a moment and made the only possible reply: "Indeed."

"How much have you forgotten?"

"About three or four months, to the best of my calculations. It's difficult," he said with a shrug, "because I cannot quite pinpoint the last thing I remember."

Margaret sat back. "Fascinating," she said again.

"Less so when it's one's own memory that has flown the coop."

"I'm sure. Forgive me. But you must confess, if this were someone else, you would be fascinated."

Edward wasn't so sure about that, but he well believed that she did. His godmother had always been interested in the scholarly and the scientific, to the point that others often criticized her as having an unfeminine mind. Predictably, Aunt Margaret had taken that as a compliment.

"Tell me," she said, her voice softening slightly. "What can I do to help?"

"About my memory? Nothing, I'm afraid. About my wife? She needs a dress."

"For the ball? Of course she does. She can have one of mine. Or May's," she added. "You'll have to get it altered, of course, but you've blunt enough to pay for that."

"Thank you," Edward said with a tip of his head. "That is exactly what I was hoping you might offer."

Margaret waved her hand. "It's nothing. But tell me, do I know this girl?"

"No, but I believe you've met her brother, Thomas Harcourt."

"I don't recall the name," she said with a frown.

"He would have come to dinner with me. Late last year, I think."

"Your friend with the blondish hair? Oh, right. Pleasant enough fellow. Convinced you to marry his sister, did he?"

"So I'm told."

Edward regretted his words the moment they left his mouth. Aunt Margaret was on them like a bloodhound.

"So you're *told*? What the devil does that mean?"

"Forget I said anything," Edward said. She would not, of course, but he had to try.

"You will explain yourself right now, Edward Rokesby, or I swear I shall write to your mother and make you sound *worse*."

Edward scrubbed at his forehead. This was all he needed. Margaret would never go through with that threat; she had far too much love for his mother to worry her needlessly. But nor would she let him out of her house until he answered her questions to her satisfaction. And given his current lack of energy, if it came down to a physical altercation, she would probably win.

He sighed. "Do you recall those months I mentioned? The ones I don't quite remember?"

"Are you telling me you don't remember marrying her?"

Edward opened his mouth, but then it just hung there. He couldn't quite bring himself to reply.

"Good God, my boy, were there any witnesses?"

Again, he had no answer.

"Are you sure you're even married to her?"

For this, he was resolute. "Yes."

She threw her arms in the air, a most out-of-character display of exasperation. "How?"

"Because I know her."

"*Do you?*"

Edward's fingers bit into the edge of his chair. Something hot and angry slithered through his veins, and it was a struggle to keep his voice clipped and even. "What do you imply, Aunt?"

"Have you seen a document? Have you consummated the marriage?"

"That is hardly your business."

"*You* are my business, and you have been since the day I stood next to your mother in Canterbury Cathedral and promised to guide you through your Christian life. Or did you forget that?"

"I confess my memory of that day is indistinct."

"*Edward!*"

If she had lost patience with him, then he was surely coming close to doing the same with her. But he kept his voice carefully regulated when he said, "I must beg of you not to call into question my wife's honor and honesty."

Margaret's eyes narrowed. "What has she done? She seduced you, didn't she? You're under her spell."

"Stop," Edward bit off, rising unsteadily to his feet. "Damn it," he growled as he grabbed the edge of the table for balance.

"Dear God, you're worse than I thought," Margaret

said. She hurried to his side and practically shoved him back in the chair. "That's it. You're staying with me."

For a moment Edward was tempted to agree. They would certainly be more comfortable here than at the Devil's Head. But at least at the inn they had privacy. They might be surrounded by strangers, but they were strangers who didn't much care what they did. Here at the Tryons' house, his every move—and more critically, Cecilia's—would be scrutinized, dissected, and then sent home to his mother in a weekly report.

No, he did not wish to move in with his godmother.

"I am quite comfortable in my current lodgings," he said to her. "I do appreciate your invitation."

Margaret scowled, clearly displeased with his behavior. "Will you permit me to ask you one question?"

He nodded.

"How do you know?"

He waited for her to elucidate, and when she did not, he said, "How do I know what?"

"How do you know that she tells you the truth?"

He did not even have to think about it. "Because I know *her*."

And he did. He may have only known her face for a few days, but he had known her heart for far longer. He did not doubt her. He could never doubt her.

"My God," Margaret breathed. "You love her."

Edward said nothing. He could not contradict her.

"Very well," she said with a sigh. "Can you make it up the stairs?"

He stared at her. What on earth was she talking about?

"You still need a dress, don't you? I don't know the first thing about what will suit the new Mrs. Rokesby, and I'd rather not order the maids to empty the wardrobes into my sitting room."

"Ah, yes, of course. And yes, I can make it up the stairs."

Still, he was grateful for the bannister.

Chapter 11

Poor ~~Lieu~~ Captain Rokesby! I hope the crossing was not as dreadful as you feared. At least your recent promotion will be of some comfort. How proud I am that you were both made captains!

We are all well here in the village. I attended the local assembly three nights ago, and per usual there were two ladies for every gentleman. I danced but twice. And the second time was with the vicar, so I do not think that counts.

Your poor sister shall be a spinster!

Ha, but do not worry. I am perfectly content. Or at the very least, imperfectly content. Is that such a thing? I think it should be.

—FROM CECILIA HARCOURT TO
HER BROTHER THOMAS

And so it was that on the afternoon of the governor's ball, Edward laid a large box upon the bed that he shared—but did not truly share—with his wife.

"Did you buy something?" she asked.

"Open it and see."

She gave him a slightly suspicious look as she perched on the edge of the mattress. "What is it?"

"Am I not allowed to bestow a present upon my wife?"

Cecilia looked down at the box, wrapped rather festively with a wide red ribbon, and then back up at him. "I wasn't expecting a gift," she said.

"All the more reason to give you one." He nudged the box a couple of inches closer. "Open it."

Her slim hands went to the ribbon, tugging the knot loose before lifting the lid of the box.

She gasped.

He grinned. It was a *good* gasp.

"Do you like it?" he asked, even though it was plain that she did.

Lips still parted with shock, she reached out to touch the whisper-soft silk that lay nestled in the dressmaker's box. It was the color of a shallow sea, just a hair too blue to match her eyes. But when Edward had seen it in May Tryon's wardrobe, he had known it was the right gown to take to the seamstress for alterations.

He wasn't sure if May Tryon yet knew that she'd made a gift of her silk gown; she'd not been home when her mother had thrown open her wardrobe doors. Edward made a mental note to thank her for her generosity before she had a chance to discover it by accident. And besides, if he knew the Tryons, May would be wearing something new, spectacular, and wildly expensive. She would not begrudge Cecilia her remade dress.

"Where did you get it?" Cecilia asked.

"I have my secrets."

Amazingly, she did not pursue the question. Instead she pulled the gown from the box, rising to her feet so that she could hold it in front of her. "We have no looking glass," she said, still sounding rather dazed.

"You shall have to trust my eyes, then," he said. "You are radiant."

In truth, Edward did not know much of ladies' fashion. Aunt Margaret had warned him that his chosen gown was not quite *au courant*, but to him it seemed as fine as anything he had ever beheld in a London ballroom.

But then again, it had been several years since he had *seen* a London ballroom, and he rather suspected that for Margaret Tryon, fashion was measured in months, not years.

"It's got two parts," he said helpfully. "The, ehrm, inside and the out."

"Petticoat and robe," Cecilia whispered. "And a stomacher. Three parts, actually."

He cleared his throat. "Of course."

She touched a reverent hand to the silver embroidery, which ran in swirls up and down the length of the skirt. "I know that I should say it's too fine," she murmured.

"Absolutely you should not say that."

"I've never owned anything so beautiful."

That, Edward thought, was a tragedy of epic proportions, but he sensed that saying so might be laying it on a bit too thick.

She looked up, her eyes snapping to his with an abruptness that signaled a sudden clarity of thought. "I thought we weren't going to the governor's ball."

"Why would you think that?"

Her lips came together in a fetching purse. "Because I had nothing to wear."

He smiled, because she so clearly realized the absurdity of her words as they passed over her lips.

She sighed. "I must be terribly vain."

"Because you like pretty things?" He leaned down, settling his mouth dangerously close to her ear. "What does that say about me, then? That I like to see pretty things on you?"

Or off her. Dear God, when he'd watched the dress-maker package the gown into its box, he could not help but keep a close eye on the fastenings. This would not be the night that he finally made love to his wife, of that he was sadly certain. He was still too weak, and far too vain to risk doing a bad job of it.

But he wanted her all the same. And he vowed that one day he would peel this dress from her body, un-wrapping her like his present. He would lay her down on the bed, part her legs, and . . .

"Edward?"

He blinked. When she came into focus, she looked somewhat concerned.

"You've gone a bit red," she said. She touched his forehead with the back of her hand. "Have you a fever?"

"It's been warm today," he lied. "Don't you think?"

"No, not really."

"You're not wearing a woolen coat." He unbuttoned his scarlet jacket and shrugged it off. "I'm sure I'll feel better if I sit down next to the window."

She watched him curiously, still holding the pale green dress in front of her. When he was settled in the chair, she asked, "Don't you want to open the window?"

Without a word, he leaned over and pushed it open.

"Are you sure you're all right?"

"Fine," he assured her. He felt like a fool. He probably looked like a fool too, but it was worth it to see her face when she looked at the pale green gown.

"It really is beautiful," she said, gazing down at it with an expression that was almost . . .

Rueful?

No, that could not be right.

"Is something wrong?" he asked.

"No," she said absently, her attention still on the gown. "No." She blinked, then looked him square in the face. "No, of course not. I just . . . Ehrm, I need to . . ."

He watched her for a moment, wondering what on earth could be responsible for her abrupt change of countenance. "Cecilia?"

"I need to get something," she said. But it sounded more like an announcement.

"All right," he said slowly.

She grabbed her reticule and hurried to the door, pausing with her fingers on the handle. "I'll only be a moment. Or a few moments. But not long."

"I will be here when you return," he said.

She gave him a little nod, cast a longing glance at the gown that now lay on the bed, and dashed from the room.

Edward stared at the door for a moment, trying to

make sense of what had just happened. His father had always told him that women were a mystery. Maybe Cecilia thought she had to buy him a gift since he'd got one for her. Silly girl. She should know better.

Still, he could not help but wonder what she'd pick out.

He got up from his chair, adjusted the window so it wasn't quite so far open, and settled down atop the bed. He didn't mean to fall asleep, but when he did . . .

He had a silly smile on his face.

Oh please oh please oh please.

Cecilia hurried down the street, praying with every ounce of her soul that the fruit cart was still at the corner of Broad Street and Pearl, where she'd seen it that morning.

She'd thought the matter of the governor's ball had been settled two days ago when they'd not been able to find a seamstress who could fashion a gown in time. If she didn't have a dress, she couldn't go. It was as simple as that.

Then the blasted man had to go and find her the most beautiful gown in the history of gowns, and dear God she wanted to weep at the injustice of it, because she *really* wanted to wear that dress.

But she couldn't go to the governor's ball. She flat-out simply could not. There would be too many people. There was no way she could contain her lie to its current small circle if she was actually presented to New York society.

Cecilia bit her lip. There was only one thing she could do that would guarantee she would not have to attend the governor's ball. It would be awful, but she was desperate.

So desperate she was willing to eat a strawberry.

She knew what would happen. It wouldn't be pretty. First her skin would go blotchy. So blotchy that the port master would likely call for a pox quarantine if he saw her. And it would itch like the devil. She still had two scars on her arms from the last time she'd accidentally eaten a strawberry. She'd scratched until she bled. She couldn't help herself.

Then her stomach would revolt. And as she'd eaten a full meal right before Edward had arrived with the dress, the revolt would be of epic proportions.

For about twenty-four hours she'd be misery personified. A swollen, itchy, vomitous mess. And then she'd be fine. Maybe a little woozy for a few days, but she'd recover. But if Edward had ever thought her attractive . . .

Well. She'd cure him of that.

She hurried around the corner onto Pearl Street, her eyes searching the length of the street. The fruit cart was still there.

Oh, thank God. Cecilia practically ran the last few yards, skidding to a halt in front of Mr. Hopchurch's cart.

Goal for today: Poison herself.

Good God.

"A fine afternoon to you," he said. Cecilia decided her eyes must not have looked as crazed as she felt, because he did not back away in fear. "What can I get you?"

She looked over his wares. It was nearing the end of his sales day, so he didn't have much. A few skinny courgettes, several ears of the sweet corn that grew so well here. And over in the corner, the biggest, fattest, most hideously red strawberry she'd ever seen. She wondered at its presence here, so late in the day. Had all his other customers sensed what she already knew? That the speckled, pocked-up, inverted red pyramid was nothing but a little bomb of misery and despair?

She swallowed. She could do this. "That's a very large strawberry," she said, eyeing it with queasy distaste. Her stomach heaved just at the thought of it.

"I know!" Mr. Hopchurch said with great excitement. "Have you ever seen one so grand? My wife was right proud of it."

"I'll take it, please," Cecilia said, practically choking on the words.

"You can't take just one," Mr. Hopchurch said. "I sell them by the half dozen."

That might explain why he had not sold it. She gave him a pathetic nod. "Six, then."

He reached out and took hold of the big one by its leafy green crown. "Do you have a basket?"

She looked down at her hands. What an idiot she was. She hadn't thought. "Never mind," she said. She didn't need six. Not with one the size of Colossus. "I'll pay you for six," she told him, "but I only need the one."

Mr. Hopchurch looked at her as if she were right crazy, but he was far too sensible to argue. He took her money and dropped the giant berry into her hands. "Fresh from the garden. Be sure to come back and tell me how you like it."

Cecilia was quite certain he would not like it if she did, but she nodded nonetheless, thanking him before making her way to a quiet spot around the corner.

Dear God, now she had to eat it.

She wondered if this was how Shakespeare's Juliet

felt, right before she took her wicked brew. The body rebelled against ingesting something it knew to be poisonous. And her body knew quite well that this strawberry was just two shades short of hemlock.

Leaning against a building for support, she lifted the red berry and held it near her face. And then, against the protests of her stomach, her nose, and honestly, every last part of her body, she took a bite.

By seven that night, Cecilia wanted to die.

Edward knew this because she said quite clearly: "I want to die."

"No, you don't," he said with more pragmatism than he felt. Logically, he knew that she would be fine, that this was probably a case of bad fish at supper— although he'd eaten what she'd eaten, and he was fine.

But it was hell to watch her suffer. She'd already retched so many times all she had left was some pinkish-yellowish bile. Even worse, her skin was beginning to rise with thick red welts.

"I think we should get a doctor," he said.

"No," she moaned. "Don't go."

He shook his head. "You're too ill."

She grabbed his hand with enough strength to startle him. "I don't need a doctor."

"Yes," he said, "you do."

"No." She shook her head, then moaned.

"What?"

She closed her eyes and lay very still. "It made me dizzy," she whispered. "Can't shake my head."

Now she had vertigo? "Cecilia, I really think—"

"It was something I ate," she cut in weakly. "I'm quite sure."

He frowned. He'd thought the same, but she was getting worse by the second. "Did you have the fish at supper?"

"Aaaahhh!" She threw her arm over her eyes, even though as far he could tell they were still closed. "Don't say that word!"

"Fish?"

"Stop!"

"What?"

"Don't mention food," she mumbled.

He thought about this. Maybe it *was* something she ate. He watched for a bit, more wary than worried. She was lying utterly still atop the bedclothes, her arms at her sides in two perfect sticks. She was still wearing the pink frock she'd had on earlier, although he supposed they were going to have to get it cleaned. He didn't think she'd got any bile on it, but she'd been sweating rather viciously. Come to think of it, he should probably loosen her stays or unfasten her buttons or something to make her more comfortable.

"Cecilia?"

She did not move.

"Cecilia?"

"I'm not dead," she told him.

"No," he said, trying not to smile. "I can see that you're not."

"I'm just lying very still," she said.

And she was doing an admirable job of it. He could barely see her lips move.

"If I lie very still," she continued, her voice coming out slightly singsongy, "it almost feels like I'm not going to . . ."

"Vomit?" he supplied.

"I was going to say die," she said. "I'm fairly certain I'm still going to vomit."

He had the chamber pot next to her in a flash.

"Not right now," she went on, reaching blindly out to push it away. "But soon."

"When I least expect it?"

"No." She let out a tired exhale. "More likely when *I* least expect it."

He tried not to laugh. He sort of succeeded, but he had a feeling she'd heard him snort. He wasn't nearly as worried about her as he'd been just a few minutes before. If she maintained her sense of humor, she was probably going to be fine. He wasn't sure how he knew this, but he'd seen enough bouts of food poisoning to decide that she was probably right; she'd eaten something that had not agreed with her.

The welts were concerning, though. He was rather glad they did not have a looking glass. She would not like what she saw.

Gingerly, he sat on the side of the bed, reaching out so that he could touch her forehead. But when the mattress dipped, Cecilia let out an unholy groan. One of her arms swung blindly through the air, connecting with his thigh.

"Ow!"

"Sorry."

"No, you're not," he said with a smile.

"Please don't rock the bed."

He pried her fingers from his leg. "I thought you didn't get seasick."

"I don't."

"If that's the case, I think you now know how the rest of us feel."

"I was perfectly happy not knowing."

"Yes," he murmured affectionately, "I expect you were."

She opened one eyelid. "Why does it sound as if you're enjoying this?"

"Oh, I'm certainly not enjoying this. But I have come to agree with you that you've a nasty case of food poisoning. So while I have the utmost sympathy and concern, I am no longer overtly worried for your health."

She grunted. Aside from the retching, it was possibly the least ladylike noise he'd heard from her lips.

He found it delightful.

"Edward?"

"Yes?"

She swallowed. "Do I have spots on my face?"

"I'm afraid so."

"They itch."

"Try not to scratch them," he said.

"I know."

He smiled. It was the most gloriously mundane conversation.

"Shall I get you a cool cloth?"

"That would be very nice, thank you."

He got up, moving carefully so that the mattress did not shift overmuch from the loss of his weight. He found a cloth near the basin, and he dipped it in the water.

"You seem stronger today," he heard Cecilia say.

"I think I am." He wrung out the cloth and made his way back to her side. Strange how that worked. He felt the strongest when he could take care of her.

"I'm sorry," she said.

"For what?"

She sighed as he placed the cloth against her forehead. "I know you wanted to go to your godmother's party this evening."

"There will be other parties. Besides, as eager as I am to show you off, it would have been exhausting. And then I would have had to watch you dance with other men."

She looked up at him. "Do you like to dance?"

"Sometimes."

"Only sometimes?"

He touched her nose. "It depends on my partner."

She smiled, and for a fleeting moment he thought he saw a tinge of sadness in her face. But it was gone so quickly he couldn't be sure, and when she spoke, her eyes were tired but clear. "I expect it's like that with many things in life."

He touched her cheek, suddenly so grateful for this moment. So grateful for *her.* "I expect so," he murmured.

He looked down. She was already asleep.

Chapter 12

I am not even able to put my pen to paper without Edward coming over to assure me that had he been at the assembly, he would have been delighted to dance with you. Oh, now he is cross. I think I might have embarrassed him.

Your brother is a menace.

He commandeered my pen! I shall forgive him if only because we have been trapped in this tent for days. It has not stopped raining since 1753, I am convinced.

My dear Miss Harcourt, pray forgive your brother. I fear the humidity has addled his brain. The rain is unrelenting, but it has brought the gift of wildflowers, quite unlike anything I have ever seen. The field is a

carpet of lavender and white, and I cannot
help but think you would like it very much.

—*FROM* THOMAS HARCOURT
(*AND* EDWARD ROKESBY) *TO*
CECILIA HARCOURT

Cecilia was soon back to her old self, save for a
few scabs on her legs where she had not been
able to keep from scratching. She resumed her search
for Thomas, and Edward often accompanied her. He'd
found that mild exercise improved his strength, so when
the weather wasn't too overbearingly hot he tucked her
arm in the crook of his elbow, and they walked about
town, running errands and asking questions.

And falling in love.

She was, at least. She refused to allow herself to
wonder if he felt the same way, although it was more
than obvious that he enjoyed her company.

And that he wanted her.

He had taken to kissing her good night. And good
morning. And sometimes good afternoon. And with
each touch, each shared glance, she felt herself slipping
further into a falsehood of her own creation.

But oh, how she wished it were true.

She could be happy with this man. She could be his

wife and bear his children, and it would be a *wonderful life* . . .

Except that it was all a lie. And when it fell apart, she wasn't going to be able to escape by swallowing a strawberry.

Goal for today: Stop falling in love.

Never had one of her little goals felt less attainable. And more destined for heartbreak.

There were already small signs that Edward's memory was returning. One morning as he was pulling on his uniform, he turned to Cecilia and said, "I haven't done this for a while."

Cecilia, who had been reading the book of poetry he'd brought with him from home, looked up. "Done what?"

He was silent for a moment before he answered, and he frowned, as if he were still working out his thoughts. "Put on my uniform."

Cecilia used a ribbon to mark her place and closed the book. "You do that every morning."

"No, before that." He paused and blinked a few times before saying, "I didn't wear a uniform in Connecticut."

She swallowed, trying to set aside her unease. "Are you sure?"

He looked down at himself, smoothing his right hand over the scarlet wool that marked him as a soldier in His Majesty's Army. "Where did this come from?"

It took her a moment to realize what he was asking. "Your coat? It was in the church."

"But I wasn't wearing it when I was brought in."

This, Cecilia was startled to realize, was a statement, not a question. "I don't know," she said. "I don't think so. I did not think to ask."

"I couldn't have been," Edward decided. "It was far too clean."

"Perhaps someone laundered it for you?"

He shook his head in the negative. "We should ask Colonel Stubbs."

"Of course," Cecilia demurred.

He did not say anything, but Cecilia knew this meant that his mind was whirring double-time, trying to find the outline of a puzzle that was still missing too many pieces. He stared sightlessly at the window, his hand tapping against his leg, and Cecilia could only wait until he seemed to suddenly come alert, turning sharply toward her to say, "I remembered something else."

"What?"

"Yesterday, when we were walking along Broad Street. A cat brushed up against me."

Cecilia did not speak. If there had been a cat, she hadn't noticed.

"It did that thing cats do," Edward continued, "rubbing its face against my leg, and I remembered. There was a cat."

"In Connecticut?"

"Yes. I don't know why, but I think . . . I think it kept me company."

"A cat," she repeated.

He nodded. "It probably doesn't mean anything, but . . ." His voice trailed off, and his eyes lost their focus again.

"It means you are remembering," Cecilia said softly.

It took a moment for him to shake off his faraway expression. "Yes."

"At least it is a happy cat memory," she offered.

He looked at her quizzically.

"You could have remembered that you'd been bitten. Or scratched." She moved off the bed and stood. "Instead you know that an animal kept you company when you were alone."

Her voice caught, and he took a step toward her.

"It comforts me," she admitted.

"That I was not alone?"

She nodded.

"I've always liked cats," he said, almost absently.

"Even more so now, I should imagine."

He looked at her with a half smile. "Let us make a summation of what I remember. I didn't wear a uniform." He ticked this off on his hand. "There was a cat."

"Yesterday you said you'd been in a boat," Cecilia reminded him. They had been out near the river, and the salty tang in the air had jogged loose a spark of memory. He'd been in a boat, he told her. Not a ship, but something smaller, something not meant to go far from shore.

"Although," Cecilia said, giving the matter more thought than she'd done the day before, "you'd have to have been in a boat, wouldn't you? How else would you have got to Manhattan? There's no bridge to this part of the island. And I don't think you swam."

"True," he murmured.

Cecilia watched him for a moment, then could not help but giggle.

"What is it?" he asked.

"You get this look," she said. "Every time you try to remember something."

"Oh really?" He made a look like he was trying to be sardonic, but she knew he was teasing.

"Yes, you go a bit like this—" She drew her brows together and let her eyes go blank. She had a feeling she was not getting it quite right, and in fact a more prickly man might think she was poking fun at him.

He stared at her. "You look unhinged."

"I believe you mean *you* look unhinged." She waved one of her hands near her face. "I am your mirror."

He burst out laughing, then reached out and tugged her toward him. "I am fairly certain I have never seen anything so delightful in the mirror."

Cecilia felt herself smiling, even as warning bells went off in her mind. It was so easy to be happy with him, so easy to be herself. But this wasn't her life. And she wasn't his wife. It was a role she'd borrowed, and eventually she'd have to give it back.

But no matter how hard she tried to keep herself from growing too comfortable in her role as Mrs. Rokesby, it was impossible to resist his smile. He pulled her closer, and then closer still, until his nose rested on hers.

"Have I told you," he said, his voice warmed with joy, "how very happy I am that you were at my side when I awakened?"

Her lips parted, and she tried to speak, but every word sat uncomfortably in her throat. He had not said this, as a matter of fact, at least not so explicitly. She shook her head, unable to take her eyes from his, drowning in the warmth of his bright blue gaze.

"If I had known," he continued, "I'm sure I would

have told you not to come. In fact I am quite sure I would have forbidden it." His mouth twisted into that wry spot halfway between a grimace and a smile. "Not, I imagine, that that would have swayed you."

"I was not your wife when I boarded the ship," she said quietly. Then she died a little when she realized this might be the most honest statement she would utter all day.

"No," Edward said, "I suppose you were not." He cocked his head to the side, and his brow drew together the way she'd been teasing him about, but his eyes stayed sharp. "Now what?" he asked, when he saw how she was studying him.

"Nothing, just that you were *almost* making the same expression as before. Your brow was the same, but your eyes didn't glaze over."

"You make me sound so appealing."

She laughed. "No, it's interesting. I think—" She paused, trying to figure just what she *was* thinking. "You weren't trying to remember something this time, were you?"

He shook his head. "Just pondering the great questions of life."

"Oh stop. What were you really thinking about?"

"Actually, I was thinking that we need to look into

the laws of proxy marriages. We ought to know the exact date of the union, wouldn't you agree?"

She tried to say yes. She couldn't quite manage it.

Edward tugged on his cuffs, smoothing out his sleeves so that his coat lay smooth on his body. "You went second, so I imagine it was whenever you got the captain to perform your side of the ceremony."

Cecilia gave a tiny nod—all she could manage with the boulder in her throat.

But Edward did not seem to notice her distress, or if he did, he must have thought she was just being emotional over the memory of her wedding, because he dropped a quick kiss on her lips, straightened, and said, "Time to greet the day, I suppose. I'm meeting with Colonel Stubbs downstairs in a few minutes, and I can't be late."

"You're meeting with Colonel Stubbs, and you did not tell me?"

His nose wrinkled. "Did I not? An oversight, I'm sure."

Cecilia did not doubt him in this. Edward did not keep secrets from her. He was remarkably open, all things considered, and when he asked for her opinion, he actually listened to her response. She supposed that to some degree he did not have much choice; with such a large hole in his memory he *had* to rely on her judgment.

Except . . . she could not imagine many other men doing the same. She'd always been proud of the fact that her father had left the running of the house in her hands, but in her heart she knew that he had not done so because he'd thought her especially capable. He just didn't want to bother with it himself.

"Do you wish to join me?" Edward asked.

"For your meeting with the colonel?" Cecilia's brows rose. "I cannot imagine he will wish to have me there."

"All the more reason for you to come. I learn far more when he's in a bad mood."

"In that case, how can I refuse?"

Edward opened the door and stepped aside, waiting for her to precede him into the hall.

"It does seem odd that he's not more forthcoming," Cecilia said. "Surely he wants you to recover your memory."

"I don't think he's trying to be secretive," Edward said. He took her arm as they descended the stairs, but unlike the week prior, it was to be a gentleman and not because he needed her physical support. It was remarkable how much he had improved in just a few short days. His head still pained him, and of course there was the memory gap, but his skin had lost the grayish pallor that had been so worrying, and if he was not ready for a fifty-mile march, he was at least able to go about his day without needing to take a rest.

Cecilia thought he sometimes still looked tired, but Edward just told her she was acting like a wife.

He smiled when he said this, though.

"I think," Edward said, still on the topic of Colonel Stubbs, "that it is his job to keep secrets."

"But surely not from you."

"Perhaps," Edward said with a small shrug. "But consider this: He does not know where I was or what I did these last few months. It is almost certainly not in the interest of the British Army to entrust me with secrets just yet."

"That's preposterous!"

"I appreciate your unwavering support," he said, giving her a wry smile as they reached the ground floor, "but Colonel Stubbs must be assured of my loyalties before revealing his hand."

Cecilia was not sold. "I cannot believe he would dare to doubt you," she muttered. Edward's honor and honesty were so clearly intrinsic to his nature. She did not understand how anyone could not see this.

Colonel Stubbs was standing by the door when they

entered the dining room, his face skewed into its usual scowl. "Rokesby," he said upon seeing them, followed by: "Your wife is here too."

"She was hungry," Edward said.

"Of course," the colonel replied, but his nostrils flared with irritation, and Cecilia saw his jaw clench as he led them to a nearby table.

"They make a fine breakfast here," Cecilia said sweetly.

The colonel stared at her for a moment, then grunted something that might have been a response before turning back to Edward.

"Do you bring any news?" Edward asked.

"Do you?"

"I am afraid not, but Cecilia has been most helpful in my quest to regain my memory. We have traversed the town many times, searching for clues."

Cecilia pasted a placid smile on her face.

Which Colonel Stubbs ignored. "I don't see how you think to find clues here in New York. It's the time in Connecticut that needs to be examined."

"About that," Edward said mildly, "I was wondering— did I have a uniform?"

"What?" The colonel's voice was curt and distracted, and he was patently irritated by the abrupt change of subject.

"I had the strangest recollection this morning. It's probably not even relevant, but as I was donning my coat, it occurred to me that I had not done so in quite a long time."

The colonel just stared at him. "I don't follow."

"The coat at the hospital . . . This one, as a matter of fact," Edward said, brushing his hand along his sleeve. "Where did it come from? It's obviously mine, but I don't think I had it with me."

"I held it for you," Stubbs said gruffly. "Wouldn't do to be labeled a lobsterback in Connecticut."

"Are they not loyal to the crown?" Cecilia inquired.

"Rebels are everywhere," Stubbs said, shooting her an irritated look. "They are sprinkled like salt, and the very devil to excise."

"Excise?" Cecilia echoed. It was a disturbing choice of words. She had not been in New York very long, but even she was able to discern that the political landscape was more complicated than the newspapers at home would have her believe. She was, and always would be, a proud British subject, but she could not help but see that the colonists had some legitimate grievances.

But before she could say anything further (not that she was intending to), she felt Edward's hand on her leg under the table, its heavy weight cautioning her not to speak.

"I beg your pardon," Cecilia murmured, casting her eyes obediently toward her lap. "I was not familiar with the term."

It *hurt* to utter such a lie, but there was clearly some benefit in having the colonel think her somewhat less than brilliant. And the last thing she wanted was for him to think that *she* was not loyal to the crown.

"Might I inquire, then," Edward asked, moving the conversation forward with smooth agility, "if my lack of a uniform in Connecticut means that I was there as a spy?"

"I wouldn't say *that*," the colonel huffed.

"What *would* you say?" Cecilia asked, biting her tongue when Edward's hand tightened on her thigh again. But it was difficult to keep her mouth shut. The colonel was so aggravating, dropping bits of information here and there, never quite telling Edward what he needed to know.

"I beg your pardon," she mumbled. Edward had turned to her with a cool glance, once again warning her not to interfere. She had to stop antagonizing Colonel Stubbs, and not just for Edward's sake. The colonel knew Thomas as well, and though he had not proved helpful in her search thus far, he might in the future.

"*Spying* is such an unsavory word," Colonel Stubbs

said, nodding in reply to her apology. "Certainly nothing to discuss in front of a lady."

"A scout, then," Edward suggested. "Would that be a more accurate description?"

Stubbs grunted in the affirmative.

Edward's lips pressed into a firm line that was oddly difficult to interpret. He did not look angry, at least not as angry as Cecilia was feeling. Rather, she had the impression that he was sifting through information in his mind, placing it in neat little piles for future reference. He had a very orderly way of looking at the world—a trait that must have made his memory deficit twice as difficult to bear.

"I realize," Edward said, steepling his hands in a contemplative motion, "that you are in an extremely delicate position. But if you truly wish for me to remember the events of the last few months, you will need to help me recall them." He leaned forward. "We are on the same side."

"I have never doubted your loyalty," the colonel said.

Edward nodded graciously.

"But nor can I feed you the information I wish to hear."

"Are you saying you *know* what Edward was doing?" Cecilia cut in.

"Cecilia," Edward said, his voice a soft warning.

Which she ignored. "If you know what he was doing, you must tell him," she insisted. "It's cruel of you not to. It could help him regain his memory."

"Cecilia," Edward said again, this time with bite.

But she could not keep silent. Ignoring Edward's warning, she locked eyes with Colonel Stubbs and said, "Surely if you want him to remember what happened in Connecticut, you will tell him everything *you* know."

The colonel met her stare with his own. "That is all very well and good, Mrs. Rokesby, but have you considered that anything I say could influence your husband's recollections? I cannot afford to color his memories with information of my own that may or may not be accurate."

"I—" Some of the fight left Cecilia as she realized the colonel had a point. But still, wasn't Edward's peace of mind worth something?

Stern lines formed at the corners of Edward's mouth. "Allow me to apologize for my wife," he said.

"No," Cecilia said. "I will apologize for myself. I am sorry. It is difficult for me to see the situation from your point of view."

"You want your husband to get well," Colonel Stubbs said with surprising gentleness.

"I do," she said fervently. "Even—"

Her heart stopped. Even if it meant her own down-fall? She was living in a house of cards, and the moment Edward regained his memory, it was all over. She almost laughed at the bitter irony of it. She'd been argu-ing nonstop with the colonel, fighting for the one thing that would break her heart.

But she couldn't help it. She wanted him to get well. She wanted it more than anything. More than—

Her heart stopped. More than finding Thomas?

No. That could not be. Maybe she was just as bad as Colonel Stubbs, withholding facts that could help Edward get his memory back. But Thomas was her brother. Edward would understand.

Or so she kept telling herself.

"Cecilia?"

She heard Edward's voice, coming to her as if through a long tunnel.

"Darling?" He took her hand, then started to rub it. "Are you all right? Your hands are like ice."

Slowly she came back to the present, blinking as she took in Edward's worried face.

"You sounded like you were choking," he said.

She looked at the colonel, who was also regarding her with worry. "I'm sorry," she said, realizing that the choking sound must have been a sob. "I don't know what came over me."

"It's quite all right," Colonel Stubbs said, much to Cecilia's—and by the looks of it, Edward's—surprise. "You are his wife. It is as God intended that you should put his welfare above all else."

Cecilia allowed a moment to pass, then asked, "Are you married, Colonel Stubbs?"

"I was," he said simply, and it was easy to know from his expression what he meant.

"I'm sorry," she murmured.

The normally stoic colonel swallowed, and his eyes flashed with pain. "It was many years ago," he said, "but I think of her every day."

Impulsively, Cecilia reached out and covered his hand with hers. "I'm sure she knows," she said.

The colonel gave a jerky nod, then made some sort of huff and puff of a noise as he regained his composure. Cecilia took her hand away; their moment of connection had passed, and anything longer would have been awkward.

"I must be going," Colonel Stubbs said. He looked at Edward. "I hope you know that I do pray for the return of your memory. And not only because you may possess information that could be crucial to our cause. I do not know what it is like to be missing entire months, but I cannot imagine it sits well within one's soul."

Edward acknowledged this with a nod, and then they both stood.

"For what it's worth, Captain Rokesby," the colonel continued, "you were sent to Connecticut to gather information about their ports."

Edward's brow pulled together. "My cartographical skills are unremarkable."

"I don't think anyone was looking for maps, although that would certainly be useful."

"Colonel?" Cecilia said, coming to her feet. When he turned to look at her she asked, "Was Edward meant to investigate something specific? Or was it more of a general fact-gathering excursion?"

"I'm afraid I cannot say."

So it was something specific. That certainly made more sense.

"Thank you," she said politely, and she bobbed into a curtsy.

He tipped his hat. "Ma'am, Captain Rokesby."

Cecilia watched as Stubbs turned to go, but before he took a step he turned back. "Have you any news of your brother, Mrs. Rokesby?"

"No," she said. "Major Wilkins has been most helpful, though. He had his man inspect the records at the hospital for me."

"And?"

"Nothing, I'm afraid. There was no mention of him."

The colonel nodded slowly. "If anyone would know how to find him, it would be Wilkins."

"We go to Haarlem soon," Cecilia said.

"Haarlem?" Stubbs looked over at Edward. "Why?"

"The infirmary," Edward said. "We know that Thomas was injured. It's possible he was brought there."

"But surely he wouldn't stay."

"Someone might know of him," Cecilia said. "It's worth looking into."

"Of course." Colonel Stubbs nodded again, both at her and at Edward. "I wish you good luck with it."

Cecilia watched him go, turning to Edward the moment the colonel exited to say, "I'm sorry."

His brows rose.

"I shouldn't have spoken. It was your place to question him, not mine."

"Do not be concerned," Edward said. "I was displeased at first, but you managed to turn the situation around. I had not realized he was a widower."

"I do not know what made me inquire," Cecilia confessed.

Edward gave her a smile and took her hand, patting

it reassuringly. "Come, let us sit back down and eat. As you said, they do a fine breakfast here."

Cecilia allowed him to lead her back to the table. She felt strangely shaky, unmoored. Food would help, she hoped. She'd always been the sort who needed a proper breakfast to face the day.

"I must say, though," Edward mused as he took his seat across from her, "I rather liked having such a staunch champion."

Cecilia looked up sharply at that. *Champion* seemed such an undeserved compliment.

"I don't think you realize just how strong you are," he said.

She swallowed. "Thank you."

"Shall we go to Haarlem today?"

"Today?" She snapped to attention. "Are you sure?"

"I've been feeling much better. I think I'm up to a journey to the top of the island."

"Only if you're certain . . ."

"I'll arrange for a carriage after breakfast." He signaled to the innkeeper that they were ready for food, then turned back to her. "Let's turn our attention to Thomas this morning. Quite honestly, I'm ready to take a break from my own sleuthing. At least for today."

"Thank you," she said. "I don't expect that we will

learn anything, but I could not live with myself if we did not at least try."

"I agree. We should—ah! Bacon." Edward's entire face lit up when the innkeeper set a plate of toast and bacon in the center of the table. It was no longer hot, but that made little difference in the face of his now ferocious appetite.

"Honestly," Edward said, crunching a piece with a decided lack of table manners, "is this not the finest thing you've ever tasted?"

"The finest?" she asked doubtfully.

He waved this off. "It's bacon. How can anything in the world seem bleak when one is eating bacon?"

"An interesting philosophy."

He gave her a cheeky grin. "It's working for me right now."

Cecilia gave in to his humor and reached for a piece of her own. If bacon truly equaled happiness, who was she to argue?

"You know," she said with a partially full mouth. (If he could dispense with proper table manners, then by heaven, so could she.) "This actually isn't very good bacon."

"But you feel better, don't you?"

Cecilia stopped chewing, tilted her head to the side, and considered this. "You're right," she had to admit.

Again with the impertinent smile. "I generally am."

But as they cheerfully munched through their break-fast, she knew it wasn't the bacon that was making her happy, it was the man across the table.

If only he was truly hers.

Chapter 13

I normally wait to receive a letter from you before writing my own, but as it has been several weeks since we last heard from you, Edward insists that we take the initiative and begin a missive. There is little to say, though. It is astonishing how much time we spend sitting about doing nothing. Or marching. But I assume you do not wish for a pageful of contemplations on the art and science of marching.

—FROM THOMAS HARCOURT
TO HIS SISTER CECILIA

Haarlem was exactly what Edward had expected. The infirmary was just as rudimentary as Major Wilkins had warned, but thankfully most of the beds were vacant. As it was, Cecilia had been visibly horrified at the conditions.

It had taken some time to find the man in charge, and then more than a little wheedling to convince him to go through the records, but as Wilkins had predicted, there was no mention of Thomas Harcourt. Cecilia had wondered if perhaps some of the patients had not been logged in, and Edward couldn't really blame her for asking—the general level of cleanliness did not inspire confidence in the infirmary's organization.

But if there was one thing the British Army never seemed to muck up, it was record-keeping. The list of patients was just about the only thing in the infirmary that was spotless. Each page in the register was organized in precise rows, and each name was accompanied by rank, date of arrival, date and type of departure, and a brief description of the injury or illness. As a result, they now knew that Private Roger Gunnerly of Cornwall had recovered from an abscess on his left thigh, and Private Henry Witherwax of Manchester had perished of a gunshot wound to the abdomen.

But of Thomas Harcourt, nothing.

It was a very long day. The roads from New York Town to Haarlem were terrible and the carriage they'd procured wasn't much better, but after a hearty supper at the Fraunces Tavern, they were both feeling restored. The day had been considerably less humid than the one before, and by evening there was a light breeze carrying the salty tang of the sea, so they took the long way back to the Devil's Head, walking slowly through the emptying streets at the bottom of Manhattan Island. Cecilia had her hand tucked in the crook of Edward's elbow, and even though they maintained a proper distance from one another, every step seemed to bring them closer.

If they were not so far from home, if they were not in the middle of a war, it would have been a perfect evening.

They walked in silence along the water, watching the seagulls dive for the fish, and then Cecilia said, "I wish—"

But she didn't finish.

"You wish for what?" Edward asked.

It took her a moment to speak, and when she did, it was with a slow, sad shake of her head. "I wish I knew when to give up."

He knew what he was supposed to do. If he were playing a role on the stage or starring in a heroic novel, he would tell her that they must never give up, that their hearts must remain true and strong, and they must search for Thomas until every last lead was exhausted.

But he wasn't going to lie to her, and he wasn't going to offer false hope, and so he just said, "I don't know."

As if by silent agreement, they came to a gentle stop and stood side by side, staring out over the water in the fading light of the day.

Cecilia was the first to speak. "You think he's dead, don't you?"

"I think . . ." He didn't want to say it, hadn't even wanted to think it. "I think he is probably dead, yes."

She nodded, with eyes that were filled with more resignation than sorrow. Edward wondered why that was somehow even more heartbreaking.

"I wonder if it would be easier," she said, "knowing for sure."

"I don't know. The loss of hope versus the certainty of truth. It's not an easy judgment to make."

"No." She thought about this for a long moment, never taking her eyes off the horizon. Finally, just when Edward thought she must have given up on the conversation, she said, "I think I would rather know."

He nodded even though she wasn't looking at him. "I think I agree."

She turned then. "You only think? You are not certain?"

"No."

"Nor I."

"It has been a disappointing day," he murmured.

"No," she surprised him by saying. "To be disappointed one has to have expected a different outcome."

He looked over at her. He didn't need to ask the question out loud.

"I knew it was unlikely we'd find word of Thomas," she said. "But we had to try, didn't we?"

He took her hand in his. "We had to try," he agreed. And then something occurred to him. "My head did not hurt today," he said.

Her eyes lit up with joy. "Did it not? That is wonderful. You should have said something."

He scratched his neck absently. "I'm not sure I even realized it until now."

"That is just wonderful," she said. "I'm so happy. I—" She rose onto her tiptoes and laid an impulsive kiss on his cheek. "I'm very happy," she said again. "I don't like seeing you in pain."

He brought her hand to his lips. "I could not bear it if our roles were reversed." It was true. The thought of her in pain was like an icy fist around his heart.

She let out a little chuckle. "You made a fine nurse when I was ill last week."

"Yes, but I'd rather not do it again, so do stay healthy, yes?"

She looked down, in an expression that almost seemed shy, and then she shivered.

"Cold?" he asked.

"A little."

"We should go home."

"Home, is it?"

He chuckled at that. "I confess I never thought to live in a place named for the devil."

"Can you imagine," she said, her face starting to light up with a mischievous smile, "a house back in England named Devil's Manor?"

"Lucifer House?"

"Satan's Abbey."

They both dissolved into laughter at that, and Cecilia even glanced up at the sky.

"Watching out for thunderbolts?"

"Either that or a plague of locusts."

Edward took her arm and nudged her back on the path toward the inn. They weren't far, a few minutes' walk at most. "We are both relatively good people," he said, leaning in as if imparting a juicy piece of gossip. "I think we are safe from biblical intervention."

"One can only hope."

"I could probably withstand the locusts," he mused, "but I cannot be held responsible for my behavior if the river turns to blood."

She snorted out a laugh at that, then countered with "I myself would like to avoid boils."

"And lice." He shuddered. "Nasty little bastards, if you pardon my language."

She looked over at him. "You've had lice?"

"Every soldier has had lice," he told her. "It's an occupational hazard."

She looked faintly repulsed.

He leaned in with a cheeky expression. "I'm quite clean now."

"I should hope so. I've been sharing a room with you for more than a week."

"Speaking of which . . ." he murmured. Neither of them had been paying much attention, but their feet had found their way back to the Devil's Head.

"Home again," she quipped.

He held the door for her. "Indeed."

The crowd in the main room seemed more raucous than usual, so he placed a hand at the small of her back and gently steered her along the perimeter to the stairs. He knew he could not hope to find better accommodations than this, but still, it was no place for a lady to take up permanent residence. If they had been in England, he would never—

He shook off the thought. They weren't in England. Normal rules did not apply.

Normal. He couldn't even remember what the word meant. There was a lump on his head that had swallowed three months of his memory, his best friend had disappeared so completely that the army hadn't even noticed he was missing, and at some point in the not-so-distant past he'd married a woman by proxy.

A proxy marriage. Good Lord, his parents would be aghast. And truthfully, so was he. Edward was not like his devil-may-care younger brother Andrew, flouting rules simply for the fun of it. When it came to the important things in life, he did them properly. He wasn't even certain a proxy marriage would be considered legal back in England.

Which brought him to another point. Something wasn't quite right about this entire situation. Edward wasn't sure what Thomas had said or done to induce him into marriage with Cecilia, but he had a feeling there was more to it than she had told him. There was likely more to it than she knew herself, but the truth would never be known unless Edward regained his memory.

Or they found Thomas.

At this point, Edward wasn't certain which was less likely.

"Edward?"

He blinked, focusing his gaze on Cecilia. She was

standing next to the door to their room, a faintly amused smile on her face.

"You had that look again," she said. "Not the re-membering one, the thinking terribly hard one."

This did not surprise him. "Thinking terribly hard about almost nothing," he lied, pulling out the key to their room. He did not want to reveal his suspicions to her, not just yet. Edward did not doubt Thomas's reasons for arranging this marriage—his friend was a good man and certainly wanted what was best for his sister—but if she had been persuaded to marry him under false pretenses she would be furious.

Maybe Edward should be trying harder to ferret out the truth, but honestly, he had bigger issues to deal with just now, and when it came right down to it, he *liked* being married to Cecilia.

Why on earth would he upset the happy balance they'd achieved?

Unless . . .

There was one reason he'd rock that boat.

He wanted to make love to his wife.

It was time. It *had* to be time. His desire . . . His need . . . They had been threatening to explode from within since the moment he'd seen her.

Maybe it was because he had figured out who she

was from her conversation with Colonel Stubbs. Maybe it was because even from his hospital bed he could sense her concern and devotion, but when he opened his eyes and saw her for the first time, her green eyes filled first with worry, then with surprise, he'd felt an incredible rush of lightness, as if the very air around him was whispering in his ear.

Her.

She's the one.

And weak as he was, he'd wanted her.

But now . . .

He might not have regained his full strength, but he was definitely strong enough.

He looked over at her. She was still smiling, watching him as if she had a delicious little secret, or maybe as if she thought *he* did. Either way, she looked terribly amused as she cocked her head to the side and asked, "Are you going to unlock the door?"

He turned the key in the lock.

"Still thinking very hard about nothing?" she teased as he opened the door for her.

No.

He wondered if she was aware of the delicate dance they played every evening when it was time for bed. Her nervous swallow, his stolen glance. Her quick grab of their one book, his studious attention to the lint that had—or more often had not—gathered on his scarlet coat. Every night Cecilia went about her business, filling the room with nervous chatter, never quite at ease until he crawled into the opposite side of the bed and bid her good night. They both knew what his words really meant.

Not tonight.

Not yet.

Did she realize that he too was waiting for a signal? A look, a touch . . . anything to let him know that she was ready.

Because he was ready. He was more than ready. And he thought . . . maybe . . . she was too.

She just didn't know it yet.

When they entered their small room, Cecilia scurried over to the basin on the table, which she'd requested the inn fill with water each evening. "I'm just going to wash my face," she said, as if he did not know what she was doing when she splashed herself with the water, as if she had not done the same thing every evening.

As she performed her ablutions, his hands went to the buttons on his cuffs, unfastening each before sitting on the edge of the bed to remove his boots.

"I thought supper was quite delicious this evening," Cecilia said, tossing the quickest of glances over her shoulder before reaching into the wardrobe for her hairbrush.

"I agree," he replied. This was part of their duet, steps in the intricate choreography that led to them entering the bed on opposite sides and then ended with him pretending he did not wake up each morning with her in his arms. She was checking to see if he was behaving differently, assessing his expression, his movements.

He did not need her to tell him this to know that it was true.

Her eyes were like glass, pale green and luminous, and she hadn't a prayer of hiding her emotions. He could not imagine her ever keeping a secret. Surely it would show on her face, on those full lips that she never quite seemed to keep still. Even when she was quiet there were hints of motion in her expression. Her brow would draw down, or her lips would part, just wide enough for a breath to pass through. He did not know if everyone else saw this in her. He supposed at first glance she might seem serene. But if you took the time to look at her, to see beyond the oval face and even features that had been captured in that second-rate miniature Edward had studied so many times . . . That was when you saw it. The tiny bits of motion, dancing in time to her thoughts.

Sometimes he wondered if he could watch her forever without being bored.

"Edward?"

He blinked. She was seated at the small vanity, regarding him with curiosity.

"You were staring," she said. She had taken her hair down. It was not quite as long as he'd thought it might be, back when pieces were falling from their pins that day at the hospital. He'd watched her brush it every night, her lips silently counting the strokes. It was almost mesmerizing how the texture and shine seemed to change as she pulled the brush through the strands.

"Edward?"

Again, she'd caught him drifting off. "Sorry," he said. "My mind keeps wandering."

"I'm sure you're very tired."

He tried not to read too much into her pronouncement.

"*I'm* tired," she said.

There were so many levels to that simple, two-word sentence. The simplest: *It was a very long day. I'm tired.*

But he knew there was more to it than that. Cecilia was always careful to make sure that he was not overtaxing himself, so there was certainly a bit of: *If I'm tired, then you must be too.*

Then there was the truth. The simplest, most basic

core of it all: *If I tell you I'm tired . . . If you think I'm not up to it . . .*

"May I?" he murmured, reaching for the brush.

"What?" Her pulse fluttered in her throat. "Oh, there is no need. I am almost done."

"Just a bit more than half."

Confusion painted a wrinkle onto her brow. "I'm sorry?"

"You've done twenty-eight strokes. You normally do fifty."

Her lips parted with surprise. He could not tear his eyes from them.

"You know how many times I brush my hair each evening?"

He gave a little shrug, even as his body tightened at the sight of her tongue moistening a dry spot just to the left of the center of her upper lip. "You're a creature of habit," he said. "And I'm observant."

She set down the hairbrush, as if cutting off her routine might somehow change who she was. "I did not realize I was so predictable."

"Not predictable," he said. He reached across her and took the silver brush in his hand. "Consistent."

"Con—"

"And before you ask," he interrupted gently, "that is a compliment."

"You don't need to brush my hair."

"Of course I do. You shaved my beard, if you recall. It's the very least I can do."

"Yes, but I don't—"

"Shhh . . ." he admonished, and then he took the brush and drew it through her already shining and un-tangled locks.

"Edward, I—"

"Twenty-nine," he said before she could complete yet another protest. "Thirty."

He could pinpoint the moment she finally surren-dered. Her steel-backed posture softened, and a soft breath—not quite a sigh—crossed her lips.

To himself he counted *thirty-two*, *thirty-three*, and *thirty-four*. "It's nice, isn't it?"

"Mmmm."

He smiled. *Thirty-five, thirty-six*. He wondered if she'd notice if he went past fifty.

"Does anyone ever take care of you?" he asked.

She yawned. "That's a silly question."

"I don't think it is. Everyone deserves to be cared for. Some, I imagine, more than others."

"Thomas does," she finally answered. "Or did. It's been so long since I last saw him."

I will, Edward vowed.

"You took great care of me when I was ill," he said.

She turned, just enough so that he could see her puzzled expression. "Of course."

"Not everyone would have done so," he pointed out.

"I am your . . ."

But she did not finish the sentence.

Forty-two, forty-three.

"You are *almost* my wife," he said softly.

He could see only the edge of her face, not even a true profile. But he knew that she had stopped breathing. He felt the instant she went still.

"Forty-eight," he murmured. "Forty-nine."

Her hand came over his, held it in place. Was she trying to prolong the moment? Freeze time so that she did not have to face their inevitable move toward intimacy?

She wanted him. He knew that she did. It was there in the soft moans he heard when they kissed, sweet sounds he doubted she even knew she made. He felt her desire when her lips moved against his, artless and curious.

He took her hand, still resting atop his, and brought it to his mouth. "Fifty," he whispered.

She didn't move.

On soft, silent feet he made his way around to her side, transferring her fingers from one hand to the other so that he could set the hairbrush back on the small vanity. Again, he brought her fingers to his lips, but this time he gave her a gentle tug, urging her to her feet.

"You are so beautiful," he whispered, but the words seemed insufficient. She was so much more than her lovely face, and he wanted to tell her that, but he was not a poet, and he did not know how, especially with the air between them growing hot and thick with desire.

He touched her cheek, marveling at the soft silk of her skin beneath his callused fingers. She was looking up at him, her eyes wide, and he could see that she was intensely nervous, far more than he would have expected, given how close they had become in the past week. But he'd never been with a virgin; maybe they were all like this.

"This isn't our first kiss," he reminded her, brushing his mouth gently against hers.

Still, she did not move, but he would swear he could hear her heart pounding. Or maybe he was hearing it *through* her, from her hand to his.

From her heart to his.

Was he falling in love with her? He could not imagine what else could make him feel like this, as if his days did not truly begin until he saw her smile.

He *was* falling in love with her. He'd already been halfway there before they had even met, and maybe he'd never remember the events that had led him to this moment, but he would remember *this*. This kiss. This touch.

This night.

"Don't be afraid," he murmured, kissing her again, this time teasing her lips with his tongue.

"I'm not afraid," she said, in a voice that was somehow just strange enough to give him pause. He touched her chin, tipped her face up to his, and searched her eyes for something he could not even define.

It would be so much easier if he knew what he was looking for.

"Has someone"—he didn't want to say it—"*hurt* you?"

She stared at him, uncomprehending, until the moment he took a breath to explain further.

"No," she said suddenly, understanding his meaning just in time to save him an explanation. "No," she said again. "I promise."

The relief Edward felt hit him like something solid. If someone had hurt her, raped her . . . It would not matter to him that she was not a virgin, but he would have to spend the rest of his life bringing the cur to justice.

His heart—nay, his soul—would not allow otherwise.

"I will be gentle," he promised, his hand lightly

tracing the line of her throat to the bare skin at her collarbone. She had not changed from her day dress to her nightgown, and so while the fabric was tighter, with meddlesome buttons and laces, it nevertheless revealed a wider swath of skin, from the curve of her shoulder to the gentle swell of her breasts.

He kissed her there, right where the lace edging of her bodice met her skin, and she gasped, her body instinctively arching toward him.

"Edward, I—"

He kissed her again, closer to the shadow between her breasts.

"I don't know if—"

And then at the other side, each kiss a soft benediction, a mere hint of the passion he was holding tightly in check.

His fingers found the fastenings at the back of her dress, and he brought his mouth back to hers as he slowly set her body free. He'd thought to distract her with kisses, but he was the one made stupid by desire, because once her lips parted beneath his, he was utterly consumed.

And so was she. What started as something playful quickly burned hot until they were both drinking of the other like this might be their only chance of union. Edward had no idea how he got her dress off without tearing it; probably the last shred of his rational mind recognized that she had only two frocks here in New York, and they needed to keep both of them in working order.

She was wearing a light chemise, knotted loosely at the front, and his fingers trembled as they grasped one end of the tie. He pulled it slowly, watching as the corresponding loop grew smaller and smaller until it finally slid through the knot.

He edged the chemise from her shoulder, his breath quickening as each inch of her peach-pale skin was exposed.

"It goes the other way," she said.

"What?" Her voice had been soft; he wasn't sure he'd got her meaning.

"The chemise," she said, her eyes not quite meeting his. "It goes over the head."

His hand went still, and he felt a smile tugging at the corners of his lips. He'd been trying to be so gentle, so gentlemanly, and here she was offering directions for her disrobement.

She was delightful. No, she was magnificent, and he could not imagine how he'd ever thought his life had been complete before this moment.

She looked up, her head tilting to the side as she said, "What is it?"

He just shook his head.

"You're smiling," she accused.

"I am."

Now she was smiling too. "Why?"

"Because you're perfect."

"Edward, no, I—"

She was still shaking her head when he pulled her into his arms. The bed was mere steps away, but she was his wife, and he was finally going to make love to her, and by God he was going to sweep her off her feet and carry her there.

He kissed her again and again, his hands roaming over her body, first through the chemise, and then daring their way underneath the hem. She was everything he'd dreamed, responsive and warm. Then he felt her ankle hooking around his leg, drawing him closer, and it was like the entire world had burst into sunshine. This was no longer him seducing her. She wanted him too. She wanted to pull him closer, to feel him against her, and Edward's heart sang with equal parts joy and satisfaction.

He pulled back, sitting up far enough so that he could tug his shirt over his head.

"You look different," she said, watching him with passion-glazed eyes.

His brows rose.

"The last time I saw you"—she reached up, touched his chest with the tips of her fingers—"was the day you left hospital."

He supposed it was true. She had always turned her back when he was changing his clothes. And he had always watched her, wondering what she was thinking, if she wanted to turn around and take a peek.

"Better, I hope," he murmured.

She gave a little eye roll at that, which he supposed he deserved. He had not yet put on all of the weight he had lost, but he was certainly more fit, and when he ran his hands over his arms, he could feel his muscles re-forming, slowly clawing their way back to strength.

But he was strong enough for this. He was definitely strong enough for this.

"I didn't think men were supposed to be so beautiful," Cecilia said.

He planted his hands on either side of her shoulders, bracing himself so he could loom over her as he warned, "If you make me blush I shall have to exert my husbandly authority over you."

"Your husbandly authority? What does that entail?"

"I'm not sure," he admitted. "But I'm fairly certain you promised to obey."

If he hadn't been so focused on her face, he might not

have seen the little twitch in her jaw. Or the awkward swallow that made a trail down her throat. He almost teased her about it. There was not a woman of his acquaintance—at least not one he liked and respected—who actually meant it when she promised to obey her husband.

He wondered if she'd crossed her fingers when she'd said the words on the ship. Or maybe she'd found some way out of saying them altogether, the little vixen. And now she was too embarrassed to admit it.

"I never expected you to obey me," he murmured, smiling as he went in for another kiss. "Merely to agree with me in all things."

She shoved him in the shoulder, but all he could do was laugh. Even when he rolled onto his side and pulled her close, he could not stop the silent mirth that shook through his body and into hers.

Had he ever laughed in bed with a woman? Who knew it would be so delightful.

"You do make me happy," he said, and then he finally took her advice and pulled the chemise from her body, her arms rising up as he slid it over her head.

His breath caught. She was nude now, and although the sheets covered her lower body, her breasts were bare to him. She was the most beautiful thing he'd ever seen, but there was more to it than that. It wasn't just that the sight of her made him dizzy with desire. Or that he was quite certain he had never been so hard with need as he was at that moment.

It was *more*. It was deeper.

It was divine.

He touched one of her breasts, grazing the pretty pink nipple with his forefinger. She gasped, and he could not help but let out a growl of masculine pride. He loved that he could make her want him, want *this*. He loved knowing that she was almost certainly growing wet between her legs, that her body was coming alive, and *he* was doing it.

"So pretty," he murmured, adjusting their bodies so that she was once again on her back, and he was straddling her. But with her chemise gone, the position took on a far more erotic air. Her breasts flattened a bit with gravity, but the nipples, pink as roses, jutted proudly upward, practically begging for his touch.

"I could look at you all day," he said.

Her breath quickened.

"Or maybe not," he said, leaning down to give her right nipple one little lick. "I don't think I could look and not touch."

"Edward," she gasped.

"Or kiss." He moved to the other breast, drawing the tip into his mouth.

She arched beneath him, a soft shriek escaping her lips as he continued his sweet torture.

"I can nibble, too," he murmured, going back to the other side, this time using his teeth.

"Oh my God," she moaned. "What are you doing? I feel it . . ."

He chuckled. "I hope you feel it."

"No, I feel it . . ."

He waited for a few seconds, and then, his words laced with wicked desire, he said, "You feel it somewhere else?"

She nodded.

Someday, after they'd made love a hundred times, he'd make her say where she felt it. He'd make her say the words that would make his already hard cock turn into something built with steel. But for now, he would be the naughty one. He would use every weapon in his arsenal to make sure that when he finally entered her she was desperate with need.

She would know what it meant to be adored. She would know what it meant to be worshipped. Because he had already realized that his greatest pleasure lay with her finding hers.

He squeezed her breast, his hand molding it into a tiny mountain as he bent down to place his lips by her ear. "I wonder where you feel it," he said, grazing her with his teeth. He rolled over onto his side, propping himself up on one elbow as his hand slid from her breast to her hip. "Could it be here?"

Her breath grew louder.

"Or maybe"—he slid across her belly, tickling her navel with his finger—"here?"

Still, she quivered beneath his touch.

"I don't think that's the spot," he said, idly drawing circles on her skin. "I think you were speaking of somewhere a little lower."

She made a sound. It might have been his name.

He flattened his palm against her abdomen, and with purposeful slowness inched his way down until his fingers met the soft thatch of hair that guarded her womanhood. He felt her grow very still, as if she wasn't sure what to do, and he could only smile as he listened to the frenzied rasps of air of passing over her lips.

Tenderly he parted her, his fingers flicking over her nub until some of the rigidity left her body, and she fell more fully open to him. "Do you like that?" he whispered, even though he knew she did. But when she nodded he still felt like king of the world. The mere act of pleasuring her seemed to be enough to make his heart swell with pride.

He continued to tease her, drawing her closer and closer to her peak, even though his own body was crying out for satisfaction. He had not intended to see to her completion first, but once he touched her, felt her body singing beneath his fingers, he knew what he had to do. He wanted her to fall apart, to utterly shatter and think there was no greater pleasure.

And then he wanted to show her that there was.

"What are you doing?" she whispered, but he thought the question might be rhetorical. Her eyes were closed, and her head was thrown back, and as her body arched, thrusting those perfect breasts to the sky, he thought he'd never seen anything so lovely and erotic.

"I'm making love to you," he said.

Her eyes opened. "But—"

He brought a finger to her lips. "Don't interrupt me." She was a clever girl; she obviously knew what happened between a man and a woman, and she knew that something much larger than his fingers was meant to find its way inside of her. But clearly no one had told her about all the delicious things that could happen along the way.

"Have you heard of *la petite mort*?" he asked her.

Her eyes clouded with confusion as she shook her head. "The little death?"

"It's what the French call it. A metaphor, I assure you. I have always thought it more an affirmation of life." He leaned down and drew her nipple into his mouth. "Or perhaps a reason for living."

And then, with all the wicked promise he felt in his soul, he looked up at her through his lashes and murmured, "Shall I show you?"

Chapter 14

I miss the days when you were in London and we could write back and forth like a conversation. I suppose we are now at the mercy of the tides. Our letters must cross each other on the ocean. Mrs. Pentwhistle said she thought it was a charming thought, that they had little hands and were waving at each other across the water. I think Mrs. Pentwhistle drank too much of Reverend Pentwhistle's Communion wine.

Please tell Captain Rokesby that the little purple flower he pressed arrived in perfect condition. Isn't it remarkable that such a little sprig is strong enough to journey from Massachusetts to Derbyshire? I am sure I will never have the opportunity

to thank him in person for it. Please do assure him
that I will treasure it always. It is so very special to
have a small piece of your world.

      —FROM CECILIA HARCOURT TO

        HER BROTHER THOMAS

T*he little death.*

  Surely the French had been onto something when they came up with that phrase. Because the tightness that was coiling in Cecilia's body . . . the pulsing, inexorable need for something she did not even understand . . . It all felt like it was leading toward something she could not possibly survive.

"Edward," she gasped. "I can't . . ."

"You can," he assured her, but it was not his words that sank into her, it was his voice, pressed up against her skin as his wicked lips made lazy discovery of her breasts.

He had touched her—kissed her—in places she herself had not dared to explore. She was bewitched. No, she was awakened. She'd lived twenty-two years in this body and was only just now learning its purpose.

"Relax," Edward whispered.

Was he mad? There was nothing relaxing about this, nothing that made her want to relax. She wanted to grab and claw and yes, scream as she fought her way to the edge.

Except she did not know what that edge was, or what might be on the other side.

"Please," she begged, and it didn't even seem to matter that she had no idea what she was begging for. Because he did. Dear God, she hoped he did. If he didn't, she was going to kill him.

With his mouth and his fingers, he brought her to the peak of desire. And then, when her hips rose up, silently begging him for more, he dipped one finger inside of her and flicked his tongue across her breast.

She came apart.

She cried his name as her hips lifted from the bed. Every muscle clenched in unison. It was like a symphony made of only one taut note. Then, after her body had grown tight as a board, she finally drew breath and collapsed onto the mattress.

Edward withdrew his finger and lay on his side next to her, propped up on his elbow. When she found the energy to open her eyes, she saw that he was smiling like a cat in cream.

"What was that?" she said, her words more breath than voice.

He brushed a damp tendril of hair from her forehead, then leaned forward to kiss her brow. "*La petite mort*," he murmured.

"Oh." There was a world of wonder in that single syllable. "That's what I thought."

This seemed to amuse him, but in that lovely way that made Cecilia flush with pleasure. She was making him smile. She was making him *happy.* Surely when she reached her final reckoning that would count for something.

But they had not yet consummated the marriage.

She closed her eyes. She had to stop thinking that way. There *was* no marriage. This was not a consummation, it was—

"What's wrong?"

She looked up. Edward was staring down at her, his eyes so bright and blue, even in the fading light of evening.

"Cecilia?" He did not sound concerned, exactly, but he knew something had changed.

"I'm just . . ." She fought for something to say, something she could say that would actually be true. And so she said, ". . . overwhelmed."

He smiled, just a little, but it was enough to change the shape of her heart forever. "That's a good thing, isn't it?"

She nodded as best as she could. It was a good thing, at least right now. As for next week, or next month, when her life would surely fall apart . . .

She would deal with that when she had to.

His knuckles brushed her cheek in a tender caress, and still, he stared down at her like he could read her soul. "What are you thinking, I wonder."

What was she thinking? That she wanted him. That she loved him. That even though she knew this was wrong, it *felt* like they were married, and she just wanted it to be real, if only for this one night.

"Kiss me," she said, because she needed to take control of the moment. She needed to be *in* this moment, not floating off into the future, into a world where Edward's smile was no longer hers.

"A little bossy all of a sudden," he teased.

But she was having none of it. "Kiss me," she said again, wrapping one of her hands behind his head. "Now."

She pulled him down, and when their lips met, her hunger exploded. She kissed him like he was her very air, her food and water. She kissed him with everything she felt inside, everything she could never tell him. It was a declaration and an apology; it was a woman clutching at bliss while she had the chance.

And he returned it all with equal passion.

She would never know what came over her, how her hands seemed to know what to do, pulling him close, reaching for the fastening of the breeches he still had not taken off.

She let out a cry of frustration when he pulled away from her, hopping from the bed to tear off the offending garment. But she did not take her eyes off him, and God above, he was beautiful. Beautiful and very, very large, enough to make her eyes widen with apprehension.

He must have seen her expression because he chuckled, and when he got back on the bed, his expression was somewhere between roguish and feral. "It'll fit," he said, his voice husky against her ear.

His hand slid down her body to the cleft between her legs, and it was only then that she realized how very hot and wet she'd gotten. Hot and wet and needy. Had he pleasured her on purpose? To make her ready for him?

If so, it had worked, because she felt an overwhelming hunger for him, a need to take him within her, to join her body to his and never let go.

She felt him press up against her, just the very tip of him, and her breath caught.

"I'll be gentle," he promised.

"I'm not sure I want you to be."

A shudder ran through his body, and when she looked up, his jaw was tightly clenched as he fought for control. "Don't say things like that," he managed to get out.

She arched against him, trying to somehow get even closer. "But it's true."

He moved forward, and she felt herself opening to him.

"Am I hurting you?" he asked.

"No," she said, "but it feels very . . . strange."

"Strange good or strange bad?"

She blinked a few times, trying to make sense of what she was feeling. "Just strange."

"I'm not so sure I like that answer," he murmured. His hands reached behind her, pulling her open wider, and she gasped as another inch of his manhood pressed forward. "I don't want this to be strange." His lips found her ear. "I think we're going to need to do this *very* often."

He sounded different, almost untamed, and something very feminine inside of her began to sparkle. *She* had made him this way. This man—this big, powerful man—was losing control, and it was all for a need of *her.*

She had never felt so strong.

The sensations weren't like the ones from before,

though. When he had been using just his hands and his lips, he had whipped her into a storm of desire and then sent her soaring with pleasure. But now it was more that she had to get used to him, accommodate his size. It didn't hurt, but it wasn't as lovely as before. At least not for her.

But for Edward . . . Everything she had been feeling before, every last clench of need she saw on his face. He was loving this. And that was enough for her.

But not, apparently, for him, because he frowned and stopped moving.

She looked up at him with questioning eyes.

"This will not do," he said, dropping a kiss on her nose.

"Am I not pleasing you?" She'd thought she was, but maybe not.

"If you pleased me any more I might perish," he said with a wry expression. "That's not the problem. I am not pleasing you."

"You did. You know you did." She blushed when she said this, but she could not bear for him to think she was not enjoying herself.

"You do not think you can be pleasured twice?"

Cecilia felt her eyes grow very wide.

Edward's hand slipped between their bodies and found the most sensitive spot of her womanhood.

"Oh!" She'd felt him moving there, but still, the sensation was so intense she could not help but let out a cry of surprise.

"That's more like it," he murmured.

And then it all began to build again. The pressure, the need . . . it was so great she did not notice how he was stretching her with each stroke. Every time she thought there could not possibly be more of him, he pulled back and then plunged forward, reaching even further into her soul.

She had not known she could be so close to another human being. She had not known she could be so close and want even more.

She arched her back, her hands clutching at his shoulders as his body finally came fully flush against hers.

"My God," he breathed, "it's like I've come home." He looked down at her, and she thought she saw the slightest sheen of moisture in his eyes before his mouth captured hers in a torrid, passionate kiss.

And then he began to move.

It began as slow, steady strokes, creating an exquisite friction inside of her. But then his breath jerked into gasps, and whatever rhythm he'd begun sped into a frenzy. She felt it growing within her too, that race toward the precipice, but she was nowhere as lost as Edward was, at least not before he adjusted his position and sucked one of her nipples into his mouth.

She cried out at the shock of it, at the impossible connection between her breast and her womb. But she felt it there . . . dear God above, when his fingers began to tease the other nipple, she felt it between her legs and she began to quiver and clench.

"Yes!" Edward growled. "My God, yes, squeeze me." He grabbed her breast, harder than she'd have ever thought she'd like, but she loved it, and with a sudden piercing jolt she came apart again.

"Oh God," Edward was grunting. "Oh God oh God oh God." His movements grew almost crazed, and he was pounding forward, and then he seemed to go almost still, caught in one last thrust before moaning her name and collapsing atop her.

"Cecilia," he said again, his voice barely a whisper. "Cecilia."

"I'm right here." She stroked his back, her fingertips making lazy circles across the indentation of his spine.

"Cecilia." And then again. "Cecilia."

She liked that he couldn't seem to say anything besides her name. Heaven knew, she wasn't thinking much beyond his.

"I'm crushing you," he mumbled.

He was, but she didn't mind. She liked the weight of him.

He rolled off her, but not all the way, leaving himself draped partly over her. "I never want to stop touching you," he said. He sounded incredibly drowsy.

She turned to look at him. His eyes were closed, and if he had not fallen asleep, he would very soon. Already his breath had begun to even out, and his eyelashes—so thick and dark—lay lazily against his cheeks.

She'd never watched him fall asleep, she realized. She had shared a bed with him for a week, but every night she'd crawled into her side and carefully turned her back. She would listen to his breathing, practically holding her own breath in an effort to keep still and quiet. And she told herself that she would listen, and then she would know when he fell asleep, but every time she somehow drifted off before that happened.

He was always up before her in the mornings, already dressed or mostly so, when she opened her eyes and yawned her way into the day.

So this was a treat. He was not a restless sleeper, but his mouth moved a little, almost as if he were whispering a prayer. She yearned to reach out and touch his cheek, but she didn't want to wake him. His recent display of strength and stamina notwithstanding, he was not fully restored to health and he needed his rest.

So she watched him and she waited. Waited for the guilt she knew would eventually wrap itself around her heart. She wanted to lie to herself and say that he had seduced her beyond reason, but she knew that was not true. Yes, she had been swept away by passion, but she could have stopped him at any point. All she had to do was open her mouth and confess her sins.

With her fist to her mouth, she stifled a grim laugh. If she'd told Edward the truth he would have been off her like a shot. He would have been furious, and then he would have probably hauled her off to a priest and married her on the spot. That was just the sort of man he was.

But she couldn't let him do that. He was practically engaged to that girl back home, the one he'd told her about—Billie Bridgerton. She knew he was very fond of her. He always smiled when he talked about her. Always. What if they really *were* engaged? What if he'd promised himself to her and had forgotten about it along with everything else in the last few months?

What if he loved her? He could have forgotten about that, too.

But even with all the guilt now coursing through her veins, she couldn't bring herself to regret this. Someday all she would have left of this man would be memories, and she was damned if she did not make those memories as brilliant as she could.

And if there was a child . . .

Her hand went to her womb, where even now his seed could be taking root. If there was a child . . .

No. That was unlikely. Her friend Eliza had been married a full year before she got pregnant. And the vicar's wife even longer. Still, Cecilia knew enough to know that she could not continue to tempt fate. Maybe she could tell Edward that she feared getting pregnant so far from home. It would be no lie to say that she did not relish the idea of an ocean journey while she was with child.

Or with a child. Good Lord, the journey had been awful enough on her own. She had not been seasick, but it had been dull, and at times frightening. To do that with an infant?

She shuddered. It would be hell.

"What's wrong?"

She twisted at the sound of Edward's voice. "I thought you were asleep."

"I was." He yawned. "Or almost." One of his legs was still pinning her down, so he moved it, then drew her up against him, her back to his front. "You were upset," he said.

"Don't be silly."

He kissed the back of her head. "Something was bothering you. I could tell."

"While you were asleep?"

"Almost asleep," he reminded her. "Are you sore?"

"I don't know," she said quite honestly.

"I should get you a cloth." He let go of her and slid from the bed. Cecilia twisted her neck so that she could watch him as he crossed the room to the basin of water. How could he be so unselfconscious in his nakedness? Was it a male thing?

"Here we are," he said, returning to her side. He'd dampened the cloth, and with tender motions he cleaned her.

It was too much. She almost cried.

When he was done, he set the cloth aside and resumed his position next to her, propping himself up on one elbow as he used his free hand to fiddle with her hair. "Tell me what is bothering you," he murmured.

She swallowed, summoning her courage. "I don't want to become pregnant," she said.

He went still, and Cecilia was glad for the dim light in the room. She wasn't sure she wanted to see whatever emotion had flashed through his eyes.

"It might be too late for that," he said.

"I know. I just—"

"You don't want to be a mother?"

"No!" she exclaimed, surprising herself with the force of her reply. Because she did. The thought of bearing his child . . . It nearly made her weep with the want of it. "I don't want to become pregnant *here*," she said, "in North America. I know there are doctors and midwives, but eventually I want to go home. And I don't want to make that crossing with a baby."

"No," he said, his brow pulling into a thoughtful frown. "Of course not."

"I don't want to do it while I'm pregnant either," she said. "What if something should happen?"

"Things happen everywhere, Cecilia."

"I know. But I just think I would feel more comfortable at home. In England."

None of this was a lie. It just wasn't the whole truth.

He continued to stroke her hair, the motion soft and soothing. "You look so distraught," he murmured.

She didn't know what to say.

"You needn't be so upset," he told her. "As I said, it might be too late, but there are precautions we can take."

"There are?" Her heart made a delighted skip before she remembered that she had far greater problems than this.

He smiled, then touched her chin, tipping her face up toward his. "Oh yes. I would show you now, but I think you need some rest. Sleep," he said. "It will all seem clearer in the morning."

It wouldn't. But she slept, anyway.

Chapter 15

A thousand apologies. I have not written in over a month, but in truth there was little to write about. Everything is boredom or battle, and I do not wish to write about either. We arrived in Newport yesterday, though, and after a good meal and a bath, I am feeling more like myself.

—FROM THOMAS HARCOURT
TO HIS SISTER CECILIA

Dear Miss Harcourt,

Thank you for your kind note. The weather has begun to take a chill again, and by the time you receive this, I suspect we will be glad for our woolen coats. Newport is more of a town than we have seen in some time, and we are both enjoying its comforts. Thomas and I have been given rooms in a private home, but our men have been billeted in houses of worship, half in a church and half in a synagogue. Several of our men were fearful that they would be smote by God for sleeping in an unholy house. I do not see how it is more unholy than the tavern they visited the night before. But it is not my job to provide religious counsel. Speaking of which, I do hope your Mrs. Pentwhistle has not been back in the wine. Although I must confess, I did enjoy your story about the "psalm that went horribly awry."

And because I know you will ask, I have never visited a synagogue before; it looks rather like a church, to be frank.

—FROM EDWARD ROKESBY TO
CECILIA HARCOURT, ENCLOSED
WITHIN THE LETTER FROM HER
BROTHER

As usual, Edward woke before Cecilia the following morning. She did not stir as he eased himself from the bed, attesting to her exceptional fatigue.

He smiled. He was happy to take credit for her fatigue.

She'd be hungry, too. She generally ate her biggest

meal of the day at breakfast, and though the Devil's Head always had eggs due to the chickens they kept in the back, Edward thought a treat might be in order. Something sweet. Chelsea buns, maybe. Or *speculaas*.

Or both. Why not both?

After dressing, he jotted a quick note and left it on the table, informing her that he would be back soon. It wasn't far to the two bakeries. He could be there and back in under an hour if he did not run into anyone he knew.

Rooijakkers was closer, so he walked there first, smiling to himself as the bell jangled over his head, alerting the proprietor to his presence. It wasn't Mr. Rooijakkers tending to the shop, though, but his red-haired daughter, the one Cecilia said she had befriended. Edward recalled meeting her himself, back before he'd gone to Connecticut. He and Thomas had both preferred the Dutch bakery to the English one around the corner.

Edward felt his smile grow wistful. Thomas had quite the sweet tooth. Much like his sister.

"Good morning, sir," the lady called out. She wiped her floury hands on her apron as she came out from the back room.

"Ma'am," Edward said with a small bow of his chin.

He wished he could remember her name. But at least this time, he came by his lapse honestly. Whatever her name was, it wasn't hiding out in the blackened portion of his memory. He'd always been bad with names.

"How nice to see you again, sir," the lady said. "You haven't been in in a very long time."

"Months," he confirmed. "I've been out of town."

She nodded, giving him a jaunty smile as she said, "Makes it hard for us to have regular customers, what with the army sending you here, there, and everywhere."

"Just to Connecticut," he said.

She chuckled at that. "And how is your friend?"

"My friend?" Edward echoed, even though he knew very well that she must be talking about Thomas. Still, it was disquieting. No one asked about him anymore, or if they did, it was with hushed, somber voices.

"I haven't seen him in some time, actually," Edward said.

"That's a shame." She cocked her head to the side in a friendly gesture. "For the both of us. He was one of my best customers. He had quite the love of sweets."

"His sister as well," Edward murmured.

She looked at him curiously.

"I married his sister," he explained, wondering why

he was telling her this. Probably just because it made him happy to say it. He'd married Cecilia. Well. He'd *really* married her now.

Mr. Rooijakkers's daughter went still for a moment, her gingery eyebrows drawing together before she said, "I'm so sorry, I'm afraid I can't recall your name . . ."

"Captain Edward Rokesby, ma'am. And yes, you've met my new wife. Cecilia."

"Of course. I'm sorry, I did not put it together when she said her name earlier. She looks rather like her brother, doesn't she? Not in the features so much but—"

"The expressions, yes," Edward finished for her.

She grinned. "You must want *speculaas*, then."

"Indeed. A dozen, if you will."

"We have probably never been introduced," she said as she bent down to retrieve a platter of biscuits from a low shelf. "I am Mrs. Beatrix Leverett."

"Cecilia has spoken most fondly of you." He waited patiently as Mrs. Leverett counted out the biscuits. He was rather looking forward to Cecilia's reaction when he brought her breakfast in bed. Well, biscuits in bed, which might be even better.

Except for the crumbs. That might present a problem.

"Is Mrs. Rokesby's brother still in Connecticut?"

Edward's lovely imaginings came to a halt. "I beg your pardon?"

"Mrs. Rokesby's brother," she repeated, looking up from her task. "I thought he went with you to Connecticut."

Edward went very still. "You know about that?"

"Should I not?"

"Thomas was with me in Connecticut," he said. His voice was soft, almost as if he were testing out the statement, trying it on like a new coat.

Did it fit?

"Wasn't he?" Mrs. Leverett asked.

"I . . ." Hell, what was he to say? He didn't particularly wish to share the details of his condition with a near stranger, but if she had information about Thomas . . .

"I have been having difficulty remembering a few things," he finally said. He touched his scalp, just under the brim of his hat. The bump was much smaller now, but the skin was still tender. "I was hit on the head."

"Oh, I'm so sorry." Her eyes filled with compassion. "That must be terribly frustrating."

"Yes," he said, but his injury was not what he wished to discuss. He looked at her directly, eyes set squarely on hers. "You were telling me about Captain Harcourt."

Her shoulders rose in a tiny shrug. "I don't really know anything. Just that the both of you went to Connecticut several months ago. You came in just before you left. For provisions."

"Provisions," Edward echoed.

"*You* bought bread," she said with a little chuckle. "Your friend has a sweet tooth. I told him—"

"—that the *speculaas* would not travel well," he finished for her.

"Yes," she said. "They crumble too easily."

"They did," Edward said softly. "Every last one of them."

And then it all came flooding back.

"Stubbs!"

The colonel looked up from his desk, visibly startled by Edward's furious bark.

"Captain Rokesby. What on earth is the matter?"

What was the matter? What was the *matter*? Edward fought to keep his fury under control. He'd stormed out of the Dutch bakery without his purchases, practically ran through the streets of New York to get here, to Colonel Stubbs's office at the building currently being used as British headquarters. His hands were fisted, his blood was pounding through his brain like he'd been in battle, and by God, the only thing that was keeping him from assaulting his superior officer was the threat of a court-martial.

"You knew," Edward said, his voice shaking with rage. "You knew about Thomas Harcourt."

Stubbs stood slowly, and his skin flushed red under his whiskers. "To what, precisely, do you refer?"

"He went to Connecticut with me. Why the hell didn't you say so?"

"I told you," Stubbs said in a stiff voice, "I could not take the risk of influencing your memories."

"That's shite and you know it," Edward spat. "Tell me the truth."

"It is the truth," Stubbs hissed, stalking around Edward to slam the door to his office shut. "Do you think I liked lying to your wife?"

"My wife," Edward repeated. He had remembered *that,* too. He wouldn't say that his memory was completely restored, but it was mostly all there, and he was fully certain that he had not participated in a proxy wedding ceremony. Nor had Thomas ever asked him to.

Edward couldn't imagine what had led Cecilia to such a deception, but he could only deal with one cocked-up disaster at a time. His eyes landed on Stubbs's with barely contained fury. "You have ten seconds to explain to me why you lied about Thomas Harcourt."

"For the love of God, Rokesby," the colonel said,

raking his hand through his thinning hair, "I'm not a monster. The last thing I wanted was to give her false hope."

Edward froze. "*False* hope?"

Stubbs stared at him. "You don't know." It wasn't quite a question.

"I believe we have already ascertained that there is a lot I don't know," Edward said, his voice clipped with tightly wound emotion. "So please, enlighten me."

"Captain Harcourt is dead," the colonel said. He shook his head, and with honest sorrow said, "He took a shot to the gut. I'm sorry."

"What?" Edward stumbled back, his legs somehow finding a chair for him to sink into. "How? When?"

"Back in March," Stubbs said. He crossed the room and yanked open a cabinet, pulling out a decanter of brandy. "It wasn't even a week after you left. He sent word to meet him up at New Rochelle."

Edward watched the colonel's unsteady hands as he sloshed amber liquid into two glasses. "Who went?"

"Just me."

"You went alone," Edward said, his tone making it clear that he found this difficult to believe.

Stubbs held forth a glass. "It was what had to be done."

Edward exhaled as memories—strangely fresh and

stale at the same time—unrolled through his mind. He and Thomas had gone to Connecticut together, entrusted with the task of assessing the viability of a naval attack on the waterfront. The command had come from Governor Tryon himself. He'd chosen Edward, he'd said, because he needed someone he could trust implicitly. Edward had chosen Thomas for the very same reason.

But the two of them had traveled together for only a few days before Thomas had headed back to New York with the information they'd gathered about Norwalk. Edward had continued east, toward New Haven.

And that was the last he'd seen of him.

Edward took the glass of brandy and downed it in a single shot.

Stubbs did the same, then said, "I take it this means you have recovered your memory."

Edward gave him a sharp nod. The colonel would want to question him immediately, he knew that, but he would say nothing until he got some answers about Thomas. "Why did you have General Garth send a letter to his family that he was only wounded?"

"He *was* only wounded when we sent that," the colonel replied. "He was shot twice, several days apart."

"What?" Edward tried to make sense of this. "What the hell happened?"

Stubbs groaned and seemed to deflate as he leaned against his desk. "I couldn't bring him back here. Not when I wasn't sure of his loyalties."

"Thomas Harcourt was no traitor," Edward spat.

"There was no way to know that for certain," Stubbs shot back. "What the hell was I supposed to think? I got up to New Rochelle, just as he'd specified, and then before he can say anything other than my name people start shooting at me."

"At him," Edward corrected. After all, Thomas was the one who'd been shot.

Stubbs downed his brandy—his second glass by now—and went back for another. "I don't know who the hell they were shooting at. For all I know, I was the target and they missed. You know most of the colonials are an untrained rabble. Half can't hit the side of the wall."

Edward took a moment to absorb this. He knew in his bones that Thomas was no traitor, but he could see how Colonel Stubbs—who did not know him well—could have had doubts.

"Captain Harcourt was hit in the shoulder," Stubbs said grimly. "The bullet went clean through. It wasn't that hard to get the bleeding stopped, but he was in a lot of pain."

Edward closed his eyes and took a breath, but it

didn't steady him. He'd seen far too many men with gunshot wounds.

"I took him to Dobbs Ferry," Stubbs continued. "We have a small outpost near the river. It's not quite behind enemy lines, but close."

Edward knew Dobbs Ferry well. The British had used it as a rendezvous point ever since the Battle of White Plains nearly three years earlier. "What happened then?" he asked.

Colonel Stubbs looked at him with a flat expression. "I returned here."

"You left him there," Edward said disgustedly. What sort of man left a wounded soldier in the middle of the wilderness?

"He was not alone. I had three men guarding him."

"You held him as a prisoner?"

"It was for his own safety as much as anything else. I didn't know if we were keeping him from escaping, or keeping the rebels from killing him." Stubbs eyed Edward with increasing impatience. "For God's sake, Rokesby, I am not the enemy here."

Edward held his tongue.

"He could not have made the trip back to New York in any case," Stubbs said with a shake of his head. "He was in far too much pain."

"You could have stayed."

"No, I could not," Stubbs retorted. "I had to return to headquarters. I was expected. No one even knew I'd slipped away. Believe me, as soon as I came up with an excuse I went back to fetch him. It was only two days." He swallowed, and for the first time since Edward's arrival, he actually went pale. "But when I got there, they were dead."

"They?"

"Harcourt, the three men holding him. All of them."

Edward looked at the glass in his hand. He'd forgotten he was holding it. He watched his hand as he set it down, almost as if this might somehow stem the shaking of his fingers. "What happened?" he asked.

"I don't know." Stubbs closed his eyes, his face replete with agonized memory as he whispered, "They'd all been shot."

Bile rose up in Edward's stomach. "Was it an execution?"

"No." Stubbs shook his head. "There had been a fight."

"Even Thomas? Wasn't he under guard?"

"We had not bound him. It was clear that he had been fighting too, even with his injury. But . . ." Stubbs swallowed. Turned away.

"But what?"

"It was impossible to tell which side he'd been fighting for."

"You knew him better than that," Edward said in a low voice.

"Did I? Did you?"

"Yes, goddamn it, I did!" The words erupted from him in a roar, and this time Edward shot to his feet.

"Well, I didn't," Stubbs returned. "And it's my bloody job to be suspicious of everyone." He grabbed his forehead, his thumb and middle finger pressing hard into his temples. "I'm just so sick of it all."

Edward took a step back. He'd never seen the colonel like this. He wasn't sure he'd ever seen anyone like this.

"Do you know what it does to a man?" Stubbs asked, his voice only just louder than a whisper. "To trust no one?"

Edward did not speak. He was still so angry, so full of rage and fury, but he no longer knew where to direct it. Not at Stubbs, though. He took the brandy glass from the colonel's trembling hand and walked over to the decanter, where he poured them each another. He did not care if it was barely eight in the morning. Neither of them needed a clear head.

He suspected neither of them wanted a clear head.

"What happened to the bodies?" Edward asked in a low voice.

"I buried them."

"All of them?"

The colonel closed his eyes. "It was not a pleasant day."

"Have you any witnesses?"

Stubbs looked up sharply. "You do not trust me?"

"Forgive me," Edward said, because he did trust Stubbs. In this . . . in everything, he supposed. He did not know how the man had kept this to himself. It must have burned a hole in his gut.

"I got help for the graves," Stubbs said. He sounded exhausted. He sounded spent. "I will give you the names of the men who aided me if you so require."

Edward looked at him for a long moment before answering, "I do not." But then he gave his head a little shake, almost as if he were trying to jostle his thoughts into place. "Why did you send that letter?"

Stubbs blinked. "What letter?"

"The one from General Garth. Saying that Thomas had been injured. I assume he did so at your request."

"It was true when we sent it," the colonel answered. "I'd wanted to notify his family with all due haste. There was a ship leaving the harbor the morning after I left him in Dobbs Ferry. When I think about it now . . ." He raked his hand through his thinning hair, and his body seemed to deflate as he sighed. "I was so pleased I'd managed to dispatch it so quickly."

"You never thought to correct your error and send another?"

"There were too many unanswered questions."

"To notify his family?" Edward asked in disbelief.

"I planned to send a letter once we had answers," Stubbs said stiffly. "I certainly didn't think his sister would cross the Atlantic for him. Although, I don't know, maybe she came for you."

Not likely.

Stubbs walked over to his desk and opened a drawer. "I have his ring."

Edward watched as he carefully removed a box, opened that, and then pulled out a signet ring.

Stubbs held it out. "I thought his family would want this."

Edward stared at the gold circle that was dropped into his palm. Truth be told, he didn't recognize it. He'd never looked closely at Thomas's signet ring. But he knew that Cecilia would know it.

It would break her heart.

Stubbs cleared his throat. "What will you tell your wife?"

His wife. There was that word again. Goddamn it.

She wasn't his wife. He didn't know what she was, but she wasn't his wife.

"Rokesby?"

He looked up. There would be time to make sense of Cecilia's dishonesty later. For now, he would search his soul for a little kindness and allow her to grieve for her brother before confronting her with her lies.

Edward took a breath and looked the colonel squarely in the eye as he said, "I will tell her that her brother died a hero. I will tell her that you regret that you were unable to tell her the truth when she first asked due to the secretive nature of his extraordinarily important work." He took a step toward the colonel, and then another. "I will tell her that you plan to speak with her directly, to apologize for the pain you have wrought upon her, and to personally give to her any and all posthumous honors he received."

"There were no—"

"Make them up," Edward snapped.

The colonel's eyes held his for several seconds before he said, "I will make the arrangements for a medal."

Edward nodded his assent and headed for the door.

But the colonel's voice stopped him. "Are you sure you wish to lie to her?"

Edward turned slowly around. "I beg your pardon?"

"I don't feel like I know much anymore," Stubbs

said with a sigh, "but I know marriage. You don't want to start it off with a lie."

"Really."

The colonel looked at him with an odd speculation. "Is there something you're not telling me, Captain Rokesby?"

Edward pushed the door open and walked out, at least three steps past the colonel's earshot before muttering, "You have no bloody idea."

Chapter 16

I have not heard from you in so long. I try not to worry, but it is difficult.

—FROM CECILIA HARCOURT TO
HER BROTHER THOMAS

When Edward did not return by nine, Cecilia grew curious.

When he did not return by half past, her curiosity gave way to concern.

And at ten, when the bells of the nearby church tolled far too loud, she picked up his note again, just to make sure she had not misread it the first time.

Gone to fetch breakfast. I shall return before you awaken.

She caught her lower lip between her teeth. It was hard to see how one could misread that.

She began to wonder if he was stuck downstairs, waylaid by a fellow officer. It happened all the time. Everyone seemed to know him, and most wished to congratulate him on his recent safe return. Soldiers could be a garrulous lot, especially when they were bored. And everyone seemed bored these days, although most were quick to point out that it was preferable to fighting.

So Cecilia headed down to the front room of the Devil's Head, fully prepared to extricate Edward from an unwanted conversation. She'd remind him of their "very important appointment," and then maybe they'd go back upstairs . . .

But he wasn't in the front room. Nor the rear.

I shall return before you awaken.

Clearly something was amiss. Edward always woke up before she did, but she was no slugabed. He knew that. She was always dressed and ready for breakfast by half eight.

She had half a mind to go out looking for him, but she just *knew* that if she did, he'd return five minutes after she left, and he'd go out looking for *her*, and they'd spend the whole morning not quite crossing paths.

So she waited.

"You're off to a late start this morning," the innkeeper said when he saw her standing about indecisively. "Nothing to eat for you?"

"No, thank you. My husband's getting—" She frowned. "Have you seen Captain Rokesby this morning?"

"Not for several hours, ma'am. Bid me good morning and then headed out. Looked right happy, he did." The innkeeper gave her a lopsided grin as he wiped out a tankard. "He was whistling."

It said something of Cecilia's level of distraction that she couldn't even manage a tinge of embarrassment over that. She glanced toward the street-facing window, not that one could make out anything other than a few blobby shapes through the warped glass. "I expected him back some time ago," she said, almost to herself.

The innkeeper shrugged. "He'll be back soon, you'll see. In the meantime, are you sure you don't need anything?"

"Quite, but thank you. I—"

The front door made its customary groan as someone pushed it open, and Cecilia whirled around, certain that it must be Edward.

Except it wasn't.

"Captain Montby," she said with a small curtsy, recognizing the young officer who had given up his room for her the previous week. He'd gone away for a few days and then come back and was now bunking with another soldier. She had thanked him several times for his generosity, but he always insisted that it was his honor and duty as a gentleman. And anyway, half a room at the Devil's Head was better than most British soldiers got for sleeping quarters.

"Mrs. Rokesby," he returned in greeting. He bowed his chin, then followed this with a smile. "A fine morning to you. Are you off to join your husband?"

Cecilia snapped to attention. "Do you know where he is?"

Captain Montby made a somewhat directionless nod over his shoulder. "I just saw him over at the Fraunces Tavern."

"*What?*"

She must have sounded shrill because Captain Montby drew back an inch or so before saying, "Er, yes. I only spied him across the room, but I was fairly certain it was he."

"At the Fraunces? You're sure?"

"I believe so," the captain said, his words taking on the wary tone of one who does not wish to get involved in a domestic dispute.

"Was he with someone?"

"Not when I saw him."

Cecilia's lips pressed into a firm line as she headed

for the door, pausing only to thank Captain Montby for his help. She couldn't imagine what Edward was doing over at the Fraunces. Even if he'd gone there to fetch breakfast (which made absolutely no sense, since they served the exact same fare as the Devil's Head), surely he'd be back by now.

With an extremely cold meal.

And he was alone. Which meant that—well, frankly she didn't know what that meant.

She wasn't *angry* with him, she told herself. He had every right to go where he pleased. It was just that he'd said he was coming back. If she'd known that he wasn't, she might have made other plans.

Just what those other plans might be, since she was stuck on a strange continent where she knew almost no one, she wasn't sure. But that wasn't the point.

The Fraunces was not far from the Devil's Head— all the local taverns were relatively close together—so it took only about five minutes in the rapidly brightening sun for Cecilia to reach her destination.

She pulled open the heavy wooden door and stepped inside, her eyes taking a moment to adjust to the dim and smoky light of the tavern. A few blinks cleared her vision, and sure enough, there was Edward sitting at a table on the far side of the room.

Alone.

Some of the fire that had been fueling her steps slid out of her, and she paused, taking in the scene. Something wasn't right.

His posture was off. He was slouching in his chair—which he never did in public, no matter how tired he was—and his hand—the one she could see from her vantage point—was bent almost into a claw. If his nails were not so neatly trimmed, he would have left gouge marks in the wood of the table.

An empty glass sat in front of him.

She took a hesitant step forward. Had he been drinking? It certainly looked like it, although again, this would be highly out of character. It wasn't even noon.

Cecilia's heart slowed . . . then pounded, and the air around her grew thick and heavy with dread.

There were two things that could render Edward so altered. Two things that could make him forget that he'd promised to return to the room they shared at the Devil's Head.

Either he'd regained his memory . . .

Or Thomas was dead.

Edward hadn't meant to get drunk.

He'd left Colonel Stubbs's office in a fury, but by the time he exited to the street, it was gone, replaced by . . . nothing.

He was empty.

Numb.

Thomas was dead. Cecilia was a liar.

And he was a damned fool.

He stood there, stock-still and staring sightlessly into space in front of the building that housed the headquarters of so many of the top British officers. He didn't know where to go. Not back to the Devil's Head; he was not ready to face her.

God above, he didn't even want to think about that right now. Maybe . . . *maybe* she'd had a good reason for lying to him, but he just . . . He just . . .

He drew in a long choke of breath.

She'd had so many opportunities to tell him the truth, so many moments when she could have broken the quiet with a soft mention of his name. She could have told him she'd lied, and she could have told him why, and bloody hell, he would probably have forgiven her because he was so damned in love with her he would have pulled the moon from the sky to make her happy.

He'd *thought* she was his wife.

He thought he'd pledged to honor and protect her.

Instead, he was the worst sort of reprobate, a true beau-nasty. It mattered not that he'd thought they were married. He'd still slept with an unmarried virgin. Worse, she was the sister of his closest friend.

He'd have to marry her now, of course. Maybe that had been her plan all along. Except that this was *Cecilia*, and he thought he knew her. Before he'd even met her he thought he knew her.

He swiped his hand across his brow, his fingers and thumbs settling into place at the indentations of his temples. His head hurt. He squeezed hard against the pain, but it did nothing. Because when he finally managed to push Cecilia out of his mind, all that was left was her brother.

Thomas was dead, and he couldn't stop thinking about it, about how no one would ever know exactly what had happened, about how he'd died among strangers, under suspicion of treason. He couldn't stop thinking about how his friend had taken a shot to the gut. It was a terrible death . . . slow, agonizingly painful.

And he couldn't stop thinking about how he would have to lie to Cecilia. Tell her it was something less gruesome. Something quick and painless.

Heroic.

The irony was not lost on him. It was his turn to lie to her.

But he knew that it was his responsibility to inform

her of Thomas's death. No matter how angry he was with her—and truth be told, he didn't know what he felt just then—Thomas had been his closest friend. Even if Edward had never met Cecilia Harcourt, he would have traveled to Derbyshire just to deliver her brother's ring into her hands.

But he wasn't ready to see her yet. He wasn't ready to see anything other than the bottom of another glass of brandy. Or wine. Or even just water, so long as he was having it alone.

So he went to the Fraunces Tavern, where he'd be far less likely to see a friend than at the Devil's Head. They didn't do a brisk business in the morning. A man could sit with his back to the room and if he was lucky, he wouldn't have to say a word for hours.

When he got there, the barkeep took one look at him and silently handed him a drink. Edward wasn't even sure what it was. Something homemade, maybe illegal, definitely strong.

He had another.

And he sat there in the back corner all morning long. Every now and then someone would come and replace his glass. At some point a maid set a slice of crusty bread in front of him, presumably to soak up the spirits. He tried a bite. It sank in his stomach like a rock.

He went back to his drink.

But try as he might, he could not seem to intoxicate himself to the point of oblivion. He could not even make himself forget. It didn't seem to matter how many times his glass was refilled. He'd close his eyes in a long, heavy blink, thinking that this time everything would go black or even just gray, and maybe Thomas would still be dead, but he at least wouldn't be thinking about that. Cecilia would still be a liar, but he wouldn't be thinking about that, either.

But it didn't work. He could never be that lucky.

Then *she* arrived.

He didn't even need to look up to know it was she when the front door opened and a bright slash of light fell across the room. He felt it in the air, in the dank, saturnine knowledge that this was the worst day of his life. And it wasn't going to get any better.

He looked up.

She was standing by the door, close enough to a window so that the filtered sunlight touched upon her hair like a halo.

It figured she'd look like an angel.

He'd thought she was *his* angel.

She didn't move for several seconds. He knew he should stand, but he thought the alcohol might finally be catching up with him, and he didn't quite trust his balance.

Or his judgment. If he stood, he might walk to her. And if he walked to her, he might take her in his arms.

He'd regret that. Later today, when he was thinking more clearly, he would regret it.

She took a wary step toward him, and then another. He saw her lips form his name, but he heard nothing. Whether it was because she made no noise or he just didn't want to hear, he'd never know, but he could see in her eyes that she knew something was wrong.

He reached into his pocket.

"What happened?" She was closer now. He had no choice but to hear her.

He pulled out the ring and set it on the table.

Her eyes followed his motions, and at first she did not seem to grasp the significance. Then she reached out with one trembling hand and took the ring within her fingers, bringing it to her face for a closer inspection.

"No," she whispered.

He remained silent.

"No. No. can't be his. It's not so unique. This could belong to anyone." She set the ring back on the table as if it had burned her skin. "That's not his. Tell me that's not his."

"I'm sorry," Edward said.

Cecilia kept shaking her head. "No," she said again, except this time she sounded like a wounded animal.

"It's his, Cecilia," Edward said. He did not move to comfort her. He should have. He *would* have, if he did not feel so dead inside himself.

"Where did you get it?"

"Colonel Stubbs." Edward paused, trying to figure out just what he wanted to say. Or not. "He asked me to apologize. And offer his condolences."

She stared at the ring, and then, as if a tiny pin had been jabbed into her, she looked up suddenly and asked, "Why would he apologize?"

It figured she would ask. She was clever. It was one of the things he loved best about her. He should have known she would immediately latch on to the part of his statement that did not quite fit.

Edward cleared his throat. "He wished to apologize for not telling you sooner. He couldn't. Thomas was involved in something very important. Something . . . secret."

She clutched the back of the chair next to him, then gave up all pretense of strength and sat. "So he knew, all this time?"

Edward nodded. "It happened in March."

He heard her gasp—a tiny sound, but filled with

shock. "He sat with me," she said in a bewildered whisper. "In the church, when you were still unconscious. He sat with me for hours one of the days. How could he do that? He knew I was looking for Thomas. He knew . . ." She brought her hand to her mouth as her breath started coming in heavier gasps. "How could he be so cruel?"

Edward didn't say anything.

Something in Cecilia's eyes sharpened, and the pale green of her irises took on a metallic edge. "Did *you* know?"

"No." He gave her a flat, direct stare. "How could I?"

"Of course," she whispered. "I'm sorry." She sat there for a moment, a hopeless statue of baffled grief. Edward could only wonder at her thoughts; every now and then she seemed to blink more rapidly, or her lips would move as if she might be forming words.

Finally, he could take no more. "Cecilia?"

She turned slowly, her brows drawing together as she asked, "Was he given a burial? A proper one?"

"Yes," he said. "Colonel Stubbs said he saw to it himself."

"Could I visit—"

"No," he said firmly. "He was buried in Dobbs Ferry. Do you know where that is?"

She nodded.

"Then you know it's far too dangerous for you to visit. Far too dangerous for *me* to visit unless I'm ordered to do so by the army."

She nodded again, but this time with less resolve.

"Cecilia . . ." he warned. God above, he could not even contemplate chasing after her into enemy territory. That area of Westchester was a sort of no-man's-land. It was why he'd been so surprised when Colonel Stubbs had said he'd gone alone to meet with Thomas. "Promise me," Edward growled, fingers biting into the edge of the table. "Promise me you won't go."

She looked at him with an expression that was almost puzzled. "Of course not. I'm not a—" She pressed her lips together, swallowing whatever she'd thought to say in favor of: "That's not the sort of thing I would do."

Edward gave a curt nod. It was all he could manage until he got his breathing back under control.

"I imagine there is no headstone," she said after a few moments had passed. "How could there be?"

It was a rhetorical question, but the pain in her voice made him answer, anyway. "Colonel Stubbs said he left a cairn."

It was a lie, but it would give her comfort to think that her brother's grave had been marked, if only with a small pile of stones.

He picked up his empty glass, fiddling it around in

his fingers. There were a few drops left in the slightly rounded bottom, and he watched as they rolled this way and that, always following the same dampened path. How hard would he have to tilt the glass to force a new rivulet? And could he do the same with his life? Could he just tilt things hard enough to change the outcome? What if he threw it all upside down? What then?

But even with all this going on inside, his expression did not change. He could feel the stasis on his face, a steady evenness, devoid of emotion. It was what he had to do. One crack, and God only knew what was going to come pouring out.

"You should take the ring," he said.

She gave a little nod and picked it up, blinking back tears as she looked down at it. Edward knew what she'd see. The Harcourts had no coat of arms that he knew of, so the flat plane of Thomas's ring bore only the letter *H*, elegantly scripted with one flourishing swirl at the base.

But then Cecilia turned it over and looked inside. Edward straightened a bit, curious now. He had not known to look for an inscription. Maybe it wasn't Thomas's ring. Maybe Colonel Stubbs had lied. Maybe—

An agonized sob burst from Cecilia's lips, the sound so sudden and harsh that she almost looked surprised that it had come from her. Her hand formed a fist around the ring, and she seemed to crumple right there in front of him, laying her head on her forearm as she cried.

God help him, he reached out and took her hand.

Whatever she had done, for whatever reason, he could not confront her about it now.

"I knew . . ." she said, gasping for breath. "I knew he was probably dead. But my head and my heart . . . They weren't in the same place." She looked up, her eyes luminous in her tear-streaked face. "Do you know what I mean?"

He didn't trust himself to do anything but nod. He wasn't sure his head and his heart would ever be in the same place again.

Edward picked up the ring, wondering about the inscription. He turned so that the inside caught a bit of the light.

THOMAS HORATIO

"All of the men in my family have the same ring," Cecilia said. "Their given names are engraved on the inside so that they can tell them apart."

"Horatio," Edward murmured. "I never knew."

"My father's grandfather was called Horace," she said. She seemed to be calming down. Ordinary conversation could do that for a person. "But my mother hated the name. And now—" She let out a choked laugh, followed by an inelegant swipe of her face with the back of her hand. Edward would have offered her a handkerchief if he'd had one. But he'd rushed out that morning, eager to surprise her with treats. He hadn't thought he'd be gone above twenty minutes.

"My cousin is named Horace," she said, almost— but not quite—rolling her eyes. "The one who wanted to marry me."

Edward looked down at his fingers and realized he'd been rolling the ring around between them. He set it down.

"I hate him," she said, with enough intensity to compel him to look up. Her eyes were burning. He wouldn't have thought the pale hue could contain such heat, but then he remembered that when fire burned hot, the color of it turned cold.

"I hate him so much," she went on. "If it hadn't been for him, I wouldn't have—" She drew in a loud, sudden sniffle. From the looks of her, she hadn't felt it coming on.

"You wouldn't have what?" Edward asked softly.

She didn't answer right away. Finally, she swallowed and said, "I probably wouldn't have come here."

"And you wouldn't have married me."

He looked up, caught her gaze directly. If she was going to come clean, now would be the time. According to her story, she had not taken part in her half of the proxy marriage until she was on the ship.

"If you had not sailed to New York," Edward continued, "when would you have married me?"

"I don't know," she admitted.

"So maybe it was for the best." He wondered if she could hear what he heard in his own voice. It was a little too low, a little too smooth.

He was baiting her. He could not help it.

She gave him an odd look.

"If Cousin Horace had not harassed you," Edward continued, "we would not be wed. Although I suppose . . ." He let his words trail off deliberately, waiting until she had to prod him to continue.

"You suppose . . ."

"I suppose *I* would think we were married," he said. "After all, I went through with the proxy ceremony months ago. Think of it, all this time, I could have been a single man and not realized it."

He looked up, briefly. *Say something.*

She didn't.

Edward picked up his glass and tossed back the last dregs, not that there was really much of anything there.

"What happens now?" she whispered.

He shrugged. "I'm not sure."

"Did he have any things? Beyond the ring?"

Edward thought back to that last day before he and Thomas had left for Connecticut. They had not known how long they would be gone, so the colonel had made arrangements to store their things. "Colonel Stubbs should have his effects," he said. "I will have them brought to you."

"Thank you."

"He had a miniature of you," Edward blurted out.

"I beg your pardon?"

"A miniature. He always had it. I mean, no, he didn't carry it with him at all times or anything like that, but when we moved he always made sure it was with him."

Her lips trembled with the hint of a smile. "I have one of him as well. Didn't I show it to you?"

Edward shook his head.

"Oh. I'm sorry. I should have done." She slumped a bit, looking utterly lost and forlorn. "They were painted at the same time. I think I was sixteen."

"Yes, you look younger in it."

For a moment she looked confused, then she blinked several times and said, "You've seen it. Of course. Thomas said that he'd showed it to you."

Edward nodded.

"Once or twice," he lied. There was no need for her to know how many hours he'd spent staring at her image, wondering if she could possibly be as kind and funny as she was in her letters.

"I never thought it was a very good likeness," she said. "The artist made my hair too bright. And I never smile like that."

No, she didn't. But to say so would be to admit he knew the painting far better than "once or twice" would imply.

Cecilia reached out and took the ring. She held it in both hands, pinched between her thumbs and fore-fingers.

She stared at it. For such a long time, she stared at it. "Do you want to go back to the inn?" she finally asked.

But she didn't look up.

And because Edward did not trust himself to be alone with her, he said, "I need to be by myself right now."

"Of course." She said it too quickly, and she lurched to her feet. The ring disappeared into her fist. "I do too."

It was a lie. They both knew it.

"I'm going back now," she said, motioning need-lessly to the door. "I think I would like to lie down."

He nodded. "If you do not mind, I will stay here."

She gestured faintly toward his empty glass. "Maybe you shouldn't . . ."

His brows rose, daring her to finish that statement.

"Never mind."

Smart girl.

She took a step away, then paused. "Do you—"

This was it. She was going to tell him. She was going to explain it all, and it would be fine, and he would not hate himself and he would not hate her, and . . .

He did not realize that he'd started to rise until his legs hit the table. "What?"

She shook her head. "It doesn't matter."

"Tell me."

She gave him an odd look, then said, "I was just going to ask if you want me to get you something at the bakery. But I don't think I wish to see anyone right now, so . . . Well, I'd rather just go straight back to the inn."

The bakery.

Edward fell back into his seat, and then before he could contain himself, a harsh, angry laugh burst forth from his throat.

Cecilia's eyes went very wide. "I can still go, if you wish. If you're hungry, I can—"

"No," he cut her off. "Go home."

"Home," she echoed.

He felt one corner of his mouth squeezing into a humorless smile. "Satan's Abbey."

She nodded, her lips trembling as if they weren't sure if they were supposed to smile in return. "Home," she echoed. She looked to the door, then back at him. "Right."

But she hesitated. Her eyes flicked to his, waiting for something. Hoping for something.

He gave nothing. He had nothing to give.

So she left.

And Edward had another drink.

Chapter 17

We have finally arrived in New York! And not a moment too soon. We traveled via ship from Rhode Island, and once again Edward proved himself a ghastly sailor. I have told him it is only fair; he is appallingly good at everything else he does.

Ah, he glares at me now. I have the bad habit of saying my words aloud as I write them, and he does not appreciate my description. But do not fret. He is also appallingly good-natured, and he does not hold a grudge.

But he glares! He glares!

I might kill your brother.

—FROM THOMAS HARCOURT (AND EDWARD ROKESBY) TO CECILIA HARCOURT

Cecilia walked back to the Devil's Head in a daze. Thomas was dead.

He was *dead*.

She'd thought she'd prepared herself for this. As the weeks had passed without a word, she had known that the chances of Thomas being found alive were growing slim. And yet, now . . . with the proof of his signet ring in her pocket . . .

She was wrecked.

She could not even visit his grave. Edward had said that it was too far outside of Manhattan, too close to General Washington and his colonial forces.

A braver woman might go. A more reckless spirit might toss her hair and stamp her foot and insist that she must lay flowers at her brother's final resting place.

Billie Bridgerton would do it.

Cecilia closed her eyes for a moment and cursed under her breath. She had to stop thinking about bloody Billie Bridgerton. It was becoming an obsession.

But who could blame her? Edward talked about her *all the time*.

Very well, maybe not all the time, but more than twice. More than . . . Well, enough that Cecilia felt she knew quite enough about Lord Bridgerton's eldest daughter, thank you very much. Edward probably didn't realize it but she came up in almost every story he told of growing up in Kent. Billie Bridgerton managed her father's lands. She hunted with the men. And when Cecilia had asked Edward what she looked like, he'd replied, "She's actually rather pretty. Not that I noticed for so many years. I don't think I even realized she was a girl until I was eight."

And Cecilia's reply?

"Oh."

Paragon of everything articulate and insightful she was. *That* was her eloquent response. But Cecilia could hardly tell him that after all of his tales of the amazing, superhuman Billie *I-Can-Ride-a-Horse-Backwards* Bridgerton, she'd pictured her as a six-foot Amazon with large hands, a mannish neck, and crooked teeth.

Not that the crooked teeth were in any way relevant to Edward's descriptions, but Cecilia had long since accepted that a little portion of her heart was petty and vengeful, and, blast it all, she *wanted* to imagine Billie Bridgerton with crooked teeth.

And a mannish neck.

But no, Billie Bridgerton was pretty, and Billie Bridgerton was strong, and if Billie Bridgerton's brother had died, *she* would have traveled into enemy lands to make sure his grave had a proper marker.

But not Cecilia. Whatever courage she possessed had

been all used up when she'd stepped on the *Lady Miranda* and watched England disappear over the eastern horizon. And if there was one thing she'd learned about herself over the past few months, it was that she was not the sort of woman to venture into a nonmetaphorical foreign territory unless someone's very life hung in the balance.

All there was to do now was . . .

Go home.

She didn't belong here in New York, that much she knew. And she didn't belong to Edward, either. Nor he to her. There was only one thing that might truly bind them together . . .

She went still, and her hand went to the flat plane of her belly, just over her womb.

She *could* be with child. It was unlikely, but it was possible.

And suddenly it felt real. She knew she probably wasn't pregnant, but her heart seemed to recognize this new person—a miraculous miniature of Edward, and maybe of her, too, but in her imagination the baby was all him, with a dusting of dark hair, and eyes so blue they rivaled the sky.

"Miss?"

Cecilia looked up and blinked, only then realizing

that she had come to a stop in the middle of the street. An older woman in a starched white bonnet was looking at her with a kind, concerned expression.

"Are you all right, miss?"

Cecilia nodded as she lurched into motion. "I beg your pardon," she said, moving to the side of the street. Her mind was foggish, and she couldn't quite focus properly on the Good Samaritan in front of her. "I just . . . I had some bad news."

The woman looked down to where Cecilia's hand rested on her abdomen. Her ringless hand. When she met Cecilia's eyes again, her own were filled with a hideous blend of compassion and pity.

"I have to go," Cecilia blurted out, and she practically ran the rest of the way back to the Devil's Head and up the stairs to her room. She threw herself onto the bed, and this time when she cried, her tears were equal parts frustration and grief.

That woman had thought that Cecilia was pregnant. Unmarried and pregnant. She'd looked at Cecilia's bare finger and made a judgment, and oh God, there had to be some sort of irony there.

Edward had wanted to get her a ring. A ring for a marriage that didn't exist.

Cecilia laughed. Right there in the middle of her tears, in the middle of her bed, she laughed.

It was an awful sound.

If she was pregnant, at least the baby's father thought they were married. Everyone did.

Except for that woman on the street.

In an instant Cecilia had gone from a young lady in need of kindness to a fallen harlot who would soon be relegated to the fringes of society.

She supposed that was an awful lot to read into a stranger's expression, but she knew how the world worked. If she was pregnant, her life would be ruined. She would never be accepted in polite society. If her friends back home wished to remain in contact, they would have to do so clandestinely, lest their own good names be tarnished.

There had been a girl in Matlock a few years earlier who had found herself with child. Her name was Verity Markham, and Cecilia had only known her a little. Not much more than her name, really. No one knew who the father was, but it mattered not. As soon as word of Verity's condition got out, Cecilia's father had forbidden her to make contact. Cecilia had been startled by his vehemence; her father never followed local gossip. But this, apparently, was an exception.

She had not defied his order. It had never occurred to her even to question it. But now she had to wonder— if Verity had been a friend, or even something slightly more than an acquaintance—would Cecilia have been brave enough to disobey her father? She'd like to think she would, but she knew in her heart Verity would have had to have been a very close friend indeed for her to have done so. It wasn't that Cecilia was unkind; she just wouldn't have thought to behave differently.

Society had its dictates for a reason, or at least she'd always thought so. Perhaps it was more correct to say that she'd never really thought *about* the dictates of society. She'd simply followed them.

But now, faced with the specter of *being* that fallen girl . . .

She wished she had been kinder. She wished she had gone to Verity Markham's house and held her hand in friendship. She wished she had made a public show of support. Verity had long since left the village; her parents told everyone she was living with her great-aunt in Cornwall, but there wasn't a soul in Matlock who believed it. Cecilia had no idea where Verity had gone, or even if she'd been allowed to keep her child.

A sob burst from Cecilia's throat, so surprising and harsh that she had to block her mouth with her fist just to hold it in. She could bear this—*maybe*—if she were the only one affected. But there would be a child. *Her* child. She did not know what it was to be a mother. She barely even knew what it was to have one. But she knew one thing: She could not subject her child to a life of illegitimacy if it was within her power to do otherwise.

She had already stolen so much from Edward—his trust, his very name. She could not steal his child, too. It would be the ultimate cruelty. He would be a good father. Nay, he would be a *great* father. And he would love being one.

If there was a child . . . he must be told.

She made herself a vow. If she was pregnant, she would stay. She would tell Edward everything, and she would accept the consequences for the sake of their child.

But if she was not pregnant—and if her courses followed their usual schedule she would know within a week—then she would leave. Edward deserved to have his life back, the one he had planned for, not the one she'd thrust upon him.

She would tell him everything, but she'd do it in a letter.

If this made her a coward, so be it. She doubted even Billie Bridgerton would be brave enough to deliver such news face-to-face.

It took several hours, but eventually Edward felt in sufficient control of himself to return to the Devil's Head.

To Cecilia.

Who wasn't his wife.

He'd long since stopped drinking, so he was sober, or nearly so. He'd had plenty of time to tell himself that he wasn't going to think about her today. Today was about Thomas. It had to be. If Edward's life was going to fall apart in a single day, he was damn well going to deal with his disasters one at a time.

He wasn't going to stew over what Cecilia had done or what she had said, and he definitely wasn't going to devote his energy to what she *hadn't* said. He wasn't going to think about that. He *wasn't* thinking about it.

He wasn't.

He wanted to scream at her. He wanted to take her by the shoulders and shake her and then beg her to tell him why.

He wanted to wash his hands of her forever.

He wanted to bind her to him for eternity.

He wanted to bloody not *think* about this today.

Today he was going to mourn his friend. And he was going to help the woman who wasn't his wife mourn her brother. Because that was the kind of man he was.

Damn it.

He reached room twelve, took a breath, and wrapped his fingers around the door handle.

Maybe he couldn't bring himself to comfort Cecilia

the way he ought, but at least he could give her the gift of a few days before he questioned her about her lies. He had never lost anyone so close to him; Thomas was a dear friend, but they weren't brothers, and Edward knew his grief could not possibly compare to Cecilia's. But he could imagine. If something happened to Andrew . . . or Mary . . . or even George or Nicholas to whom he was not nearly so close . . .

He'd be decimated.

Besides, he had a lot to figure out. Cecilia wasn't going anywhere; nothing but foolishness lay in the path of rash decisions.

He opened the door, blinking against the sunlight that streamed out into the dim hall. *Every time,* he thought stupidly. Every time he opened this damned door he was surprised by the sunlight.

"You're back," Cecilia said. She was sitting on the bed, propped up against the headboard with her legs stretched in front of her. She was still wearing her blue frock, which he supposed made sense, since it wasn't even yet time for dinner.

He'd have to leave the room when she decided to change into that nunnish white cotton nightgown of hers. Surely she'd prefer privacy to disrobe.

Since she wasn't really his wife.

There had been no proxy wedding ceremony. He

had signed no papers. Cecilia was the sister of a dear friend and nothing more.

But what did she have to gain by claiming that she was his wife? It made no sense. She couldn't have known that he would lose his memory. She could tell the world she was married to an unconscious man, but she had to have been aware that when he woke up her lies would be exposed.

Unless she'd been taking a gamble . . . betting her future on the likelihood that he *wouldn't* wake up. If he died while all the world thought they were married . . .

It wasn't such a bad thing to be a Rokesby wife.

His parents would have welcomed her when she returned to England. They knew of his friendship with Thomas. Hell, they'd met Thomas. Had him for Christmas supper, even. They would have no reason to doubt Cecilia's word if she showed up claiming to have married their son.

But all of that was so calculating. It wasn't like her to be that way.

Was it?

He shut the door behind him, giving her a small nod before sitting down in their one chair so that he could remove his boots.

"Do you need help?" she asked.

"No," he said, then looked down before he could see

her swallow. That was what she did at times like these, when she wasn't sure what she wanted to say. He used to love watching her, the delicate line of her throat, the graceful curve of her shoulder. Her lips pressed together when she swallowed—not quite like a kiss, but close enough that he always wanted to lean forward and transform it into one.

He didn't want to watch this tonight.

"I—"

He looked up sharply at the sound of her voice. "What is it?"

But she just shook her head. "Never mind."

He held her gaze, and he was glad that the light had gone flat with the approach of nightfall. If it was too dark to see her eyes, he couldn't lose himself in them. He could pretend they weren't the color of a shallow sea, or—when the light was still tinged with the orange stripes of dawn—of the first unfurled leaf of spring.

He worked off his boots, then rose to place them neatly in the space next to his trunk. The room was heavy with silence, and he could feel Cecilia watching him as he went about his usual movements. Normally, he would be chatting with her, asking idle questions about her afternoon, or, if they had spent the day together, commenting about what they'd seen and done. She might recall something that had amused her, and he would laugh, and then, when he turned away to hang his coat in the wardrobe, he'd wonder about the odd tingle that fluttered through his body.

But he'd only wonder for a moment. Because it was obvious what it was.

Happiness.

Love.

Thank God he'd never told her.

"I—"

He looked up. There she was again, starting a sentence with a halting pronoun. "What is it, Cecilia?"

She blinked at his tone. He had not been unkind, but he had been brusque. "I don't know what to do with Thomas's ring," she said quietly.

Ah. So that was what she'd been about to say. He shrugged. "You could put it on a chain, wear it as a necklace."

She fingered the threadbare blanket beneath her. "I suppose."

"You could save it for your children."

Your children, he realized he'd said. Not *our* children.

Had she noticed the slip of his tongue? He didn't think so. Her expression had not changed. She still looked pale, and numb, and exactly how one would expect a woman who'd just been informed of a beloved brother's death would look.

Whatever Cecilia had lied about, it had not included her devotion to Thomas. That he knew was true.

All of a sudden he felt like the worst kind of heel. She was grieving. She *hurt.*

He wanted to hate her. And maybe he would in time. But for now, he could do nothing but try to absorb her pain.

With a soul-weary sigh, he walked over to the bed and sat beside her. "I'm sorry," he said, putting his arm around her shoulders.

Her body did not soften right away. She was stiff with grief and probably with confusion, too. He had not been playing the part of a loving husband, and Lord knew, that was what he'd been until his meeting with Colonel Stubbs that morning.

He tried to think of what might have happened if the news of Thomas's death had not been accompanied by the revelation of Cecilia's deception.

What would he have done? How would he have reacted?

He would have put his own grief aside.

He would have comforted her, soothed her.

He would have held her until she slept, until all her

tears were gone, and then he would have laid a whispered kiss on her brow before pulling the blankets over her.

"How can I help you?" he asked roughly. It took everything in him to form the words, and at the same time, it was the only thing he knew how to say.

"I don't know." Her voice was muffled; she'd turned her face into the crook of his shoulder. "Can you just . . . stay here? Sit next to me?"

He nodded. He could do that. It hurt somewhere deep in his heart, but he could do that.

They sat that way for hours. Edward had a tray brought up for supper, but neither of them ate. He left the room so she could change for bed, and she turned to face the wall when he did the same.

It was as if their single night of passion had never happened.

All the fire, all the wonder . . . it was gone.

Suddenly he thought about how much he hated opening the door to the room, how he never seemed to be prepared for the burst of light.

What a fool he'd been. What a damned fool.

Chapter 18

This letter is for both of you. I am so glad you have each other. The world is a kinder place when one's burdens can be shared.

—FROM CECILIA HARCOURT
TO THOMAS HARCOURT AND
EDWARD ROKESBY

The next morning, Edward woke first.

He always woke first, but he'd never been quite so grateful for it before. It was past dawn, although not much, based on the hint of light filtering in around the curtains. Outside the window, New York was already coming to life, but the sounds of daily living were still intermittent and muted. A wagon creaked by, a rooster crowed. Every now and then, someone let out a shout of greeting.

It was enough to pass through the thick walls of the inn, but not enough to wake a sound sleeper like Cecilia.

For most of his life Edward had used his sparsely populated mornings to get up and attack the day. He had always found it remarkable how much more one could achieve without so many other people around.

But more recently—or more specifically, in the brief time since Cecilia had entered his life—he found himself taking advantage of the early morning quiet to settle into his thoughts. It helped that the bed was so comfortable. And warm.

And that Cecilia was there.

She gravitated to him in the night, and he loved taking a few minutes to enjoy her soft presence before sliding quietly out of bed to don his clothes. Sometimes it was her arm, thrown over his chest and shoulders. Sometimes it was her foot, tucked curiously under his calf.

But he always left the bed before she awakened. He wasn't entirely certain why. Maybe it had been because he wasn't prepared for her to see just how much he adored the closeness. Maybe he wasn't willing to admit just how much peace he found in these stolen moments.

And then there had been the day before, when he'd

been so eager to hop out and buy her some treats at the bakery.

That had worked out well.

This morning, though, he was the one with the wandering limbs. She was curled up against him, her face burrowed near his chest. His arm held her in her place, close enough so that he could feel her breath against his skin.

He'd been stroking her hair in his sleep.

His hand stilled when he realized what he'd been doing, but he did not pull away from her. He couldn't bring himself to. If he lay perfectly still, he could almost imagine that the day before had not happened. If he did not open his eyes, he could pretend that Thomas was alive. And his marriage to Cecilia . . . It was real. She belonged here in his arms, the delicate scent of her hair tickling his nose. If he rolled her over and took comfort in her body it would be more than his right, it would be a blessing and a sacrament.

Instead, he was the man who'd seduced an innocent gentlewoman.

And she was the woman who'd made him that way.

He wanted to hate her. Sometimes he thought he did. Most of the time he wasn't sure.

Next to him, Cecilia began to stir. "Edward?" she whispered. "Are you awake?"

Was it a lie if he pretended to be asleep? Probably. But in the lexicon of recent falsehoods, it was pretty damned small.

He didn't make a conscious decision to feign slumber. It was nothing so calculating as that. But when her whispered words blew softly across his ear, something resentful woke up inside of him, and he didn't want to answer her.

He just didn't.

And then, after she made a sound of mild surprise and scooted herself into a more upright position, he started to feel an odd sense of power. She thought he was asleep.

She thought he was something he wasn't.

It was the same thing she'd done to him, albeit on a much smaller scale. She had withheld the truth, and in doing so, she had possessed all the power.

And maybe he was feeling vengeful. Maybe he was feeling wronged. There was nothing particularly noble about his reaction, but he liked pulling one over on her, just as she had done to him.

"What am I going to do?" he heard her murmur. She rolled onto her side, facing away from him. But her body remained close.

And he still wanted her.

What would happen if he didn't tell her he'd regained his memory? Eventually he'd have to reveal the truth, but there was no reason he had to do so immediately. Most of what he remembered had nothing to do with her, anyway. There was the journey to Connecticut, made on horseback in a miserable cold rain. The heart-stopping moment when a farmer by the name of McClellan had caught him skulking around the Norwalk waterfront. Edward had reached for his weapon, but when two more men emerged from the shadows—McClellan's sons, as it happened—he quickly realized the futility of resistance. He'd been marched at gunpoint and pitchfork to the McClellans' barn, where he'd been tied up and held for weeks.

That was where he'd found the cat—the one he'd told Cecilia he thought he remembered. The bedraggled little mop had been his only companion for about twenty-three hours of each day. The poor thing had been forced to listen to Edward's complete life history.

Multiple times.

But the cat must have enjoyed Edward's storytelling prowess, because it'd rewarded him with a multitude of dead birds and mice. Edward tried to appreciate the gifts in the spirit they were given, and he always waited until the little fur ball wasn't watching before he kicked the dead animals toward the barn door.

That Farmer McClellan stepped on no fewer than

six mangled rodents was an added bonus. He'd proved oddly squeamish for a man who worked with animals all day, and indeed, his yelps and shrieks every time the tiny bones crunched under his boots were some of Edward's few sources of entertainment.

But McClellan didn't bother to check on him in the barn very often. Indeed, Edward never did figure out what he'd thought to do with him. Ransom, probably. McClellan and his sons didn't seem overly devoted to Washington's cause. And they certainly weren't Loyalists.

War could make mercenaries of men, especially those who were greedy to begin with.

In the end it had been McClellan's wife who had let Edward go. Not because of any great charm on Edward's part, although he had gone out of his way to be courtly and polite to the females of the family. No, Mrs. McClellan told him she was sick and tired of sharing her family's food. She'd borne nine children and not a one had bothered to die in infancy. It was too many mouths to feed.

Edward had not pointed out that not a whole lot of food had gone into his mouth during his stay. Not when she was loosening the ropes that bound his ankles.

"Wait until dark before you go," she'd warned him. "And head east. The boys will all be in town."

She didn't tell him why they were all heading to the village center, and he didn't ask. He'd done as she'd instructed, and he'd gone east, even though it was the exact opposite direction he needed to go. Traveling on foot and by night, the journey had taken a week. He'd crossed the sound to the Long Island and made it all the way to Williamsburg without incident. And then . . .

Edward frowned until he remembered he was still feigning sleep. But Cecilia didn't notice; she was still facing away from him.

What *had* happened in Williamsburg? That was where his memory was still hazy. He'd traded his coat to a fisherman for passage across the river. He'd got into the boat . . .

The fisherman must have clobbered him over the head. To what end, Edward wasn't sure. He'd had nothing worth stealing.

Not even a coat.

He supposed he should be grateful he'd been left on the shores of Kip's Bay. The fisherman could have easily slid him over the edge of the dinghy and into a watery grave. No one would have ever known what had happened to him.

He wondered how long his family would have waited to declare him dead.

Then he berated himself for being so morbid. He was alive. He ought to be happy.

He would be, he decided. But probably not this morning. He'd earned that right.

"Edward?"

Damn. His face must have been echoing the twisting journey of his thoughts. He opened his eyes.

"Good morning," Cecilia said. But there was something slightly cautious about her tone. It wasn't shyness, or at least he didn't think so. He supposed it might stand to reason that she'd feel self-conscious and awkward now that they had slept together. By all rights she should have felt self-conscious and awkward the morning before. She probably would have done if he hadn't left before she woke up.

"You were still asleep," she said. She smiled, although just a little. "You never wake up after I do."

He gave a little shrug. "I was tired."

"I expect so," she said softly. She looked down, and then away, and then she sighed and said, "I should get up."

"Why?"

Her eyes made a few startled blinks, then she said, "I have things to do."

"Do you?"

"I—" She swallowed. "I must. I can't . . . not."

But what did she have to do if she wasn't searching for Thomas? He was the only reason she'd come to New York.

Edward waited, and it cut his heart to watch her face begin to crumple as she realized that all the things she'd been doing, all the errands and tasks—they'd all been for the purpose of finding her brother.

And now that purpose was gone.

But, Edward reminded himself, she had also spent a great deal of time caring for him. Whatever her misdeeds, she had nursed him faithfully, both in hospital and out.

He probably owed her his life.

He couldn't hate her. He wanted to, though.

Cecilia's brow puckered. "Are you all right?"

"Why do you ask?"

"I don't know. You had a funny expression."

He didn't doubt it.

Once it became obvious that he wasn't going to comment, Cecilia let out a little sigh. It seemed to deflate her. "I should still get up. Even though I have nothing to do."

Not nothing, he thought.

They were in bed. There were lots of things to do in bed.

"I can keep you busy," he murmured.

"What?"

But before she could get out more than a single word, he leaned over and kissed her.

He hadn't thought about it. In fact, if he *had* stopped to think, he would have certainly told himself not to do it. That way lay madness, surely, and right then it felt like the only thing he still possessed was his sanity.

He kissed her because in that moment every instinct he possessed was crying for it. Some primitive part of him still thought she was his wife, that he had every right to touch her this way.

She'd told him they were married. She'd told him he'd said his vows.

Edward had attended enough wedding ceremonies to know the solemnization of marriage by heart. He knew what he would have said.

With my body I thee worship.

He wanted to worship her.

He wanted to worship her so damned much.

His hand wrapped around the back of her head, pulling her against him, holding her in place.

But she didn't struggle. She didn't try to escape. Instead, her arms came around him, and she kissed him back. She *knew* they weren't married, he thought angrily, but she returned his passion with equal fervor. Her lips were eager, and she moaned with desire as her back arched, pressing her body even more tightly against his.

The spark that had been lit within him raged out of control. He rolled her beneath him, and his lips moved roughly along her neck, down to the neckline of that awful nightgown.

He wanted to bite the damned thing off.

"Edward!" she gasped, and all he could think was that she was *his*. She had said so, and who was he to deny it?

He wanted her under his dominion, in his thrall.

He shoved the hem of her nightgown up, growling with satisfaction as she parted her legs for him. He might be a brute, but as his mouth found her breast through the thin cotton of her nightgown, her fingers were digging into his shoulders hard enough to leave bruises. And the noises she was making . . .

They were the noises of a woman who wanted more.

"Please," she begged.

"What do you want?" He looked up. Smiled like the devil.

She looked at him in confusion. "You know."

His head moved in a slow shake. "You have to say it." He was wearing his smalls, but when he ground himself against her, he knew she could feel the hard length of his desire. "Say it," he demanded.

Her face colored, and he knew it wasn't just from the passion. "I want you," she cried. "You know it. You know it."

"Well, then," he drawled. "You shall have me."

He yanked the nightgown over her head, leaving her bare in the morning light. For a moment he forgot all that had happened. His rage . . . his urgency . . . it seemed to melt in the face of her beauty. He could only gaze upon her, drinking in her perfection.

"You are so lovely," he whispered. His kisses turned soft—still desperate, but without the anger that had been fueling him before. He tasted her skin, the salty-sweet essence of her as he traveled down her shoulder, along the planes of her chest.

He wanted all of her. He wanted to lose himself.

No, he wanted *her* to do so. He wanted to bring her to the excruciating brink of pleasure, and then he wanted to send her over the edge.

He wanted her to forget her very name.

He skimmed his palm along the tip of her breast, delighting as it pebbled with desire, but he did not stop there. His lips traveled to her ribs, to her belly, to the gentle jut of her hipbone.

"Edward?"

He ignored her. He knew what he was doing. He knew she'd like it.

And he knew he'd die if he didn't taste her.

She gasped his name again, this time with urgency. "What are you doing?"

"Shhh . . ." he crooned, using his big hands to spread her legs wider. She squirmed, settling herself closer to his face. Her body seemed to know what it wanted, even if her mind was in a quandary.

"You can't look at me there," she gasped.

He kissed her just below her navel, just because he knew it would shock her. "You're beautiful."

"Not there!"

"I disagree." He ran his fingers through her soft thatch of hair, skimming closer to her womanhood, parting her to his intimate gaze. Then he blew softly on her tender skin.

She let out a soft shriek of pleasure.

He let one of his fingers draw a lazy circle on her skin. "Do you like it?"

"I don't know."

"Let me try one more thing," he murmured, "then you can decide."

"I don't—oh . . ."

He smiled. Right up against her. Right where he'd licked her. "Do you like it?" he asked again.

And she whispered, "Yes."

He licked her again, this time with a broad, hungry

stroke, his body humming with satisfaction as her hips bucked off the mattress. "You need to hold still," he purred, knowing he was tormenting her. "If you want to do this properly."

"I can't," she gasped.

"I think you can." But just to be helpful, he moved his hands to the creases between her torso and her legs, where he could increase the pressure and hold her firm.

Then he kissed her. He kissed her like he kissed her mouth, hard and deep. He drank her in, and he gloried in the shivers and shakes of her body beneath him. She was drunk on desire.

She was drunk on him. And he loved it.

"Do you want this?" he murmured, lifting his head so that he could see her face.

And also so that he could torture her. Just a little.

"Yes," she gasped. "Yes! Don't stop."

He let his fingers take the place of his mouth, tickling her while he spoke maddening words. "How much do you want it?"

She didn't answer, but she didn't have to. He could see the confusion on her face.

"How much, Cecilia?" he asked. He kissed her again, but only briefly, only enough to flick her nub with his tongue.

"So much!" she practically screamed.

That was more like it.

He went back to work, worshipping her with his mouth.

He worshipped her so damned much.

He kissed her until she fell apart beneath him, her body rising from the bed with almost enough force to push him away. She grabbed his head with frantic fingers, clamped her legs around him like a vise.

She held him there until she was through with him, and he loved every moment. When she finally went limp, he moved above her, propping himself on his elbows as he gazed down upon her. Her eyes were closed, and she shivered in the morning air.

"Are you cold?" he whispered. She made a tiny nod, and he covered her sweat-sheened body with his own.

Her head lolled back at the contact, as if the weight of him had been the final pleasure before oblivion. He kissed along the taut column of her neck, down to the indentation of her collarbone. She tasted like desire.

Her desire.

His, too.

He reached between them to unfasten his undergarments. It seemed a sacrilege to have anything between them, even a thin layer of linen. Within seconds it joined her nightgown on the side of the bed, and he settled back down into the warm cradle of her body.

He poised at her entrance, held himself there, and then pressed forward until he was home.

He forgot everything. Nothing existed except this moment, in this bed. He moved without thought, acted with nothing but instinct. She moved to his rhythm, her hips meeting his with each thrust. The pleasure built inside, so sharp and deep it could almost be pain, and then suddenly she flinched, and with panic in her eyes she said, "Wait!"

He jerked back, and something like fear raced through his heart. "Did I hurt you?"

She shook her head. "No, but we have to stop. I—I can't be pregnant."

He stared at her, trying to make sense of her words.

"Remember?" She swallowed miserably. "We talked about it."

He remembered. It had meant something completely different before, though. She'd said she didn't want to be pregnant on the journey back to England. And she didn't want to have a baby in New York.

What she'd really meant was she *couldn't* have a baby. Couldn't allow herself to have one. Not without a marriage license.

For a moment he thought about denying her plea. He could finish inside of her, try to create a new life.

That would make this marriage real.

But then she whispered, "Please."

He pulled out. It went against every instinct in his body, but he did it. He rolled onto his side, away from her, and focused all of his energy on simply remembering how to breathe.

"Edward?" She touched his shoulder.

He shook her off. "I need—I need a moment."

"Yes, of course." She edged away from him, her nervous movements rocking the mattress until he heard her feet land on the floor.

"Is . . . Is there something I can do?" she asked hesitantly. Her eyes fell on his manhood, still jutting ruthlessly out from his body. "To help?"

He thought about that.

"Edward?"

Her breath whispered through the silence, and he was amazed that he could hear her over the pounding of his own heart.

"I'm sorry," she said.

"Don't apologize," he snapped. He didn't want to hear it. He rolled on his back and took a deep breath. He was still hard as a rock. He'd been so close to spilling inside of her, and now . . .

He swore.

"Maybe I should go," she said hastily.

"That would probably be a wise idea." His tone was

not gentle, but it was the best he could manage. He might have to finish himself with his hand, and he was quite certain this would not suit her tender sensibilities.

He couldn't believe he still cared about her tender sensibilities.

She dressed quickly and shot out of the room like a bolt, but by then the urgency of his situation had diminished, and there seemed no point in trying to see to himself.

Honestly, it would have felt pathetic.

He sat up and swung his legs over the side of the bed, leaning his elbows on his knees and his chin in his hands. His entire life, he'd known what to do. He wasn't perfect, not by any means. But the path between right and wrong had always been clearly defined.

He put his country before family.

His family before self.

And where had that got him? In love with a mirage.

Married to a ghost.

No, *not* married. He needed to remember that. He was not married to Cecilia Harcourt. What had just happened . . .

She was right about one thing. It couldn't happen again. At least not until they wed for real.

He *would* marry her. He had to, or so he told himself. He didn't particularly wish to examine the corner of his heart that *wanted* to marry her. It was the same corner that had been so desperately glad to *be* married to her.

That little corner of his heart . . . It was gullible, far too trusting. He didn't have particular faith in its judgment, especially when another little voice was telling him to wait, take his time.

Let her squirm for a few days.

A frustrated shout tore from his throat, and he jammed his fingers into his hair, pulling hard. This was not his finest hour.

With another groan, he heaved himself up and off the bed, stalking forward to the wardrobe to fetch his clothing. Unlike Cecilia, he *did* have things to do today.

First on the agenda: a visit to Colonel Stubbs. Edward did not think he had learned much of use about the Connecticut seaports, but he was a soldier to his bones, and it was his duty to report what he had discovered. Not to mention he needed to tell the colonel where he'd been for so long. Tied up in a barn with a cat for company wasn't particularly heroic, but it was a far cry from treason.

Plus, there was the matter of Thomas's belongings. His trunk had been stored alongside Edward's when they'd both left for Connecticut. Now that he had been officially declared dead, his things should be turned over to Cecilia.

Edward wondered if the miniature would be there.

His stomach rumbled, reminding him that he hadn't eaten in nearly a day. Cecilia had probably ordered breakfast. With luck, it would be hot and waiting for him when he went down to the dining room.

Food first, then Colonel Stubbs. This was good, having some structure to the day. He felt a bit more like himself when he knew what he needed to do.

For today, at least.

Chapter 19

We are finally seeing the first signs of spring, and I am thankful. Please give Captain Rokesby one of these crocuses. I hope I pressed them correctly. I thought you both would enjoy a small piece of England.

—FROM CECILIA HARCOURT TO
HER BROTHER THOMAS

Later that morning, Cecilia took a walk down to the harbor. Edward had told her at breakfast that he was meeting with Colonel Stubbs, and he did not know how long he would be busy. She'd been left to her own devices, possibly for the entire day. She'd gone back up to their room with the intention of finishing the book of poems she'd been plodding through for the past week, but after only a few minutes it was clear that she needed to go outside.

The room felt too tight, the walls too close, and every time she tried to focus on the typeset words on the page, her eyes filled with tears.

She was raw.

For so many reasons.

And so she decided a walk was in order. The fresh air would do her good, and she'd be far less likely to spontaneously burst into tears if there were witnesses.

Goal for today: Don't cry in public.

It seemed manageable.

The weather was very fine, not too hot, with a light breeze coming off the water. The air smelled of salt and seaweed, which was a pleasant surprise, considering how often the wind carried on it the stench of the prison ships that moored just a little ways off the coast.

Cecilia had been in New York long enough to have learned a little something about the patterns of the port. Ships arrived almost daily, but very rarely did they carry civilian travelers. Most were merchant vessels, bringing in much-needed supplies for the British Army. A few of these had been fitted to carry paying passengers; that was how Cecilia had made it across from Liverpool. The *Lady Miranda*'s main purpose had been to bring foodstuffs and armaments for the soldiers stationed in

New York. But she had also borne fourteen passengers. Needless to say, Cecilia had gotten to know most of them quite well on the five-week voyage. They'd had little in common except that they were all making a dangerous voyage across a temperamental ocean into an embattled coastal area of a landmass at war.

In other words, they were all plumb crazy.

It almost made her smile. She still couldn't quite believe she'd had the gumption to make the crossing. She'd been fueled by desperation, to be sure, and she hadn't had many other options, but still . . .

She was proud of herself. For that, at least.

There were several ships in the harbor that day, including one that Cecilia had heard belonged to the same fleet as the *Lady Miranda*. The *Rhiannon*, it was called, and it had journeyed to New York from Cork, in Ireland. The wife of one of the officers who took his supper at the Devil's Head had sailed in on it. Cecilia had not met her personally, but her arrival in town had been the source of much gossip and good cheer. With all the gossip that rang through the dining room each night, it would have been impossible *not* to have heard of it.

She wandered closer to the docks, using the tall mast of the *Rhiannon* as her North Star. She knew the way, of course, but it felt almost whimsical to be led there using her primitive navigation. How long had the *Rhiannon* been in New York? Not yet a week, if she recalled correctly, which meant that it would probably remain at dock for at least a few more days before heading back across the ocean. The holds needed to be unloaded and then loaded with new cargo. To say nothing of the sailors, who surely deserved time on dry land after a long voyage.

As Cecilia reached the harbor, the world seemed to open up like a spring flower. Bright midday light poured forth, unhindered by the three- and four-story buildings that had been blocking the sun. There was something about the water that made the earth seem endless, even if the docks weren't quite at the open ocean. It was easy to see Brooklyn in the distance, and Cecilia knew how quickly a ship could navigate through the bay and out to the Atlantic.

It was really rather pretty, she thought, even if the tableau was far too different from home to ever etch itself permanently on her heart. But she liked it all the same, especially the way the water whipped up into foam-crested waves, then slapped the retaining wall like an impatient nanny.

The ocean was gray here, but out over the horizon it would darken to a deep, fathomless blue. Some days— the turbulent ones—it had even looked green.

Another little fact she'd never have known if she had not ventured from her safe little home in Derbyshire. She was glad she'd come. Truly, she was. She would be leaving with a broken heart—for more reasons than one—but it would be worth it. She was a better person—no, she was a *stronger* person.

A better person would not have lied for so long.

Still, it was a good thing she'd come. For herself, and maybe even for Edward. His fever had risen dangerously high two days before he woke up. She'd remained by his side throughout the night, placing cooling cloths on his skin. She would never know if she'd actually saved his life, but if she had, then this all would have been worth it.

She had to hold on to that notion. It would keep her company for the rest of her life.

It was then that she realized she was already thinking in terms of leaving. She glanced down to her waist. She could be pregnant; she'd not yet had proof otherwise. But it was unlikely, and she knew she had to prepare herself for the logistics of travel.

Hence her trip to the harbor. She had not consciously considered why her feet were leading her to the water, but now, as she watched two longshoremen loading crates into the hold of the *Rhiannon*, it was quite obvious that she was there to make inquiries.

As for what she'd do once she was home . . . She supposed she'd have plenty of time in her ship's cabin to figure that out.

"Good sir!" she called out to the man who was directing the cargo. "When do you leave?"

His bushy brows rose at her question, then he cocked his head toward the ship and said, "You mean the *Rhiannon?*"

"Yes. Do you head back to Britain?" She knew that many ships detoured to the West Indies, although she thought they usually did so on the way *to* North America.

"To Ireland," he confirmed. "Cork. We leave Friday evening, if the weather holds."

"Friday," she murmured in response. It was only a few days away. "Do you carry passengers?" she asked, even though she knew that they had done so for the westward voyage.

"We do," he said with a brusque nod. "Are you looking for a spot?"

"I might be."

This seemed to amuse him. "You *might* be? Shouldn't you know by now?"

Cecilia did not dignify this with an answer. Instead she employed a cool stare—the sort she'd once thought befitting of the wife of the son of an earl—and waited until the man jerked his head toward another fellow farther up the embankment. "Ask Timmins. He'll know if we have space."

"Thank you," Cecilia said, and she made her way to a pair of men who were standing close to the bow of the ship. One had his hands on his hips while the other gestured toward the anchor. Their stances did not indicate that their conversation was urgent, so as Cecilia approached, she called out, "Your pardon, sirs. Is one of you Mr. Timmins?"

The one who'd been pointing toward the anchor doffed his hat. "I am, ma'am. How may I help you?"

"The gentleman over there"—she motioned back to where the cargo was being loaded—"mentioned that you might have room for another passenger?"

"Man or woman?" he asked.

"Woman." She swallowed. "Me."

He nodded. Cecilia decided she liked him. His eyes were honest.

"We've room for one woman," he told her. "It would be in a shared cabin."

"Of course," she said. She doubted she could afford a private cabin, anyway. Even a shared one was going to be a stretch, but she'd been careful to keep enough funds to pay for her passage home. It had been difficult; she'd had almost nothing to live on before Edward woke up. She'd never been so hungry in all her life, but she'd kept herself to one meal per day.

"Might I know the cost, sir?" she asked.

He told her, and her heart sank. Or maybe it soared. Because the fare was almost one and one half times what she'd paid to come to New York. And that was more than she had saved. She didn't know why it was more expensive to sail east than west. Probably the ships charged more simply because they could. The people of New York were loyal to the crown; Cecilia imagined that passengers tended to be more desperate to leave New York than to arrive.

But it didn't matter, because she didn't have enough.

"Do you want to purchase passage?" Mr. Timmins asked.

"Ehrm, no," she said. "Not yet, anyway."

But maybe on the next ship. If she siphoned off a bit of money every time Edward gave her some for shopping . . .

She sighed. She was already a liar. She might as well be a thief, too.

Thomas's trunk was heavy, so Edward had made arrangements to have it transported to the Devil's Head by wagon. He knew there were plenty of people in the front room to help him get it up the stairs.

When he reached room twelve, though, he saw that Cecilia was not there. He was not entirely surprised; she hadn't said anything about going out at breakfast, but he couldn't imagine that she'd want to hole herself up in the room all day. Still, it felt rather anticlimactic, sitting here in the room with her brother's trunk. She was the reason he'd gone to get it, after all. He had imagined something of a heroic return, brandishing Thomas's trunk like a hard-won prize.

Instead, he sat on the bed, staring at the damned thing taking up half the available floor space.

Edward had already seen the contents. Back at the army office, Colonel Stubbs had thrown open the lid before Thomas could even stop to think if they were invading someone's privacy.

"We need to make sure everything is there," Stubbs had said. "Do you know what he kept in it?"

"Some," Thomas said, even though he was better acquainted with Thomas's trunk than he had any right to be. He'd hunted through it on far too many occasions, searching out Cecilia's letters so that he could reread her words.

Sometimes he didn't even do that. Sometimes he'd just stared at her handwriting.

Sometimes that was all he'd needed.

God, he was such a fool.

A fool? Much worse.

Because when Stubbs had opened the trunk and asked Edward to inspect the contents, the first thing his eyes fell upon was the miniature of Cecilia. The one he now realized didn't look like her. Or maybe it did, if one didn't really *know* her. It did not capture the life in her smile, or the extraordinary color of her eyes.

He wasn't sure a paint existed that could capture that color.

The colonel had returned to his desk, and when Edward looked up, it was clear that his attention was on the documents before him and not the trunk across the room.

Edward slid the miniature into his pocket.

And that was where it remained, even when Cecilia returned from her walk. In the pocket of his coat, which hung neatly in the wardrobe.

So now Edward was a fool and a thief. And while he felt like an ass, he couldn't bring himself to regret his actions.

"You got Thomas's trunk," Cecilia softly exclaimed when she entered the room. Her hair was a little mussed from the wind, and he was momentarily mesmerized by a thin tendril that fell over her cheek. It curled into a soft blond wave, holding far more curl than it did when her hair was fully down.

How nice to defy gravity.

And what an odd, nonsensical thought.

He rose from the bed, clearing his throat as he pulled himself to attention. "Colonel Stubbs was able to retrieve it quickly."

She moved toward the trunk with a strange hesitancy. She reached out, but paused before her hand touched the latch. "Did you look?"

"I did," he said with a nod. "Colonel Stubbs asked me to make sure it was all in order."

"And was it?"

How did he answer such a question? If it had been all in order, it wasn't now, not with the miniature in his pocket.

"As far as I could tell," he finally told her.

She swallowed, the gesture nervous and sad and wistful all at once.

He wanted to hold her. He almost did; he stepped forward before he realized what he was doing, then he stopped.

He could not forget what she had done.

No, he could not *allow* himself to forget.

It wasn't the same thing.

And yet when he watched her, standing in front of her dead brother's trunk with hopelessly sad eyes, he reached out and took her hand.

"You should open it," he said. "I think it will help."

She nodded gratefully and slid her fingers from his so that she could lift the lid with both hands. "His clothes," she murmured, touching the white shirt that lay neatly folded at the top. "What should I do with them?"

Edward didn't know.

"They won't fit you," she mused. "He wasn't as broad in the shoulders. And yours are more finely tailored, anyway."

"I'm sure we can find someone in need," Edward said.

"Yes. That's a good idea. He would like that." Then she let out a little laugh, shaking her head as she brushed that rebellious bit of hair from her eyes. "What am I saying? He wouldn't have cared."

Edward blinked in surprise.

"I love my—" She cleared her throat. "I *loved* my brother, but he did not give much thought to the plight of the poor. He did not think ill of them," she hastened to add. "I just don't think he thought of them at all."

Edward nodded, mostly because he didn't know how else to respond. He was probably guilty of the same sin of indifference. Most men were.

"But it will make *me* feel better to find a home for his shirts," Cecilia said firmly.

"He would like that," Edward said, then clarified, "Making you happy."

She gave him a wry almost-smile, then turned back to the trunk. "I suppose we'll have to find someone to take his uniform, as well. Someone will need it." She ran her hand along Thomas's coat, her slim fingers pale against the scarlet wool. "When I was in hospital with you, there were other soldiers. I . . ." She looked down, almost as if paying her respects. "I sometimes helped. Not as much as I should have done, I'm sure, but I didn't want to leave you unattended."

Edward started to thank her, but before he could, she'd straightened her shoulders and was continuing in a brisker voice. "I saw their uniforms. Several were beyond repair. So, surely, someone will need it."

Her words held a hint of a question, so Edward nodded. Soldiers were expected to keep their uniforms in perfect condition, no easy feat considering the amount of time they were traipsing through the muddy countryside.

And being shot at.

Bullet holes were a nuisance to mend, but bayonet wounds were the absolute devil. In skin as well as fabric, he supposed, but he focused on the fabric, since it was the only way to hold on to one's sanity.

It was kind of her to give Thomas's uniform to another soldier. Many families wanted it back, a tangible symbol of heroism and duty.

Edward swallowed and stepped back, suddenly needing to put a little space between them. He did not understand her. And he hated that he could not maintain his rage. It had been only a day. Just over twenty-four hours since his memory had returned in a rush of color and light and words and places—none of which had included Cecilia Harcourt.

She wasn't his wife. And he should be angry. He had a right to be angry.

But his questions—the ones beating a relentless tattoo in his mind—he couldn't ask them now. Not when she was lovingly unpacking her brother's trunk. Not when she turned her face away, trying to hide the swipe of her hand at her tears.

She set Thomas's coat to the side, then delved deeper. "Do you think he saved my letters?"

"I know he did."

She glanced up briefly. "Oh, of course. You've been through the trunk already."

It wasn't how he knew, but she didn't need to know that.

Edward leaned against the edge of the bed and watched as she continued her exploration of Thomas's belongings. At some point she had dropped to her knees for easier access, and now she was going through it all with a smile on her face that he'd never thought to see again.

Or maybe it was that he'd never thought he'd want to see it so bloody badly.

He was still in love with her.

Against all better judgment, against his own damned sanity, he was still in love with her.

He sighed.

She looked up. "Is something wrong?"

Yes.

"No."

But she'd turned back to the trunk before he answered the question. He wondered . . . if she had not, if she had been looking at his face . . .

Would she have seen the truth in his eyes?

He almost sighed again.

She made a curious *hmmm,* and he found himself leaning forward to get a better look at what she was doing. "What is it?" he asked.

She frowned as she delved her hands into the neatly folded shirts and breeches. "I don't see the miniature."

Edward's lips parted, but he did not speak. He meant

to. He'd thought he was about to, but he could not put voice to words.

He wanted that damned painting. Call him a tyrant, call him a thief. He wanted it for himself.

"Perhaps he took it with him to Connecticut," Cecilia said. "I suppose there is something nice about that."

"You were always in his thoughts," Edward said.

She looked up. "It's very sweet of you to say."

"It's the truth. He talked about you so much I felt that I knew you."

Something in her eyes turned warm, even as they took on a faraway look. "Isn't that funny," she said softly. "I felt the same way about you."

He wondered if he should tell her now that he'd got back his memory. It was the right thing to do; by everything that made him a gentleman, he knew this to be true.

"Oh!" she exclaimed, neatly puncturing his thoughts. She hopped to her feet. "I nearly forgot. I never showed you my miniature of Thomas, did I?"

There was no need for Edward to respond; she'd already started rifling through her one and only satchel. It was large, but still, Edward was amazed she'd made the voyage to New York with so few belongings.

"Here it is," she said, pulling out the small cameo.

She peered down at it with a wistful smile, then held it out. "What do you think?"

"I can tell it's the same artist," he said without thinking.

Her chin drew back with some surprise. "You remember the other one that well?"

"Thomas liked to show it to people." It wasn't a lie; Thomas did like to show the miniature of Cecilia to his friends. But that wasn't why Edward remembered it so well.

"Did he?" Her eyes lit with happiness. "That's very . . . I don't know what it is. Sweet, I suppose. It's nice to know he missed me."

Edward nodded, not that she was looking at him. She'd returned to her task, carefully examining her brother's effects. Edward felt very odd and awkward, very much a spectator.

He didn't like it.

"Hmmm, what's this?" she murmured.

He leaned forward for a better look.

She pulled out a little purse, and twisted around to face Edward. "Would he have kept money in his trunk?"

Edward had no idea. "Open it and see."

She did, and to her obvious surprise several gold

coins tipped out. "Oh my goodness," she exclaimed, looking down at the windfall in her palm.

It wasn't much, at least not to Edward, but he remembered how pressed for funds she'd been when he had woken up. She'd tried to hide the extent of her poverty, but she wasn't—or at least he hadn't thought she was—an accomplished liar. She'd let slip little details, like how she'd been eating only one meal per day. And he knew of the boardinghouse from which she'd rented a room; it was barely one step above sleeping on the street. He shuddered to think what would have become of her if she had not found him in hospital.

Maybe they'd saved each other.

Cecilia was strangely quiet, still staring down at the gold in her hand as if it were something mysterious.

Perplexing.

"It's yours," he said, figuring she was trying to decide what to do with it.

She nodded absently, gazing at the coins with the most peculiar expression.

"Put it with the rest of your money," he suggested. He knew she had a little. She kept it carefully tucked away in her coin purse. He'd seen her counting it twice, and both times she'd looked up with a sheepish expression when she saw that he was watching her.

"Yes, of course," she murmured, and she rose awkwardly to her feet. She opened the wardrobe and reached into her bag. He presumed she'd pulled out the coin purse, but he couldn't really see what she was doing with her back to him.

"Are you all right?" he asked.

"Yes," she said, perhaps a touch more suddenly than he would have expected. "I just . . ." She turned partway back around. "I did not think Thomas would have money in his trunk. It means I have . . ."

Edward waited, but she did not finish the sentence. "It means you have what?" he finally prodded.

She blinked at him, and an odd beat of silence passed before she answered. "It's nothing. I just have more than I thought I did."

That seemed to Edward the very definition of obvious.

"I think . . ."

He waited, but her words trailed off as she turned and looked at the open trunk. A few shirts lay on the floor next to it, and Thomas's red coat was draped over the side, but other than that, she'd left everything in place.

"I'm tired," she said abruptly. "I think . . . Would you mind if I lie down?"

He stood. "Of course not."

She looked down, but he caught a glimpse of unbearable sadness on her face as she brushed past him and curled up on the bed, drawing her knees up until she curved away from him like a sickle.

He stared at her shoulders. He didn't know why, except that they were so obviously tight with sorrow. She wasn't crying, or at least he didn't think she was, but her breathing was hitched, as if it took some effort to keep herself under regulation.

He reached out a hand, even though he was too far away to touch her. But he couldn't stop himself. It was instinct. His heart beat, his lungs drew breath, and if this woman was in pain, he reached out to comfort her.

But he didn't take the final step. His hand fell back against his side, and he stood like a statue, helpless against his own tumult.

From the moment he saw her, he'd wanted to protect her. Even when he was so weak he could barely walk unassisted, he'd wanted to be her strength. But now, when she finally needed him, he was terrified.

Because if he allowed himself to be strong for her, to shoulder her burden the way he so desperately needed to do, he would lose himself completely. Whatever thread still hung inside him, keeping him from loving her completely, it would snap.

And his heartbreak would be complete.

He whispered her name, softly, almost daring her to hear him.

"I think I should be alone," she said, never once turning to face him.

"No, you shouldn't," he said roughly, and he laid himself down behind her, holding her tight.

Chapter 20

*Father has been especially irritable lately. But then,
so have I. The month of March is always cold and
damp, but it's been worse than usual this year. He
takes a nap each afternoon. I think I might do the
same.*

—*from* Cecilia Harcourt
to her brother Thomas
(*letter never received*)

Two days later, Cecilia bled.

She'd known it was coming. Her courses were
always preceded by a day of lethargy, a bit of cramping
in her belly, and a feeling like she'd eaten too much salt.

And yet she'd told herself that maybe she was mis-
reading the signs. Maybe she felt tired because she *was*

tired. She wasn't sleeping well. How was she to rest properly with Edward on the other side of the bed?

As for the cramping, they'd been serving pie all week at the Devil's Head. They'd told her there were no strawberries in the filling, but could she really trust the sixteen-year-old barmaid who couldn't keep her eyes off the brightly clad soldiers? There could have been a strawberry in that pie. Even a single seed could explain Cecilia's discomfort.

And as for the salt, she had no earthly clue. She was near the ocean. Maybe she was breathing the stuff in.

But then she bled. And as she carefully washed out her rags, she tried not to examine the spark of pain in her chest that came with the realization that she was not with child.

She was relieved. Surely she was relieved. A child would have meant that she would have to trap Edward into marriage. And while a very large part of her would always dream of a cottage in Kent with adorable blue-eyed children, she was coming to realize that this dream had even less of a basis in reality than she'd thought.

It was hard to imagine that a fake marriage could have a honeymoon period, but nothing had been the same since they had received word of Thomas's death. Cecilia was not an idiot; she knew that they were both grieving, but she did not understand how that alone might account for the intractably awkward chasm that had cracked the world beneath them.

The thing about Edward was, it had all seemed so *easy*. As if she'd been waiting all of her life to understand who she really was, and then, when he opened his eyes—no, it was later, with their first real conversation—she *knew*. It was bizarre, since her entire time with him had been built upon a lie, but she'd felt more honestly herself in his company than at any other time in her life.

It wasn't the sort of thing one even realized right away. Maybe not until it was gone.

And it *was* gone. Even when he'd tried to comfort her after she'd unpacked Thomas's trunk, something had been off. She had been unable to relax in his arms, probably because she knew that this too was a lie. He'd thought she was upset about her brother, but what had really pierced her heart was the realization that she now had enough money for a ticket on the *Rhiannon*.

And now that she knew she wasn't pregnant . . .

She walked over to the window and balanced her hip on the ledge. There was a slight breeze to the air, a blessed addition to the humidity that had settled over the region. She watched the leaves ruffling in the trees. There weren't many of them; this part of New York was fairly well built up. But she liked the way one side of the leaves was darker than the other, liked watching the colors flip back and forth, dark to light, green to green.

It was Friday. And with the sky a carpet of unending blue, which meant the *Rhiannon* would be sailing away that evening.

She should be on it.

She had no business remaining in New York. Her brother was dead, buried up in the woods of Westchester. She couldn't go visit the grave. It was not safe, and anyway, according to Colonel Stubbs there was no proper marker—nothing with Thomas's name and age, nothing proclaiming him a beloved brother or dutiful son.

She thought back to that awful day when she'd received the letter from General Garth. Which had turned out to be from Colonel Stubbs, actually, but that mattered little. She had just lost her father, and in the moments before she opened the missive, she'd been so terrified. She remembered exactly what she had been thinking—that if Thomas was dead, there would be no one left in the world whom she loved.

Now Thomas *was* dead. And there was no one else in the world she was allowed to love.

Edward would eventually regain his memory. She was certain of that. Already the bits and pieces were beginning to sift themselves out. And when he did . . .

It was better if she told him the truth before he discovered it himself.

He had a life back in England, one that did not include her. He had a family who adored him and a girl he was supposed to marry. A girl who, like him, was an aristocrat through and through. And when he remembered her—the inimitable Billie Bridgerton—he'd remember why they made such a good match.

Cecilia pushed herself away from the window ledge, grabbing her coin purse before she headed out the door. If she was leaving tonight, she had a great deal to do, and all of it needed to be done before Edward returned from army headquarters.

First and foremost, she needed to purchase her passage. Then she needed to pack, not that that would take very long. And finally, she needed to write Edward a letter.

She needed to let him know that he was free.

She would leave, and he could get on with his life, the one he was meant to lead. The one he *wanted* to lead. He might not realize this yet, but he would, and she didn't want to be anywhere near him when that happened. There were only so many ways a heart could break. Seeing his face when he realized he belonged with someone else?

That might do her in entirely.

She checked the pocket watch Edward kept on the table to serve as their clock. She still had time. He'd gone out earlier that morning—a meeting with Colonel Stubbs, he'd said, one that would last all day. But she needed to get moving.

This was good, she told herself as she hurried down the stairs. This was right. She'd found the money, and she wasn't pregnant. Clearly they weren't meant to be.

Goal for today: Believe in fate.

But when she reached the front room of the inn, she heard her name, called out in urgent tones.

"Mrs. Rokesby!"

She turned. Fate, it seemed, looked an awful lot like the innkeeper at the Devil's Head.

He'd come out from behind his counter and was walking toward her with a strained expression. Behind him was a finely attired woman.

The innkeeper stepped to the side. "This great lady was hoping to see Captain Rokesby."

Cecilia tilted to the side to better see the woman, who was still somewhat obscured behind the innkeeper's portly form. "May I help you, ma'am?" she said with a polite curtsy. "I am Captain Rokesby's wife."

Strange how easily the lie still slipped from her tongue.

"Yes," the woman said briskly, motioning for the innkeeper to be gone.

The innkeeper quickly complied.

"I am Mrs. Tryon," the lady said. "Captain Rokesby's godmother."

When Cecilia was twelve years old, she'd been forced to play the part of Mary in her church's Nativity play. This had required her to stand in front of all her friends and neighbors and recite no fewer than twenty lines of prose, all of which had been religiously drummed into her by the vicar's wife. But when the time came to open her mouth and announce that she was not married and didn't understand how she could be with child, she froze. Her mouth opened, but her throat closed, and it didn't matter how many times poor Mrs. Pentwhistle hissed the lines at her from offstage. Cecilia just couldn't seem to move the words from her ears to her head to her mouth.

That was the memory that blazed through Cecilia's head as she stared into the face of the estimable Margaret Tryon, wife of the Royal Governor of New York, and godmother to the man Cecilia was pretending to be married to.

This was much worse.

"Mrs. Tryon," Cecilia finally managed to squeak out. She curtsied. (Extra deep.)

"You must be Cecilia," Mrs. Tryon said.

"I am. I . . . ah . . ." Cecilia looked helplessly around at the tables of the half-filled dining room. This was not her home, and thus she was not the hostess here, but it seemed like she ought to offer to entertain. Finally, she pasted as bright a smile as she could manage on her face and said, "Would you like to sit down?"

Mrs. Tryon's expression flicked from distaste to resignation, and with a little jerk of her head, she motioned for Cecilia to join her at a table at the far side of the room.

"I came to see Edward," Mrs. Tryon said once they were settled.

"Yes," Cecilia replied carefully. "That is what the innkeeper said."

"He was ill," Mrs. Tryon stated.

"He was. Although not so much ill as injured."

"And has he regained his memory?"

"No."

Mrs. Tryon's eyes narrowed. "You are not taking advantage of him, are you?"

"No!" Cecilia exclaimed, because she wasn't. Or

rather, she wouldn't be soon. And because the thought of taking advantage of Edward's generosity and honor burned like a poker in her heart.

"My godson is very dear to me."

"He is dear to me, too," Cecilia said softly.

"Yes, I imagine he is."

Cecilia had no idea how to interpret that.

Mrs. Tryon began to remove her gloves with military precision, pausing only to say, "Were you aware that he had an arrangement with a young lady in Kent?"

Cecilia swallowed. "Do you mean Miss Bridgerton?"

Mrs. Tryon looked up, and a grudging flash of admiration—possibly for Cecilia's honesty—passed through her eyes. "Yes," she said. "It was not a formal engagement, but it was expected."

"I am aware of that," Cecilia said. Best to be honest.

"It would have been a splendid match," Mrs. Tryon went on, her voice becoming almost conversational. But only almost. There was a hint of standoffishness to her words, a vaguely bored note of warning, as if to say—*I have control, and I shall not relinquish it.*

Cecilia believed her.

"The Bridgertons and the Rokesbys have been friends and neighbors for generations," Mrs. Tryon went on. "Edward's mother has told me on many occasions that it was her dearest wish that their families be united."

Cecilia held her tongue. There wasn't a thing she could say to that that wouldn't cast her in a bad light.

Mrs. Tryon finished with her second glove, and let out a little sound—not really a sigh, more of an I-am-regrettably-changing-the-subject sort of noise. "But alas," she said, "it is not to be."

Cecilia waited for an impossibly long moment, but Mrs. Tryon did not say more. Finally, Cecilia forced herself to ask, "Was there anything in particular I might help you with?"

"No."

More silence. Mrs. Tryon, she realized, wielded it like a weapon.

"I . . ." Cecilia motioned helplessly toward the door. There was something about this woman that left her utterly inept. "I have errands," she finally said.

"As do I." Mrs. Tryon's words were crisp, and so were her motions when she rose to her feet.

Cecilia followed her to the door, but before she could bid her farewell, Mrs. Tryon said, "Cecilia—I may call you Cecilia, may I not?"

Cecilia squinted as her eyes adjusted to the sunlight. "Of course."

"Since fate has brought us together this afternoon, I

feel it my duty as your husband's godmother to impart some advice."

Their eyes met.

"Do not hurt him." The words were simple, and starkly given.

"I would never want to," Cecilia said. It was the truth.

"No, I don't suppose you would. But you must always remember that he was once destined for someone else."

It was a cruel statement, but it was not cruelly meant. Cecilia wasn't sure why she was so certain of this. Perhaps it was the thin veil of moisture in Mrs. Tryon's eyes, perhaps it was nothing more than instinct.

Maybe it was just her imagination.

It was a reminder, though. She was doing the right thing.

It was midafternoon before Edward finished up with his meetings at the British Army headquarters. Governor Tryon himself had wanted a complete recounting of Edward's time in Connecticut, and the written account he'd submitted just one day prior for Colonel Stubbs had not been deemed sufficient. So he'd sat with the governor and told him everything he'd already said three times before. He supposed there was some usefulness to it, since Tryon hoped to lead a series of raids on the Connecticut coast in just a few short weeks.

The big surprise, however, occurred right when Edward was leaving. Colonel Stubbs intercepted him at the door and handed him a letter, written on good paper, folded into an envelope, and sealed with wax.

"It's from Captain Harcourt," Stubbs said gruffly. "He left it with me in case he did not return."

Edward stared down at the envelope. "For me?" he asked dumbly.

"I asked him if he wanted us to send something to his father, but he said no. It doesn't matter, anyway, I suppose, since the father predeceased the son." Stubbs let out a tired, frowning sigh, and one of his hands came up to scratch his head. "Actually, I don't know which of them passed on first, but it hardly makes a difference."

"No," Edward agreed, still looking down at his name on the front of the envelope, written in Thomas's slightly untidy script. Men wrote such letters all the time, but usually for their families.

"If you want some privacy to read it, you can use the office across the hall," Stubbs offered. "Greene is out for the day, and so is Montby, so you should not be bothered."

"Thank you," Edward said reflexively. He did want privacy to read his friend's letter. It was not every day one received messages from the dead, and he had no idea how he might react.

Stubbs escorted him to a small office, even going so far as to open the window to alleviate the heavy, stuffy air. He said something as he departed and shut the door, but Edward didn't notice. He just stared down at the envelope, taking a deep breath before finally sliding his fingers underneath the wax seal to open it.

Dear Edward,

If you are reading this, I am surely dead. It is strange, really, to write these words. I have never believed in ghosts, but right now the notion is a comfort. I think I should like to come back and haunt you. You deserve it after that episode in Rhode Island with Herr Farmer and the eggs.

Edward smiled as he remembered. It had been a long, boring day, and their quest for an omelet had ended with their getting pelted by eggs from a fat farmer screaming at them in German. It should have been a damned tragedy—they hadn't had a meal in days that wasn't bland and boring—but Edward couldn't remember a time he'd laughed so hard. It had taken Thomas a full day to get the yolk out of his coat, and Edward had been picking bits of shell from his hair all night.

But I shall have the last laugh, because I am going to be wretchedly maudlin and sentimental, and maybe I will even force you to shed a tear over me. That would make me laugh, you know. You've always been such a stoic. It was only your sense of humor that made you bearable.

But bearable you were, and I wish to thank you for the gift of true friendship. It was something you bestowed without thinking, something that simply came from within. I am not ashamed to say that I spend half my life in the colonies terrified out of my skull. It is far too easy to die here. I cannot express the comfort it gave me to know that I always had your support.

Edward sucked in a breath of air, and it was only then that he realized how close he was to tears. He could have written the exact same words to Thomas. It was what had made the war bearable. Friendship, and the knowledge that there was at least one other person who valued your life as much as his own.

And now I must impose upon that friendship one last time. Please have a care for Cecilia. She will be alone now. Our father hardly counts. Write to her, if you will. Tell her what happened to me

414 · JULIA QUINN

so that the only word she receives is not from the army. And should you have the opportunity, go visit her. See that she is well. Perhaps you could introduce her to your sister. I think Cecilia would like that. I know that I will rest easier knowing that she might have the opportunity to meet new people and find a life outside of Matlock Bath. Once our father passes, there will be nothing for her there. Our cousin will take ownership of Marswell, and he has always been an oily sort. I should never want Cecilia to be dependent on his generosity and goodwill.

Nor Edward. Cecilia had told him all about Horace. *Oily* was an apt modifier.

I know this is a great deal to ask of you. Derbyshire isn't quite the end of the earth—I believe we both know that's right here in New York—but I am sure that once you return to England, the last thing you will wish to do is travel north to the midlands.

No, but he wouldn't have to. Wouldn't Thomas be surprised to know that Cecilia was just a quarter mile away, in room twelve at the Devil's Head. It was truly a remarkable thing she'd done, crossing an ocean to find her brother. Somehow Edward thought that even Thomas wouldn't have imagined her capable of it.

So this is farewell. And thank you. There is no one I would trust my sister's welfare to more than you. And perhaps you will not mind the task so very much. I know you used to read her letters when I was gone. Honestly, did you think I wouldn't notice?

Edward laughed. He couldn't believe Thomas had known all along.

I bequeath to you the miniature I have of her. I think she'd want you to have it. I know that I do.
  Godspeed, my friend.
    Yours most truly,
    Thomas Harcourt

Edward stared down at the letter for so long his vision blurred. Thomas had never let on that he knew of Edward's infatuation with his sister. It was almost mortifying to think of it. But clearly he'd been amused by it. Amused, and maybe . . .

Hopeful?

Had Thomas been a matchmaker at heart? It had

certainly sounded that way in his letter. If he'd wanted Edward to marry Cecilia . . .

Could Thomas have written to her about it? She'd said that he had made the arrangements for the marriage. What if . . .

Edward felt the blood drain from his face. What if Cecilia really *did* think they were married? What if she hadn't been lying at all?

Edward searched the letter frantically, looking in vain for a date. When had Thomas written this? Could he have told Cecilia to make arrangements for a proxy ceremony but then died before asking Edward to do the same?

He stood. He had to get back to the inn. He knew this was farfetched, but it would explain so much. And it was well past time that he told her that his memory had returned. He needed to stop stewing in his misery and simply ask her what was going on.

He didn't run to the Devil's Head, but it was a damned fast walk.

"Cecilia!"

Edward pushed open the door to their room with more force than was necessary. But by the time he'd reached the upper floor of the inn, his blood was rushing so fast and so hard he was practically jumping out of his skin. His head was full of questions, and his heart was full of passion, and at some point he'd decided he didn't care what she'd done. If she had tricked him, she must have had a reason. He knew her. He *knew* her. She was as good and fine a person as had ever walked on this earth, and maybe she hadn't said the words, but he knew she loved him.

Almost as much as he loved her.

"Cecilia?"

He said her name again even though it was obvious she wasn't there. Damn it. Now he was going to have to sit on his hands and wait. She could be anywhere. She frequently went out and about, running errands and taking walks. There had been less of this since her search for her brother had ended, but still, she didn't like to stay cooped up all day.

Maybe she'd left a note. She sometimes did.

His eyes swept over the room, moving more slowly along the flat planes of the tables. There it was. A thrice-folded piece of paper tucked partway under the empty washbasin so it wouldn't blow away.

Cecilia always did like to leave the window open.

Edward unfolded the paper, and for a split second he was confused by the sheer number of words on the page, far more than was needed to let him know when she'd be back.

Then he started to read.

Dear Edward,

I am a coward, a terrible one, for I know I should say these words in person. But I cannot. I do not think I could make it through the speech, and also, I do not think I will have the time.

I have so much to confess to you, I hardly know where to start. I suppose it must be with the most salient fact. We are not married.

I did not mean to carry out such a falsehood. I promise you, it began for the most unselfish of reasons. When I heard you were in hospital, I knew that I must go and care for you, but I was turned away, told that due to your rank and position, only family members would be allowed to see you. I am not sure what came over me—I did not think I was so impulsive, but then again, I did throw caution to the wind and come to New York. I was so angry. I wanted only to help. And before I knew it, I shouted that I was your wife. To this day, I am not sure why anyone believed me.

I told myself that I would reveal the truth when you awakened. But then everything went wrong.

No, not wrong, just strange. You woke up and had no memory. Even odder, you seemed to know who I was. I still do not understand how you recognized me. When you regain your memory—and I know you will, you must have faith—you will know that we had never met. Not in person. I know that Thomas showed you his miniature of me, but truly, it is not a good likeness. There is no reason you should have recognized me when you opened your eyes.

I did not want to tell you the truth in front of the doctor and Colonel Stubbs. I did not think they would allow me to stay, and I felt you still needed my care. Then later that night, something became very clear. The army was far more eager to aid Mrs. Rokesby in the search for her brother than it was for Miss Harcourt.

I used you. I used your name. For that I apologize. But I will confess that while I shall carry my guilt to the end of my days, I cannot regret my actions. I needed to find Thomas. He was all I had left.

But now he is gone, and so is my reason for being in New York. As we are not married, I think it is appropriate and best that I return to Derbyshire. I will not marry Horace; nothing shall sink me that low, I assure you. I buried the silver in the garden before I left; it was my mother's and thus not part of the entail. I shall find a buyer. You need not worry for my welfare.

Edward, you are such a gentleman—the most honorable man I have ever known. If I remain in New York, you will insist that you have compromised me, that you must marry me. But I cannot ask this of you. None of this was your fault. You thought we were wed, and you behaved as a husband would. You should not be punished for my trickery. You have a life waiting for you back in England, one that does not include me.

All I ask is that you not speak of this time. When the day shall come that I might marry, I will tell my intended what happened here. I could not live with myself if I did not. But until then, I think it best if the world continues to see me simply as

> *Your friend,*
> *Cecilia Harcourt*

Postscript—You need not worry about lasting repercussions from our time together.

Edward stood in the center of the room, utterly frozen. What the bloody hell was that? What did she mean by—

He scrambled to find the part of the letter he was looking for. There it was. She did not think she would have the time to tell him in person.

The blood drained from his face.

The *Rhiannon*. It was in the harbor. It was leaving that eve.

Cecilia had booked passage on it. He was certain of it.

He checked the pocket watch he'd left out on the table to serve as their clock. He had time. Not a lot, but enough.

It would have to be enough. His whole world depended on it.

Chapter 21

I have not heard from you in so long, Thomas. I know I should not worry, that there are dozens of ways for your letters to be delayed, but I cannot help myself. Did you know that I mark a calendar to keep track of our correspondence? A week for my letter to be put on a ship, five weeks to cross the Atlantic, another week to reach you. Then a week for your letter to be put on a ship, three weeks to cross the Atlantic (see? I was listening when you told me it is faster to journey east), then a week for it to reach me. That is three months to receive an answer to a simple question!

But then again, maybe there are no simple questions. Or if there are, they lack simple answers.

—FROM CECILIA HARCOURT TO HER BROTHER THOMAS (LETTER NEVER RECEIVED)

The *Rhiannon* was remarkably similar to the *Lady Miranda*, and Cecilia had no difficulty locating her cabin. When she'd purchased her ticket a few hours earlier, she'd been told that she would be sharing her cabin with a Miss Alethea Finch, who had been serving as a governess to a prominent New York family and was now returning home. It was not uncommon for total strangers to share accommodations on such journeys. Cecilia had done so on the way over; she'd got on quite well with her fellow traveler and had been sorry to say good-bye when they had docked in New York.

Cecilia wondered if Miss Finch was Irish, or like her, simply eager to get on the first ship back to the British Isles and did not mind having to make a stop before reaching England. Cecilia herself wasn't sure how she was going to get home from Cork, but that hurdle seemed tiny compared with the greater challenge of getting herself across the Atlantic. There would probably be ships sailing from Cork to Liverpool, or if not that, she could travel up to Dublin and sail from there.

She'd got herself from Derbyshire to New York, for heaven's sake. If she could do that, she could do anything. She was strong. She was powerful.

She was crying.

Damn it, she needed to stop crying.

She paused in the narrow corridor outside her cabin

to take a breath. At least she wasn't sobbing. She could still comport herself without attracting too much attention. But every time she thought she had hold of her emotions, her lungs seemed to lurch, and she drew in an unexpected breath, but it sounded like a choke, and then her eyes got all prickly, and then—

Stop. She needed to stop thinking about it.

Goal for today: Don't cry in public.

She sighed. She wanted a new goal.

Time to move on. With a fortifying breath, she brushed her hand over her eyes and pushed down on the handle to the door of her cabin.

It was locked.

Cecilia blinked, momentarily nonplussed. Then she knocked, reckoning that her cabinmate had arrived before she had. It was prudent for a woman alone to lock her door. She would have done the same.

She waited a moment, then knocked again, and finally the door opened, but only partway. A thin woman of middling years peered out. She filled most of the narrow opening, so Cecilia could not see much of the cabin behind her. There appeared to be two bunks, one up and one down, and a trunk was open on the floor. On the lone table, a lantern had been lit. Clearly Miss Finch had been unpacking. "May I help you?" Miss Finch asked.

Cecilia affixed a friendly expression to her face and said, "I believe we are sharing this cabin."

Miss Finch regarded her with a pinched mien, then said, "You are mistaken."

Well. That was unexpected. Cecilia looked back at the door, which was propped open against Miss Finch's hip. A dull brass "8" had been nailed into the wood.

"Cabin eight," Cecilia said. "You must be Miss Finch. We are to be bunkmates." It was difficult to muster the energy to be sociable, but she knew she must try, so she bobbed a polite curtsy and said, "I am Miss Cecilia Harcourt. How do you do?"

The older woman's lips flattened. "I was led to believe I would not be sharing this stateroom."

Cecilia glanced first at one bunk, then at the other. It was clearly a room for two. "Did you reserve a cabin for yourself?" she asked. She had heard that people sometimes did so, despite having to pay double.

"I was *told* that I had no cabinmate."

Which was not the answer to the question Cecilia had asked. But even though her own mood was rattling between black and blue, she held her temper in check. She was going to have to share an extremely small cabin with this woman for at least three weeks. So she summoned her best approximation of a smile and said, "I only booked passage this afternoon."

Miss Finch drew back with obvious disapproval. "What sort of woman books passage across the Atlantic on the day of departure?"

Cecilia's jaw tightened. "My sort of woman, I suppose. My plans changed rather abruptly, and I was fortunate enough to find a ship departing immediately."

Miss Finch sniffed. Cecilia wasn't sure how to interpret this, aside from the obvious fact that it was not complimentary. But Miss Finch finally took a step back, allowing Cecilia entry into the tiny cabin.

"As you can see," Miss Finch said, "I have unpacked my belongings on the bottom berth."

"I am more than happy to sleep on top."

Miss Finch sniffed again, a little louder. "If you get seasick, you will have to exit the room. I will not have the smell in here."

Cecilia felt her resolve toward politeness slipping away. "Agreed. Just so long as you do the same."

"I hope you do not snore."

"If I do, no one has told me of it."

Miss Finch opened her mouth, but Cecilia cut her off with "I'm sure *you* will tell me if I do."

Miss Finch opened her mouth again, but Cecilia added, "And I will thank you for it. It does seem the sort of thing one ought to know about oneself, would you not agree?"

Miss Finch drew back. "You are most impertinent."

"And you are standing in my way." The room was very small, and Cecilia had not fully entered; it was nearly impossible to do so while the other woman had her trunk open on the floor.

"It is my room," Miss Finch said.

"It is *our* room," Cecilia nearly growled, "and I would appreciate it if you would move your trunk so that I might enter."

"Well!" Miss Finch slammed her trunk shut and shoved it under her bed. "I don't know where you will put your trunk, but don't think you can take up the middle of the floor if I cannot."

Cecilia didn't have a trunk, just her large traveling bag, but there seemed little reason to make a point of that.

"Is that all you have?"

Especially since Miss Finch seemed eager to make the point for her.

Cecilia tried to draw a calming breath. "As I said, I had to leave most suddenly. There was no time to pack a proper trunk."

Miss Finch stared down her bony nose and made another one of those sniffing sounds. Cecilia resolved to spend as much time as possible on deck.

There was a small table nailed to the foot of the bed,

with enough space underneath for Cecilia's bag. She removed the few things she thought she might wish to have in her bunk and then edged past Miss Finch so that she could climb up and see where she would be sleeping.

"Don't step on my bed getting up to your bunk."

Cecilia paused, counted in her head to three, then said, "I shall restrict my movements to the ladder."

"I am going to complain to the captain about you."

"By all means," Cecilia said with a grandiose wave of her arm. She made her way up another rung and took a peek. Her bunk was neat and tidy, and even if she didn't have much headroom, at least she wouldn't have to look at Miss Finch.

"Are you a harlot?"

Cecilia whirled around, nearly losing her footing on the ladder. "What did you just ask?"

"Are you a harlot?" Miss Finch repeated, punctuating each word with a dramatic pause. "I can think of no other reason—"

"No, I am not a harlot," Cecilia snapped, well aware that the odious woman would most likely disagree if she knew the events of the past month.

"Because I won't share a room with a whore."

Cecilia lost it. She simply lost it. She'd held her composure through the death of her brother, through the revelation that Colonel Stubbs had lied in the face of her grief and worry. She'd even managed not to fall apart while leaving the only man she would ever love, and now she was putting a bloody ocean between them, and he was going to hate her, and this awful wretched woman was calling her a *whore*?

She jumped off the ladder, strode to Miss Finch, and grabbed her by the collar.

"I don't know what sort of poison you ingested this morning," she seethed, "but I have had enough. I paid good money for my half of this cabin, and in return I expect a modicum of civility and good breeding."

"Good breeding! From a woman who does not even possess a trunk?"

"What the devil does that mean?"

Miss Finch threw up her arms and screeched like a banshee. "And now you invoke the name of Satan!"

Oh. Dear. God. Cecilia had entered hell. She was sure of it. Maybe this was her punishment for lying to Edward. Three weeks . . . maybe even a full month with this shrew.

"I refuse to share a cabin with you!" Miss Finch cried.

"I assure you I would like nothing more than to grant your wish, but—"

A knock sounded on the door.

"I hope that's the captain," Miss Finch said. "He probably heard you screaming."

Cecilia gave her a disgusted look. "Why on earth would the captain be here?" They lacked a porthole, but she could tell from the movement of the ship that they had already left the dock. Surely the captain had better things to do than arbitrate a catfight.

The crisp rap of knuckles on wood was replaced by the pound of a fist, followed by a bellow of "Open the door!"

It was a voice Cecilia knew quite well.

She went pale. Truly, she felt the blood leave her face. Her mouth went slack with shock as she turned toward the pulsing flat of the door.

"Open the damn door, Cecilia!"

Miss Finch gasped and whirled to face her. "That's not the captain."

"No . . ."

"Who is it? Do you know who it is? He could be here to attack us. Oh dear God, oh dear heavens . . ." Miss Finch moved with surprising agility as she leapt behind Cecilia, using her as a human shield for whatever monster she thought was going to come barreling through the door.

"He's not going to attack us," Cecilia said in a dazed voice. She knew she should do something—shake off

Miss Finch, open the door—but she was frozen, trying to make sense of what was clearly an impossibility.

Edward was here. On the ship. On the ship that had *left the harbor.*

"Oh my God," she gasped.

"Oh, *now* you're worried," Miss Finch snapped.

The ship was moving. It was *moving.* Cecilia had watched the crew unwrap the thick ropes from the moorings as she made her way across the deck. She'd felt them push away from the dock, recognized the familiar pitch and sway as they set out across the bay and into the Atlantic.

Edward was on the ship. And as he was hardly likely to swim back to shore, that meant he had deserted his post, and—

More pounding, louder this time.

"Open this door right now or I swear I will break it down!"

Miss Finch whimpered something about her virtue.

And Cecilia finally whispered Edward's name.

"You know him?" Miss Finch accused.

"Yes, he's my . . ." What was he? Not her husband.

"Well, then open the door." Miss Finch gave her a hard shove, catching Cecilia sufficiently off guard to send her tumbling against the far wall. "But don't let him in," she barked. "I won't have a man in here. You take him out and do your . . . your . . ." Her fingers made disgusted piano-like motions in front of her. "Your *business*," she finally finished. "Do it elsewhere."

"Cecilia!" Edward bellowed.

"He's going to break the door!" Miss Finch shrieked. "Hurry!"

"I'm hurrying!" The cabin was only eight feet across—hardly enough for hurrying to make a difference—but Cecilia made her way to the door and put her fingers on the deadbolt lock.

And she froze.

"What are you waiting for?" Miss Finch demanded.

"I don't know," Cecilia whispered.

Edward was here. He'd followed her. What did that *mean*?

"*CECILIA!*"

She opened the door, and for one blessed moment, time stopped. She drank in the sight of him standing across the threshold, his fisted hand still raised to pound against the door. He wore no hat, and his hair was badly mussed and ruffled.

He looked . . . wild.

"You're wearing your uniform," she said stupidly.

"You," he said, jabbing his finger toward her, "are in so much trouble."

Miss Finch let out a gleeful gasp. "Are you going to arrest her?"

Edward wrenched his gaze away from Cecilia for just long enough to snap an incredulous "What?"

"Are you going to arrest her?" Miss Finch scurried up until she was just behind Cecilia. "I think she's a—"

Cecilia elbowed her in the ribs. For her own good. There was no telling how Edward would react if Miss Finch called her a whore in front of him.

Edward flicked an impatient look at Miss Finch. "Who is that?" he demanded.

"Who are *you*?" Miss Finch shot back.

Edward jerked his head toward Cecilia. "Her husband."

Cecilia tried to contradict. "No, you're—"

"I will be," he growled.

"This is highly irregular," Miss Finch said with a sniff.

Cecilia whirled around. "Will you kindly step back?" she hissed.

"Well!" Miss Finch said with a huff. She made a great show of the three mincing steps it took to reach her bunk.

Edward tipped his head toward the older lady. "Your friend?"

"No," Cecilia said emphatically.

"Certainly not," Miss Finch said.

Cecilia shot her an irritated look before turning back to Edward. "Didn't you get my letter?"

"Of course I got your letter. Why the hell else would I be here?"

"I didn't say which ship—"

"It wasn't that difficult to figure it out."

"But you—your commission—" Cecilia fought for words. He was an officer in His Majesty's Army. He couldn't just leave. He'd be court-martialed. Dear God, could he hang? They didn't hang officers for deserting, did they? And certainly not those from families like the Rokesbys.

"I had enough time to settle matters with Colonel Stubbs," Edward said in a curt tone. "*Just.*"

"I—I don't know what to say."

His hand wrapped around her upper arm. "Tell me one thing," he said in a very low voice.

She stopped breathing.

And then he looked over her shoulder at Miss Finch, who was following the proceedings with *avid* interest. "Would you mind granting us some privacy?" he ground out.

"This is my cabin," she said. "If you wish for privacy, you'll have to find it elsewhere."

"Oh for the love of God," Cecilia burst out, whirling around to face the hateful woman, "can you find enough kindness in your stony heart to give me a moment with—" She swallowed, her throat closing on her words. "With him," she finally finished, jerking her head toward Edward.

"Are you married?" Miss Finch asked primly.

"No," Cecilia replied, but this did not hold much traction given that Edward said, "Yes," at the exact same time.

Miss Finch turned her beady gaze from one to the other. Her lips pressed together, and her brows rose into two unattractive arches. "I'm going to get the captain," she announced.

"Do," Edward said, practically shoving her out the door.

Miss Finch shrieked as she stumbled into the hall, but if she had anything more to say, it was cut off when Edward slammed the door in her face.

And locked it.

Chapter 22

I am coming to find you.

—FROM CECILIA HARCOURT
TO HER BROTHER THOMAS
(LETTER NEVER SENT)

Edward was not in a good mood.

A man generally required more than three hours to uproot his life and decamp to another continent. As it was, he'd barely had time to pack his trunk and secure authorization to leave New York.

By the time he made it to the docks, the crew of the *Rhiannon* was preparing for departure. Edward had to practically leap across the water to board the ship, and he would have been forcibly removed had he not shoved the colonel's hastily written order in the face of the captain's second in command, securing himself a berth.

Or maybe just a spot on the deck. The captain's man said he wasn't even sure they had a spare hammock.

No matter. Edward didn't need much room. All he had were the clothes on his back, a few pounds in his pockets . . .

And a big black hole where his patience used to be.

So when the door to Cecilia's cabin opened . . .

One might have thought he'd have been relieved to see her. One might have thought, given the depth of his feelings, given the panic that had propelled him all afternoon, he would have sagged with relief at the sight of those beautiful seafoam eyes, staring up at him with astonishment.

But no.

It was all he could do not to throttle her.

"Why are you here?" she whispered, once he'd finally got the damnable Miss Finch out of the room.

For a moment he could only stare. "You're not seriously asking me that."

"I—"

"You left me."

She shook her head. "I set you free."

He snorted at that. "You've had me locked up for over a year."

"What?" Her response was more motion than sound, but Edward didn't feel like explaining. He turned away, his breath ragged as he raked his hand through his hair. Bloody hell, he wasn't even wearing his hat. How had that happened? Had he forgotten to put it on? Had it flown off as he ran for the ship?

The godforsaken woman had him tied in knots. He wasn't even sure if his trunk had made it aboard. For all he knew he'd just embarked on a monthlong voyage without a change of undergarments.

"Edward?" Her voice came from behind him, small and hesitant.

"Are you pregnant?" he asked.

"What?"

He turned around and said it again, with even more precision. "Are. You. Pregnant."

"No!" She shook her head in an almost frantic motion. "I told you I wasn't."

"I didn't know if—" He stopped. Cut himself off.

"You didn't know what?"

He didn't know if he could trust her. That was what he'd been about to say. Except it wasn't true. He did trust her. On this, at least. No, on this, especially. And his initial instinct—the one goading him to question her word—that was nothing but a devil on his shoulder, wanting to lash out. To wound.

Because she'd *hurt* him. Not because she'd lied—he supposed he could understand how all that had happened. But she had not had faith. She had not trusted him. How could she have thought that running away was the right thing to do? How could she have thought he didn't *care*?

"I am not with child," she said in a voice so low with urgency it was almost a whisper. "I promise you. I would not lie about such a thing."

"No?" His devil, apparently, refused to give up its voice.

"I promise," she said again. "I would not do that to you."

"But you would do *this*?"

"This?" she echoed.

He stepped toward her, still seething. "You left me. Without a word."

"I wrote you a letter!"

"Before you fled the *continent*."

"But I—"

"*You ran away.*"

"No!" she cried. "No, I didn't. I—"

"You are on a boat," he exploded. "That is the very definition of running away."

"I did it for you!"

Her voice was so loud, so full of keening sorrow that

he was momentarily silenced. She looked almost brittle, her arms sticklike at her sides, her hands pressed into desperate little fists.

"I did it for you," she said again, softer this time.

He shook his head. "Then you should have damn well consulted me to see if it was what I wanted."

"If I stayed," she said, with the slow and heavy cadence of one who was desperately trying to make the other understand, "you would have insisted upon marrying me."

"Indeed."

"Do you think this was what I wanted?" she practically shouted. "Do you think I *liked* sneaking away while you were gone? I was sparing you from having to do the right thing!"

"Listen to yourself," he bit off. "Sparing me from having to do the right thing? How could you even think I would want to do anything else? Do you know me at all?"

"Edward, I—"

"If it's the right thing," he snapped, "then I should be doing it."

"Edward, please, you must believe me. When you recover your memory, you will understand—"

"I got my memory back days ago," he cut in.

She froze.

He was not such a noble man that he did not experience a small pang of satisfaction at that.

"*What?*" she finally said.

"I got my—"

"You didn't tell me?" Her voice was calm, dangerously so.

"We had just found out about Thomas."

"You didn't *tell* me?"

"You were grieving—"

She smacked him on the shoulder. "How could you keep that from me?"

"I was angry!" he roared. "Didn't I have the right to keep something from *you?*"

She stumbled back, hugging her arms to her body. Her anguish was palpable, but he couldn't stop himself from advancing, jabbing his forefinger hard against her collarbone. "I was so bloody furious with you I could hardly see straight. But speaking of doing the right thing, I thought it would be kinder if I waited to confront you until after you'd had a few days to grieve for your brother."

Her eyes grew large, and her lips trembled, and her posture—somehow tense and slack at the same time—brought to Edward's mind a deer he'd almost shot years ago, while hunting with his father. One of them had stepped on a twig, and the animal's large ears had perked and turned. It didn't move, though. It stood there for what felt like an eternity, and Edward had had the most bizarre sense that it was contemplating its existence.

He had not taken the shot. He had not been able to bring himself to do so.

And now . . .

The devil on his shoulder slunk away.

"You should have stayed," he said quietly. "You should have told me the truth."

"I was scared."

He was dumbfounded. "Of me?"

"No!" She looked down, but he heard her whisper, "Of myself."

But before he could ask her what she meant, she swallowed tremulously and said, "You don't have to marry me."

He couldn't believe she was still thinking *that* was possible. "Oh, I don't, don't I?"

"I won't hold you to it," she half babbled. "There's nothing to hold you to."

"Isn't there?" He took a step toward her, because it was long past time they eliminated the distance between them, but he stopped in place when he realized what he saw in her eyes.

Sorrow.

She looked so unbearably sad, and it *wrecked* him.

"You love someone else," she whispered.

Wait . . . *What?*

It took him a moment to realize he hadn't said it aloud. Had she gone mad? "What are you talking about?"

"Billie Bridgerton. You're supposed to marry her. I don't think you remember, but—"

"I'm not in love with Billie," he interrupted. He ran his hand through his hair, then turned to face the wall as he let out a shout of frustration. Good God, was *that* what this was all about? His neighbor back home?

And then Cecilia said—she *actually* said, "Are you sure?"

"Of course I'm sure," he retorted. "I'm certainly not going to marry her."

"No, I think you are," she said. "I don't think you've recovered your full memory, but you said as much in your letters. Or at least Thomas did, and then your godmother—"

"What?" He whirled around. "When did you speak to Aunt Margaret?"

"Just today. But I—"

"Did she seek you out?" Because by God, if his godmother had insulted Cecilia in any way . . .

"No. It was entirely by chance. She'd come to see

you, and I happened to be leaving to purchase my ticket—"

He growled.

She backed up a step. Or rather she tried. She'd clearly forgotten that she was already up against the edge of the bunk.

"I thought it would be rude not to sit with her," she said. "Although I must say, it was very awkward to play the hostess in a public house."

Edward went still for a moment, then to his amazement he felt his lips cracking into a smile. "God, I would have loved to have seen that."

Cecilia gave him a bit of a sideways glance. "It is much more amusing in retrospect."

"I'm sure."

"She's terrifying."

"She is."

"*My* godmother was a dotty old woman in the parish," Cecilia muttered. "She knit me socks every year for my birthday."

He considered this. "I am quite certain Margaret Tryon has never knit a pair of socks in her life."

A little grumbling sound formed in Cecilia's throat before she said, "She'd probably be ridiculously competent at it if she tried."

Edward nodded, his smile by now reaching his eyes.

"Probably." He gave her a little nudge so that she sat on the bunk, and then he sat beside her. "You know I'm going to marry you," he said. "I can't believe you thought I would do otherwise."

"Of course I thought you'd insist upon marrying me," she replied. "That's why I left. So you wouldn't *have* to."

"That's the most ridic—"

She placed her hand on his shoulder to silence him. "You would never have taken me to bed if you thought we weren't married."

He did not contradict her.

She shook her head sadly. "You slept with me under false pretenses."

He tried not to laugh, he really did, but within seconds the bed was shaking with his mirth.

"Are you laughing?" she asked.

He nodded, clutching his middle as her question set off another wave of glee. " 'Slept with me under false pretenses,' " he chortled.

Cecilia frowned disgruntledly. "Well, you did."

"Perhaps, but who cares?" He gave her a friendly nudge with his elbow. "We're getting married."

"But Billie—"

He grabbed her by the shoulders. "For the last time, I don't want to marry Billie. I want to marry *you.*"

"But—"

"I love you, you little fool. I've been in love with you for years."

Maybe he was a little too full of himself, but he would swear he heard her heart skip a beat. "But you didn't know me," she whispered.

"I knew you," he said. He took her hand and brought it to his lips. "I knew you better than—" He paused for a moment, needing the time to collect his emotions. "Do you have any idea how many times I read your letters?"

She shook her head.

"Every letter . . . my God, Cecilia, you have no idea what they meant to me. They weren't even written to me—"

"They were," she said softly.

He went still, but his eyes held hers, silently asking her what she meant.

"Every time I wrote to Thomas I was thinking of you. I—" She swallowed, and although the light was too dim to see her blush, somehow he knew her face had gone pink. "I scolded myself every time."

He touched her cheek. "Why are you smiling?"

"I'm not. I—well, maybe I am, but it's because I'm embarrassed. I felt so silly, pining over a man I'd never met."

"No sillier than I," he said. He reached into the pocket of his coat. "I have a confession."

Cecilia watched as he unfurled his fingers. A miniature—*her* miniature—lay in his palm. She gasped, and her eyes flew to his. "But . . . how?"

"I stole it," he said plainly, "when Colonel Stubbs asked me to inspect Thomas's trunk." He'd tell her later that Thomas had wanted him to have it. It didn't really matter, anyway; he hadn't known this when he'd slipped it into his pocket.

Her eyes went from the tiny painting to his face and back again.

Edward touched her chin, raising her eyes to his. "I've never stolen anything before, you know."

"No," she said in an amazed murmur, "I can't imagine you would."

"But this—" He pressed the miniature into her palm. "This I could not do without."

"It's just a portrait."

"Of the woman I love."

"You love me," she whispered, and he wondered how many times he would have to say it for her to believe him. "You *love* me."

"Madly," he admitted.

She looked down at the painting in her hand. "It doesn't look like me," she said.

"I know," he said, reaching a shaky hand out. He tucked a lock of her hair behind her ear, his large palm coming to rest against her cheek. "You're so much more beautiful," he whispered.

"I lied to you."

"I don't care."

"I think you do."

"Did you do so with intent to hurt me?"

"No, of course not. I only—"

"Did you wish to defraud—"

"No!"

He shrugged. "As I said, I don't care."

For a second it seemed she might stop protesting. But then her lips parted again, and she took a little breath, and Edward knew it was time to put a stop to this nonsense.

So he kissed her.

But not for terribly long. Much as he wanted to ravish her, there were other, more important matters at hand. "You could say it back, you know," he told her.

She smiled. No, she beamed. "I love you too."

Just like that, all of the pieces of his heart settled into place. "Will you marry me? For real?"

She nodded. Then she nodded again, faster this time. "Yes," she said. "Yes, oh yes!"

And because Edward was a man of action, he stood,

grabbed her hand, and hauled her to her feet. "It's a good thing we're on a ship."

She made an inarticulate noise of confusion but was immediately drowned out by an unfortunately familiar shriek.

"Your friend?" Edward said, with an amused arch of his brow.

"Not my friend," Cecilia replied immediately.

"They're in there," came the grating voice of Miss Finch. "Cabin eight."

A crisp knock sounded on the door, followed by a deep male voice. "This is Captain Wolverton. Is aught amiss?"

Edward opened the door. "My apologies, sir."

The captain's face lit with delighted recognition. "Captain Rokesby!" he exclaimed. "I did not realize you were sailing with us."

Miss Finch gaped. "You know him?"

"We were at Eton together," the captain said.

"Of course you were," Cecilia heard herself murmur.

"He was attacking her," Miss Finch said, jolting her finger in Cecilia's direction.

"Captain Rokesby?" the captain said, with palpable disbelief.

"Well, he almost attacked me," she sniffed.

"Oh please," Cecilia scoffed.

"It's good to see you, Kenneth," Edward said, reaching out and enveloping the captain's hand in a hearty shake. "Might I impose upon you for a marriage ceremony?"

Captain Wolverton grinned. "Now?"

"As soon as you're able."

"Is that even legal?" Cecilia asked.

He gave her a look. "*Now* you're quibbling?"

"It's legal as long as you're on my ship," Captain Wolverton said. "After that, I'd recommend redoing it on dry land."

"Miss Finch can be our witness," Cecilia said, her lips pressed together in a blatant attempt not to laugh.

"Why, well . . ." Miss Finch blinked about seven times in the space of a second. "I suppose I would be honored."

"We'll get the navigator to be the second witness," Captain Wolverton said. "He loves this sort of thing." Then he eyed Edward with a decidedly fraternal expression. "You'll take my cabin, of course," he said. "I can bunk elsewhere."

Edward thanked him—profusely—and they all filed out of the cabin, heading up to the deck, which, the captain insisted, was a much more suitable backdrop for a wedding.

But when they stood beneath the mast, with all the

crew gathered to celebrate with them, Edward turned to the captain and said, "One question before we get started . . ."

Captain Wolverton, clearly amused, motioned to him to continue.

"May I kiss the bride *first*?"

Epilogue

Cecilia Rokesby was nervous.

Correction, she was *really* nervous.

In approximately five minutes, she was going to meet her husband's family.

His very aristocratic family.

Who did not know he'd married her.

And it was most definitely legal now. It turned out the Bishop of Cork and Ross did a brisk business in special licenses—theirs was not the first shipboard marriage needing a more legally binding ceremony. The bishop had a stack of licenses ready to be filled out, and they were married on the spot, with Captain Wolverton and the local curate as witnesses.

After that, she and Edward had decided to proceed

straight to Kent. His family would be desperate to see him, and she had no one left in Derbyshire. There would be time enough to return to Marswell and gather her personal belongings before ceding the house to Horace. Her cousin couldn't do anything without confirmation of Thomas's death, and since Cecilia and Edward were the only people in England who could presently make such a confirmation . . .

Horace would have to learn the fine art of patience.

But now they were here, coming up the drive at Crake House, the ancestral home of the Rokesbys. Edward had described it to her in great detail, and she knew it would be large, but when they rounded the corner, she could not help but gasp.

Edward squeezed her hand.

"It's huge!" she said.

He smiled distractedly, his attention fully on his home, which loomed larger through the window with each rotation of the carriage wheels.

He was nervous too, Cecilia realized. She could see it in the constant tapping of his hand against his thigh, in the little flash of white every time he caught his lower lip with his teeth.

Her big, strong, capable man was nervous.

It made her love him even more.

The carriage came to a halt, and Edward hopped down before anyone could come to assist them. Once he had Cecilia safely on the ground beside him, he tucked her hand in his arm, and led her toward the house.

"I'm surprised no one has come out yet," he murmured.

"Maybe no one was watching the drive?"

Edward shook his head. "There is always—"

The door swung open, and a footman stepped out.

"Sir?" the footman said, and Cecilia realized he must be new, because he had no idea who Edward was.

"Is the family at home?" Edward asked.

"Yes, sir. Who may I say is calling?"

"Edward. Tell them Edward is home."

The footman's eyes widened. Clearly he'd been employed long enough to know what *that* meant, and he practically ran back into the house. Cecilia stifled a grin. She was still nervous. Correction, she was still *very* nervous, but there was something almost fun about this, something made her slightly giddy.

"Should we wait inside?" she asked.

He nodded, and they entered the grand foyer. It was empty, devoid of even a single servant until—

"*Edward!*"

It was a shriek, a loud feminine shriek, exactly the sound one might expect from someone so happy she might burst into tears at any moment.

"Edward Edward Edward! Oh my God I can't believe it's really you!"

Cecilia's brows rose as a dark-haired woman virtually *flew* down the stairs. She took the last half dozen steps in a single leap, and it was only then that Cecilia saw that she was wearing men's breeches.

"Edward!" With one last cry, the woman hurled herself into Edward's arms, hugging him with enough intensity and love to bring tears to Cecilia's eyes.

"Oh, Edward," she said again, touching his cheeks as if she needed to reassure herself it was really he, "we've been in such despair."

"Billie?" Edward said.

Billie? Billie Bridgerton? Cecilia's heart sank. Oh dear God. This was going to be awful. She probably still thought Edward was going to marry her. He'd said they had no formal understanding, that Billie didn't want to marry him any more than he did her, but Cecilia suspected that that was the obtuse male in him talking. How could any woman not want to marry him, especially one who'd been told since birth that he was hers?

"It's so good to see you," Edward said with a brotherly kiss on her cheek, "but what are you doing here?"

At that Billie laughed. It was a watery, through-her-tears sort of laugh, but her joy was there in every note. "You don't know," she said. "Of course you don't know."

"I don't know what?"

And then another voice entered the conversation. A male one.

"I married her."

Edward whirled around. "George?"

His brother. It had to be. His hair wasn't quite the same shade of brown, but those eyes, those incandescently blue eyes . . . He had to be a Rokesby.

"You married Billie?" Edward still looked . . . quite honestly, *shocked* really wasn't quite strong enough a word.

"I did." George looked right proud of it too, although Cecilia had less than a moment to gauge his expression before he enveloped Edward in a hug.

"But . . . but . . ."

Cecilia watched with interest. It was impossible not to smile. There was a story here. And she couldn't help but be a little bit relieved that Billie Bridgerton was clearly in love with someone else.

"But you hate each other," Edward protested.

"Not nearly so much as we love each other," Billie said.

"Good God. You and Billie?" Edward looked from one to the other and back again. "Are you certain?"

"I recall the ceremony quite distinctly," George said with dry humor. He tipped his head toward Cecilia. "Are you going to introduce us?"

Edward took her arm and drew her close. "My wife," he said with obvious pride. "Cecilia Rokesby."

"Formerly Harcourt?" Billie asked. "You were the one who wrote to us! Oh, *thank you*. Thank you!"

She threw her arms around Cecilia and hugged her so tightly that Cecilia could hear every catch in her voice as she said, "Thank you again and again. You have no idea how much that meant to us."

"Mother and Father are in the village," George said. "They should be back within the hour."

Edward smiled broadly. "Excellent. And the rest?"

"Nicholas is at school," Billie said, "and of course Mary has her own home now."

"And Andrew?"

Andrew. The third brother. Edward had told Cecilia that he was in the navy.

"Is he here?" Edward asked.

George made a sound that Cecilia could not interpret. One might have called it a chuckle . . . if it weren't so liberally laced with something better described as awkward resignation.

"Shall you tell him or shall I?" Billie said.

George took a breath. "Well, now *that* is quite a story . . ."